Roxanne Sydney knew something was afoot, and had every intention of sharing in the fun . . .

Robert Lymond smiled his melting smile at me. "I would be devastated if anything happened to you."

"Stop trying your tricks on me, Lymond," I said, on guard. I recognized that persuasive tone he used when he wanted something. "I intend to stay here in Cairo. And I plan to be careful. I realize that the ordinary rules of law and order do not apply here."

"An understatement," Lymond said. "Do you have any idea of what's out there? People have disappeared here and never been heard from again. People have been murdered in their beds."

"I realize that, Lymond. I've purchased pistols for my butler and me."

Lymond put his head in his hands. "That's even worse. You're likely to blow your own foot off. Can't you be reasonable? This is no place for you and you know it. It's time for you to go home and think about getting married like your sisters."

Cold fury swept over me as I sat there, trying to decide which of his ridiculous statements to answer first. "You are just like every other man in the universe. Adventures are for men while women are good for nothing except staying home and having children!"

Before I thought, I picked up the pitcher of lemonade and threw the remainder of the contents right in his face.

He walked out the door, closing it softly behind him. It was a very effective exit—I would have been most impressed, except the slice of lemon dangling from his hair over his ear detracted from the effect.

It was just the beginning of a beautiful relationship!

ZEBRA'S REGENCY ROMANCES
DAZZLE AND DELIGHT

A BEGUILING INTRIGUE (4441, $3.99)
by Olivia Sumner

Pretty as a picture Justine Riggs cared nothing for propriety. She dressed as a boy, sat on her horse like a jockey, and pondered the stars like a scientist. But when she tried to best the handsome Quenton Fletcher, Marquess of Devon, by proving that she was the better equestrian, he would try to prove Justine's antics were pure folly. The game he had in mind was seduction—never imagining that he might lose his heart in the process!

AN INCONVENIENT ENGAGEMENT (4442, $3.99)
by Joy Reed

Rebecca Wentworth was furious when she saw her betrothed waltzing with another. So she decides to make him jealous by flirting with the handsomest man at the ball, John Collinwood, Earl of Stanford. The "wicked" nobleman knew exactly what the enticing miss was up to—and he was only too happy to play along. But as Rebecca gazed into his magnificent eyes, her errant fiancé was soon utterly forgotten!

SCANDAL'S LADY (4472, $3.99)
by Mary Kingsley

Cassandra was shocked to learn that the new Earl of Lynton was her childhood friend, Nicholas St. John. After years at sea and mixed feelings Nicholas had come home to take the family title. And although Cassandra knew her place as a governess, she could not help the thrill that went through her each time he was near. Nicholas was pleased to find that his old friend Cassandra was his new next door neighbor, but after being near her, he wondered if mere friendship would be enough . . .

HIS LORDSHIP'S REWARD (4473, $3.99)
by Carola Dunn

As the daughter of a seasoned soldier, Fanny Ingram was accustomed to the vagaries of military life and cared not a whit about matters of rank and social standing. So she certainly never foresaw her *tendre* for handsome Viscount Roworth of Kent with whom she was forced to share lodgings, while he carried out his clandestine activities on behalf of the British Army. And though good sense told Roworth to keep his distance, he couldn't stop from taking Fanny in his arms for a kiss that made all hearts equal!

The Mummy's Mirror

Dawn Aldridge Poore

ZEBRA BOOKS
KENSINGTON PUBLISHING CORP.

ZEBRA BOOKS are published by

Kensington Publishing Corp.
850 Third Avenue
New York, NY 10022

First Printing: August, 1995

Printed in the United States of America

Glossary

Aba or Abah—a Bedouin cloak

Afreet—a devil or demon

Baksheesh—gratuity, alms

Dahabeeah or Dahabeeyah—houseboat

Effendi—sir

Fiman—a passport from the Sultan entitling the holder to special honors

Galabeeah or Galabeeyah—loose robe worn by men

Keffiyah or Khafiya—Arab kerchief used as a headdress

Korbash—a knotted whip

Marhaha—welcome

Sytt or Sitt—Princess, Lady

Suk—bazaar, market

Tacterwan—a litter drawn by mules

One

I threw down the rest of the letters. "I can't take this any more, Aunt Hen," I said. "I'm going to hire the next person who shows up at the door, no matter how unsuitable. A companion for me is merely for show anyway." I sat back down in my chair and put my feet up on Bucephalus's broad back. There was plenty of room—Bue is a mastiff and he has gained enough weight lately to become an extraordinarily huge dog. I was going to have to put him on a diet and I intended to do that just as soon as I had a companion of some sort installed in the house.

"Now, now, Roxanne," Aunt Hen said mildly. "With all your sisters married and gone, you know you need someone here. Just think of the company a genteel woman of mature years would provide for you."

Visions of long nights spent discussing embroidery stitches floated through my head and I was hard pressed not to gnash my teeth. Aunt Hen was oblivious and kept on chattering. "After all, just think of all the wonderful times you and I have had. If only you'd move to London with Harley and me whenever we return from Italy . . ." She let her words trail off.

"Aunt Hen, you know I can't do that. You and Uncle Harley are newlyweds." Aunt Hen blushed. Not by any stretch of my imagination could I see Aunt Hen and Uncle

Harley in any sort of intimate situation. They were both past sixty and Uncle Harley was as gruff as an old bear. They had been married for all of a month.

I had hoped to keep on living at Bellerophon, my home in Brighton. I wanted to live by myself since Aunt Hen had moved into Uncle Harley's house in London, but she was having none of that. She'd insisted that I hire a companion and, when she discovered that I had not, she'd left Uncle Harley's side to come stay with me until I filled the vacancy. I was trying. After all, Uncle Harley threatened to come stay with us at Bellerophon unless Aunt Hen came back to London immediately. The threat of Uncle Harley in residence had been known to spur even the most vacillating into action.

"If only Miss Rowe had been able to stay with you," Aunt Hen said with a sigh.

"Yes, that would have solved everything," I agreed. I had hired a suitable companion, Miss Flora Rowe, who was just the sort of person for whom I was searching. Miss Rowe was close to my own age—she had said she was six and twenty. Furthermore, she was quiet and agreed with me in every instance, no matter what I said. I was sure that if I suggested to her that black was white, she would say "Quite so, Miss Sydney." Unfortunately, Miss Rowe's brother had discovered that I was to be her employer and had sent me a curt letter informing me that Miss Rowe would not be joining me after all. He didn't say so in that many words, but it was clear that he didn't want his sister in my company. Aunt Hen was incensed and, although I really wasn't bothered by his implications, I couldn't imagine letting some male bully me that way. But then, I wasn't Miss Rowe.

"Why don't you go back to London, Aunt Hen?" I suggested, sipping my tea and stretching. "I'll be fine here. I promise I'll hire the next person who comes for an interview." Bue snuffled and moved, knocking my feet to the floor. I propped them again on his back and he didn't even notice.

"I wouldn't think of leaving you alone, dear!" Aunt Hen paused. "After all, dear Robert might come to Bellerophon to stay and that would be beyond scandalous. What would the neighbors say?"

"Probably no more than they've ever said," I answered. Back in the days before we discovered Papa's hidden treasure—the Treasure of Agamemnon he called it—we had been in almost dire financial straits. Since none of us wanted to sell Bellerophon, we took the next best option: we decided to let part of the house. Robert Lymond had been our first—and only—lodger. We didn't need to let the house now, but Lymond had signed a five year lease. That meant he had four years remaining on his contract. Lymond showed no signs at all of being chivalrous and negating the lease. In fact, he seemed rather gleeful that he would be around for four more years to plague me. I really couldn't say very much since I certainly wouldn't be alive if Lymond hadn't come to my rescue when I was in danger of being burned alive. He would carry scars from that day on the backs of his hands forever.

"Don't say such, Roxanne," Aunt Hen said with an injured look. "You know I've taken care of you girls since poor George first asked me. You've been my only family until Harley . . ." She let her voice trail off just enough to make me feel guilty. Aunt Hen, bless her, was absolutely dying to get back to Uncle Harley and we both knew it. That was fine with everyone else—all we asked was that we be allowed to stay as far as possible from Uncle Harley.

The thoughts of Uncle Harley precipitated Aunt Hen into

a letter writing mood—no matter that she'd written him one letter already today, and she decided to go to her room and write her beloved before she went to bed. I bade her good night, opened a handsome wooden presentation case, and removed my book from it. My sister, Olivia, a converted Methodist, had given me a book of sermons before she went off to the wilds of the Americas with her missionary husband. The book had been elegantly placed in a velvet-lined presentation box that was trimmed with brass fretwork. Olivia was quite proud of her selection and had made me promise to read each and every one of the sermons. "These will bring peace to your soul," she had said as she kissed me goodbye. I had tried to read the things, God knew I had, but the only thing they brought me was excessive boredom. Still, because I had promised Olivia, I was determined to get through them. I had also made a promise to myself: as soon as I finished the sermons, I would donate the book to charity and keep the box to use for small jewelry.

I opened the book to a sermon I had been trying to read for the better part of two days: "Moral Principles of the Submissive Woman." I certainly hoped Olivia wasn't in agreement with such drivel. I wanted to throw the book against the wall, but that was hardly the way to treat a book of sermons. Besides, I thought with a sigh, I had promised.

I grimly began reading again. After one or two very didactic, very boring paragraphs, the words began to blur. The dullness of the reading material, the warmth of the small fire, the lateness of the hour, and Bue's gentle snoring at my feet combined to create a lazy mood. I felt myself slipping into sleep.

Sounds from Bue pulled me back to reality from a very pleasant dream. For some reason, I had been dreaming about Robert Lymond. In my dream, Lymond was as I had first seen him—almost. When I had first seen him, Bue was sitting on top of him, pinning him to the ground. Still, even in that position, he was extraordinarily handsome. As soon as he stood, I had been struck by him. He was a little taller than average and had a well-formed body that was emphasized by excellent tailoring. Lymond had never needed padding in his garments—his shoulders were broad and the rest of his body muscular. He had dark brown hair that had a touch of curl in it and always seemed to be ready for a trip to the barber's. I was always divided on his best feature: his eyes were fine, a startling, clear blue, but I liked his smile, a rather lopsided grin that lit up his whole face.

The only thing wrong with my dream was that I really didn't seem to be myself. Oh, the person was blond all right, just as I am, but the person in the dream was tiny. I am, as Chaucer so gallantly puts it, "not undergrown." Not huge, mind you, but certainly not someone who would be mistaken for a flitting fairy princess.

Still, for the most part, my dream was quite nice. Lymond and I were walking around Bellerophon, talking. He seemed to be telling me that he cared for someone. Then he took me into his arms and I could have sworn that I felt his touch on my skin. Next, he seemed to be kissing me and the sensation was not at all unpleasant. Actually, in my dream it seemed quite enjoyable. From the back of my mind I heard another noise, rather like Lymond's voice saying my name in soothing and affectionate tones. That, too, was pleasant and I heard myself say his name lazily, then he kissed me again, the touch of his lips no heavier than a butterfly's touch.

Bue started wriggling and making snuffling noises. My

feet fell from his back and hit the floor with a thud and I had to catch myself to keep from falling from the chair. My eyes flew open and it took me a moment to orient myself. Actually, I was confused beyond measure. Robert Lymond was sitting in the chair right in front of me, gently scratching Bue behind the ears. Bue was clearly enjoying this and was snuffling against Lymond's leg.

I blinked my eyes, not sure if I was still dreaming. "Are you really here?" I asked.

Lymond laughed and I caught a glint of a gray hair in the candlelight. Lymond wasn't much older than when he had first come to Bellerophon looking for a place to rent, but he seemed older than he had in my dream. It took me a moment to shake off the feeling that there were two Robert Lymonds—the one in my dream and the one in front of me. Two Lymonds were just one too many for the world—perhaps two too many.

"Good evening, my dear Miss Sydney." He began scratching Bue on the chest and Bue fell to the floor, all four paws straight up. The dog was right on my feet and it took me a moment to extricate myself. I was glad for the time as it gave me a moment to compose myself. I was still feeling the effects of my dream. My lips were actually tingling. "Do you know you snore, Roxie?" Lymond asked conversationally.

"I most certainly do not, Lymond!" I put my book of sermons on the table beside me. My list of prospective companions fell from the table and landed on Bue's nose. Lymond picked it up and started to hand it to me. "What's this, Roxie? A list of people you don't like?"

I snatched the list but he drew it away. "Of course not, Lymond. You know I'm probably the most agreeable person around. This happens to be—" I had to pause to wait for

Lymond to stop laughing. I didn't find the comment at all humorous. "As I was saying," I continued icily as he mopped at his eyes with his handkerchief, "that happens to be a list of prospective companions."

Lymond made a show of looking at the list. "Ah, yes, you do need someone to lock you in your room, don't you?" He laughed again. "I don't see Gentleman Jackson's name on this list."

"Very funny, Lymond." I snatched the list from him and cached it in the presentation box. I was getting quite a collection of slips of paper in there—soon there wouldn't be room for the book. "I'm sifting through these names trying to find someone congenial. Not that I need a companion," I added, "but Aunt Hen refuses to leave me alone until I have one. I'm doing this for Uncle Harley."

"Who, by the way, came with me and is no doubt greeting his beloved right now," Lymond said. "I'm sure you'll enjoy his company."

I shuddered. "Here? Uncle Harley is here? Gad, Lymond, I had no idea he'd actually leave London and come to Brighton. I'll hire someone tomorrow."

Lymond, who knew Uncle Harley better than I, laughed. "I thought you had hired a companion, Roxanne. Where's Miss Rowe? I saw her in London when?" He frowned as he tried to recall. "Two days ago, I think, and she gave me the impression that she was coming straight to Bellerophon. Something about her brother."

I made a face. "She is not coming here. I had already employed her but her brother would not allow her to be in my employ. He seemed to feel I would be a bad influence. Imagine!"

Lymond laughed again and touched the back of my hand with his. The scars on his hands looked less raw than they did at first, but they still were prominent. Lymond had had beautiful hands, long, slim, with tapered fingers. The shape was still beautiful, but I could cry every time I looked at them. Lymond caught me looking.

"Stop berating yourself, Roxie. You know I'd do whatever I had to in order to save you. I don't think about it at all." He put a finger under my chin and tilted my face up. "Now smile." Before I thought, I obediently forced my mouth into a grin. It was only a surface smile, however.

"That's better," Lymond said, leaning back in his chair as I rang for some tea. "Back to Miss Rowe—I'm *sure* she said she was coming to Bellerophon immediately. Something about her brother just wanting her around to watch his children and be an unpaid housekeeper."

"I knew it!" I said triumphantly. "I knew there had to be some motive that would make him invite Miss Rowe into his house. After all, the poor woman had been shunted from post to post for years and he hadn't offered once to take her in, then, all of a dash, he simply must protect her from such an 'unsuitable influence.' "

"I think you're right, Roxanne. I really don't know if she's coming, however. That may just be something she told her brother. Miss Rowe seemed a quiet sort, so I don't really think she'd come down here on her own," Lymond said as Meggie brought in tea. Bue had shifted so that he was across both Lymond's and my feet. I wiggled my feet out and propped them on Bue's back again. Lymond left his where they were—he evidently didn't realize how much Bue weighed.

"I agree, Lymond." I poured a cup of tea for each of us and put sugar and lemon in his, just as he liked it. "And what brings you to Bellerophon, Lymond? Surely you didn't bring Uncle Harley down here just because you felt sorry for him being separated from Aunt Hen?"

Lymond nibbled on a macaroon. "Actually, I felt sorry for myself. I was having to entertain Uncle Harley, you know. Do you want me to go to London and fetch Miss Rowe for you so Uncle Harley and Aunt Hen won't have to be separated again?"

"It's that bad?"

He nodded, then changed the subject. "When are you off to Egypt? Now that you have the money from the jewels we found, I would have thought you'd been away traveling the globe."

"I intend to, Lymond, just as soon as I get this companion business out of the way. I'll write Miss Rowe tomorrow and let her know the post is still open. With any luck, I should be ready to leave in a fortnight or so." I paused and sipped my tea. "Didn't you tell me you were going to Egypt as well?"

Lymond nodded. "I hadn't planned on it, but Uncle Harley asked me, so I shall. He wanted to go, but since he promised Aunt Hen to take her to Italy for a honeymoon, he couldn't. So, I volunteered."

I laughed at him, reading between his words. "Don't sound so altruistic, Lymond. I know you'd do anything to get as far from Uncle Harley as possible. I'm surprised you aren't in Cairo already."

"I would have been there, but I was waiting for—" He stopped. "You never did tell me why you decided to travel to Egypt, Roxanne." He looked at me casually over the rim of his teacup. "Are you looking for anything in particular?"

I knew that tone. Whenever Lymond got too casual, it meant he was either fishing for information or he was trying to hide something. This time, I suspected both. "No,"

I answered, just as casually, "I merely wanted to go there because Papa told me so many stories about it. I thought I'd look up Mohammed if he's still alive. I heard from him some time ago but he must be old by now. He was somewhat older than Papa, you know. I'm sure he could tell me many wonderful stories about their travels together. Papa always said the two of them traversed Egypt from one end to the other, going where few Englishmen had ever been. They had adventures by the dozens, and I'd like to hear some of them."

"Perhaps Mohammed will think most of those adventures unsuitable for feminine ears." There was that grin again. "Anything else? No new searches for antiquities?"

"I have all the antiquities I need, thank you." I looked at him and raised my eyebrows. "Come to the point, Lymond. You're not here for just a casual visit, are you? What are you trying to ask me?"

He smiled that smile that always melted every woman in sight—except me. I was quite immune to his wiles. "Now, Roxanne, what a thing to say! Of course this is a casual visit—I'm merely here to bring Uncle Harley down to see his wife. He's an old man and I don't like the thought of him traveling alone."

"Balderdash. Why are you really here?"

Lymond shook his head. "O, ye of little faith. You always think I have some kind of ulterior motive. I'm merely being the dutiful nephew." He grinned again, only this time it was that slightly rakish grin that came close to melting me. "Besides, Francis and the rest of the family promised to pay me if I'd get Uncle Harley out of their hair. A bonus if I could get him out of town. The sum is not inconsiderable."

We both knew Uncle Harley well enough to laugh. We

chatted idly for a while, drinking our tea, and Lymond told me the on-dits of the *ton*. I had been lulled into comfort when Lymond leaned towards me.

"Roxanne, have you thought about postponing your trip? From what I've heard, it's not a particularly good place for travel, especially a female alone."

I sat up, instantly aware. "Now we come to it, don't we, Lymond. Is this the real reason you're here—to warn me off?"

Lymond sighed. "I wish you wouldn't go. Cairo's all right, but I hear the hinterlands can be dangerous."

"Horsefeathers. This is the modern age. Perhaps travel was once dangerous, but I don't believe it's so today. Besides, you know I can take care of myself." I pinned him with a look. "Now tell me why you really came here."

"Would you believe that I come to see you? That I missed your gorgeous face and flashing eyes?"

"No, I wouldn't." I paused. "Perhaps I would believe that for as long as it took you to say it." I glanced at him as he smiled. "You didn't tell me when you were leaving for Egypt."

"Soon." He leaned further towards me and put down his teacup. "Enough of trivialities and trips. I have been worried about you, Roxanne." He put his hand on mine. "Tell me, Roxanne, how have you been getting along? Do you miss your sisters?"

"Very much, Lymond." I tried to smile, but it was wavering. I felt my chin begin to quiver and quickly stood up. "However, I'm sure they're all very happy. Cassie's baby will be here soon—by the time I return from Egypt, I'll be an aunt. Julia and Olivia promised to come back from the United States as soon as they could. They may have children by then." In spite of my best efforts, I felt my voice catch and I got up and walked to the window. I heard Lymond move behind me and thought for a moment that he might come clasp my shoulders, hold me, and offer comfort. Instead, there was a tremendous crash, then a howl from Bue. I jumped and wheeled around.

Lymond had attempted to rise. True, he seemed to have remembered to get his feet from under the dog, but then he had sprawled all over the tea things and onto the floor. At present, he was rather inelegantly spread on the floor, arms and legs akimbo. There were macaroons in his hair.

I dashed to his side and jerked up his head. "Are you hurt, Lymond? Answer me!"

"Roxanne," he said slowly through gritted teeth, "you're pulling my hair out. Will you please let go?"

I removed my hand, possibly more quickly than Lymond intended, and his head banged down on the floor again. He cursed a bit—Lymond's vocabulary in that area is quite fluent—and sat up, rubbing his legs and feet. "Damn dog," he said, as I brushed macaroon crumbs from his coat of dark gray superfine.

"Don't blame Bue for your own shortcomings, Lymond," I said. "He didn't do anything at all. From what I can see, you fell right over him."

"All right, I admit that I did. Never mind." He stood up and started stamping his feet. It took me a moment to realize that he was trying to get the feeling back into them. After all, Bue had been sprawled on his feet for the better part of half an hour. I was definitely going to have to put Bue on a diet. "Damned dog," Lymond muttered again.

"It certainly isn't Bue's fault," I said again. I started to say more but Aunt Hen and Uncle Harley came to the door to investigate the commotion. Aunt Hen looked decidedly unkempt. One might almost say she was disheveled.

"Lymond fell," I explained.

Uncle Harley peered around. "I hope he didn't hurt any valuables," he said.

"None of the tea things are broken," I said briefly, picking up the tray and the rest of the macaroons. I put them on the table and straightened everything up. Lymond didn't help.

"Roxanne, you really should lock up some of these artifacts. What's this?" Uncle Harley asked.

"That's a book of sermons in a presentation box. Olivia gave it to me before she left." As I had expected, Uncle Harley tossed it down. Then he picked up a small vase from the table. "Did he?"

"Did he what, dear?" Aunt Hen asked.

"Did the young whelp break any damn thing! I'm not talking about sermons or tea things, dammit!" Uncle Harley roared. "I'm talking about valuables!"

"A whelp?" Aunt Hen looked around the room vaguely. "You must be mistaken, dear. There are no whelps here. Bue is full grown. Actually, there's no one here except dear Robert and Roxanne." She looked faintly shocked at the thoughts of Lymond and me alone in the room. I could almost see her mind working as she turned to me. "Roxanne, I've had the most wonderful idea! Since you can't locate a suitable companion, why don't you go to Italy with Harley and me? I don't know why you want to go to Egypt anyway—it's full of flies and disease. People die there every day, you know."

I felt myself go pale at the thought of weeks with Aunt Hen and Uncle Harley. "Thank you so much, Aunt Hen, but I'm sure I'll find a companion. Lymond was just telling me that Miss Rowe might be available after all." I looked at Lymond for confirmation, but he was still wiggling his feet and brushing crumbs from his coat.

"Didn't hurt yourself, did you?" Uncle Harley growled, walking over to Lymond. "No broken bones that would stop you from going on your trip?" He didn't wait for a reply, but pounded Lymond on the back a time or two, then told him to be sure to get enough rest. With a gleam in his eye, he then turned to Aunt Hen, "Are you ready for bed, love?"

Aunt Hen blushed and giggled as she and Uncle Harley went up the stairs. I stared after them.

"Roxanne," Lymond said gently. "Close your mouth."

I shut my mouth with a snap, searching for a suitable rejoinder, but came up with nothing. "Well!" I finally said.

"I love it when you're speechless," Lymond said with a rakish grin. "Remember, they're newlyweds." He stifled a yawn.

"It appears you're ready for bed as well."

His grin became even more rakish. "Yes, but we aren't newlyweds."

I sat down in my chair again. "No, and never will be." I busied myself with opening my book of sermons. Lymond looked at me a moment and then started for the door. Just as he was almost out of the room, I remembered what Uncle Harley had said to him. "Rest? What was that about rest, Lymond. What's going on?"

Lymond looked at me and I could see that he was think-ing of prevaricating, but I had him pinned down. "Did I forget to mention that I'm leaving for Egypt soon?" Ly-mond looked innocently at me. "I thought I told you."

"Don't equivocate, Lymond," I said sharply. "You know very well that you didn't say you were leaving so soon. I knew you were planning the journey, but I certainly didn't know it was immediately."

"I promised Uncle Harley I'd go," he said with a sigh, sitting down across from me again. "You know Uncle Harley—once he gets one of these maggoty notions in his head, all hell couldn't blow it loose."

I nodded and Lymond continued. "Uncle Harley's on the track of a cache of rare papyri that have been hidden in some sort of golden casket. It seems that a friend of a friend told him about it. The original word came from your father's old friend, Mohammed. The friend of the friend wanted a sum of money up front before the details of the papyri's whereabouts was even discussed. Uncle Harley, of course, couldn't decide if it was a legitimate business deal or some sort of scheme to help him dispense with some of his money. As usual, he's decided not to pay out any money. Instead, he wants me to go to Egypt immediately, look up Mohammed, and find out about it."

"I hope you have an enjoyable trip, Lymond," I said politely. "Remember to watch out for the flies and disease."

He gave me a devilish look. "I'm planning to enjoy myself, Roxanne."

"Really? How nice for you, Lymond." I refused to take the bait, but there was a strange, sinking feeling in my stomach. "I do hope I see you before you leave. If not, have a good trip." I picked up my book of sermons and swept out of the room. As usual, when I wanted to make a good exit, there was a problem. Bue heard me leaving and dashed out by me, almost knocking me down in the process. I heard Lymond chuckling to himself as I left.

Two

I slept later than usual the next morning. Since my sisters married and went away and the issue of the treasure was resolved, I seemed to have become indolent. I didn't get up and go in for breakfast until almost nine, early by London standards, but quite late by mine. I didn't see Lymond around anywhere, so ate alone and conferred with Woodbury, the butler, about the household tasks for the day. I much preferred to leave the entire running of the house to Woodbury, but he's a stickler for formality. It comes, I suppose, from his days in the Army. Everything must be done by the book. That's Woodbury's book, not mine.

Imagine my surprise when I finally went into the library and discovered Lymond and Uncle Harley deep in conversation. They didn't see me for a moment, but when they did, Lymond quickly swept some papers under some others. I certainly didn't want to pry, so I sat down to chat. After a moment I realized they were obviously just sitting there waiting for me to leave them alone. Although I can certainly take a hint, I was determined to thwart whatever devious plans they were plotting. I settled back in my chair and began to chatter about the weather. I had gone on for about three or four minutes when Lymond interrupted me.

"Spit it out, Roxanne. What's on your mind?"

I gazed at him with wide eyes. "Why, Lymond, whatever

are you talking about? I'm merely concerned about the weather. I do know poor Holmwood is in such a state about it. Gardeners always plan their days around the weather and Holmwood is no exception." I smiled brightly.

"Damn the weather," Lymond growled. Clearly he wasn't having one of his better days.

"Why don't you go to your room and read?" Uncle Harley asked. He attempted to be jovial. Uncle Harley attempting joviality was a pathetic sight.

"How kind of you to suggest that," I said, smiling at him. "As it so happens, I stayed up late last night reading a book of sermons Livvy left for me. There was one particularly interesting passage I wanted to share with you." I launched into a discussion of theology of the sort I thought was in the book. To tell the truth, I hadn't been able to stay awake long enough to get much out of any of the sermons.

Lymond looked at Uncle Harley and gathered up the papers. "We might as well go to my room," he said to Uncle Harley.

I glared at him. "That isn't necessary, Lymond. Please feel free to continue your conversation. After all, I'm sure mere females such as I aren't capable of listening to such weighty matters as the two of you seem to want to discuss." I stood up, waiting for him to apologize and ask me to join them.

"Thank you, Roxanne," he said absently, putting his papers back down on the table. "I certainly appreciate you allowing us our privacy." There was nothing for it except for me to leave. It was difficult to resist slamming the door behind me as I went out, but I managed it. Lymond would certainly pay for this later, I thought.

I was back in my quarters fuming when Woodbury appeared. "There is a rather distraught woman at the door

demanding to see you," he said stiffly. "I wasn't sure . . . ?"
He let his voice trail off in stiff disapproval.

Having nothing better to do, I told him to show her in.
To my surprise, he brought in Miss Rowe. Certainly not
the starchy, proper Miss Rowe I had met and engaged in
London. This Miss Rowe looked positively frowsy. She
appeared to have slept in her clothes and her hair was falling
down in little wisps around her face. There was a streak of
dirt on her face as well as dirt on her clothing.

"My dear Miss Rowe," I said, getting up and assisting
her, "do come in. Whatever has happened to you?"

Good breeding always tells. Miss Rowe drew herself up,
smiled slightly at me, and spoke. "I have come, Miss Sydney, to inquire if you have yet filled the post I relinquished."

"No, I haven't." I propelled her towards a chair and she
sat down.

"Then I would like to reapply, if possible. If you don't
wish to have me, I would like to know if you know of any
posts available." The poor dear was trying so hard to be
brave, but her chin was quivering. I thought about patting
her shoulder, but knew if I touched her, she would simply
dissolve. Sheer will was all that was holding her together.
So I did what I usually do under such circumstances—I
rang for tea.

I sat across from her. "My dear Miss Rowe, whatever
has happened?" I said as gently as possible.

She looked at me with stricken eyes. "Then you don't
wish to employ me now? I was so afraid of that."

"No, no, not at all." I paused as Meggie brought in tea
and I gave Miss Rowe a restorative cup with a great deal
of sugar. I took another look at her and sent Meggie back
for some cold meats and cheese. I would have wagered that

Miss Rowe hadn't eaten in a while. "There," I said as the color began to return to her cheeks. "Do you feel better?"

She nodded. Meggie brought in another tray of meat, cheese, and fruit and I plied Miss Rowe with food. "No, Miss Rowe," I continued, "I haven't filled the post although I have been searching. I particularly wished you as a companion and I simply haven't found anyone with your qualifications. If you're sure you're available and would like the position, I'd be delighted to have you join me."

Her reaction was much different than I expected. She burst into tears.

"I do apologize, Miss Sydney," she said. "I was just overcome with relief."

"Perhaps, Miss Rowe, you should begin your tenure by doing two things," I told her with a smile as I offered her more tea. "First, please call me Roxanne, and second, please tell me why you have appeared here in such a state."

There was a long pause while she gathered her strength and then the words came out in a rush. "My brother turned me out."

I jumped to my feet. "The cad! How could he?"

"Please, Miss Syd—Roxanne, no matter how either of us feel, he is still my brother."

"My apologies, Miss Rowe." I sat back down. "Do you wish to tell me the story?"

For the first time, she smiled. "Flora, please." She paused. "If you recall, at our last meeting you told me that my brother wished only to turn me into an unpaid housekeeper. Well, there was that, but he also wished to marry me off to one of his business partners—a local tradesman who is, if I must say so, completely odious."

I almost bit my tongue to keep from calling her brother

a cad again, but accomplished it. "So you left?" I prompted gently.

She nodded. "My brother gave me an ultimatum. Either marry Edward Higgins or be cast out with only the clothes on my back." She looked down at her muddy shoes and clothes. "I chose to leave. One of the children tossed my cloak and my reticule to me from a window." She glanced down at a worn reticule. "Not that it mattered, it was empty."

"So you came here." The full meaning of her story came upon me. "Flora, do you mean you *walked* all the way here?"

She nodded. "It's taken days. I saw Mr. Lymond and thought of asking for assistance, but I hesitated. I decided to come directly to Brighton after Mr. Lymond told me you were here." She paused. "I was forced to take shelter in haystacks and barns. I was afraid to go to houses and ask. A woman alone . . ." Her voice trailed off.

This time I couldn't contain myself. "The cad!" Poor Flora looked so shocked that I hastily apologized. "You're here now, and here you'll stay, Flora," I told her as I rang for Meggie to prepare a bath and some clean clothes for her. "I want no arguments about it. I think we'll rub along quite well together."

After getting Miss Rowe settled in, I went through some of the clothing my sisters had left, searching for some suitable things. It broke my heart to actually see and touch the things they had worn and then think that they were now away from me, out leading their own lives. In the privacy of their room, I finally broke down and cried for a long time. I do own I felt much better afterwards, although I had to sit in there for another quarter hour or so to get my face back to respectability. I certainly didn't wish to walk out advertising that I had been crying my eyes out. I was quite myself by the time I returned to Miss Rowe. I saw her to a room and the poor thing fell asleep on the bed almost immediately.

That accomplished, I was at loose ends and decided to take Bue out for some air since the day was gloriously sunny.

I was sitting on a garden bench, Bue at my feet. I had turned my face up to the sun and was enjoying the feeling of the warmth on my skin. My eyes were closed and I didn't see Lymond walking towards us. The only thing that alerted me was Bue's happy wriggling.

Lymond sat down beside me and began scratching Bue absently behind the ears. "You're the only woman I know who sits in the sun," Lymond said, doing much as I was, turning his face to the sun and breathing deeply. "Every other woman in the kingdom is terrified she'll ruin her complexion."

"That's the least of my worries," I told him. "However, don't tell Aunt Hen I'm doing this. She'll be after me with lemon juice and buttermilk." I gave him a cursory look. "Did you complete your important business?"

"Yes." He sighed. "I didn't mean to be rude, but Uncle Harley was giving me my instructions." He said nothing more and I would have died before I questioned him further. We sat in silence for a few minutes.

"I suppose Aunt Hen and Uncle Harley will be able to leave for Italy immediately," I said, "since I've hired a companion." I looked at him to gauge his reaction. I was disappointed. He didn't even open his eyes. "Good," he said. We sat in silence a few minutes longer. "I think I'll be leaving on my trip within a fortnight," I said.

"Good," he said, then turned and gave me a flashing

smile. "Good for you, at any rate. I don't know about the Egyptians. You are still planning your trip to Egypt, I take it?"

"I certainly am." It was my turn to say nothing more.

He stood up and smiled down at me. "I hope you have a wonderful time," he said insincerely. "Perhaps we'll run into each other, although I doubt it. You'll probably be staying in Cairo doing all the tourist things while I imagine I'll be chasing all over the country for Uncle Harley's casket of papyri."

I nodded, absolutely dying to ask him some questions. "I imagine I'll stay primarily in Cairo. I've always wanted to tour the pyramids." I couldn't resist one question. "And you, Lymond. Where do you plan to make your base?"

"Oh, here and there. Uncle Harley wants me to check into several things, of course, and Debenham has asked me, since I'll be in Egypt anyway, to check into the political situation. As Home Secretary, he's concerned about Egypt. Politics there are really volatile."

"I know. Even the post is sporadic. I wrote to Papa's friend Mohammed a while back and I have yet to receive a reply." I stood up. Bue got up and stretched lazily. "Bue will miss you," he said.

I smiled and patted Bue on the head. We had been through much together. "I'm taking him with me," I said. I smiled at Lymond.

Lymond looked doubtfully down at Bue. "I don't know, Roxanne. He might get lost or come to harm in an unfamiliar place. I know you want him for companionship, but his very size might terrify someone."

"Exactly my point." We began strolling back to the house. "I think he'll take well to the leash when we're there.

I've been taking him out for walks almost every day to accustom him to it."

"Still . . ." Lymond frowned as he looked again at Bue. "There will be unfamiliar faces and especially unfamiliar smells. He could create a scene."

"I'm sure I'll be able to handle him," I said firmly.

Aunt Hen met us as we went inside. "Dear Roxanne, why didn't you tell me Miss Rowe was here? I just saw the poor dear and she told me her terrible story! I'm so glad you've taken her in, Roxanne!"

"Have I missed another interesting episode here?" Lymond asked, lifting his brows.

"Hardly. As I recall, Lymond, you and Uncle Harley were quite busy in the library with private matters."

"And I'm sure I'll hear about that for several months. You won't be able to resist," he said with a laugh. "Aunt Hen, you're going to have to tell me about Miss Rowe."

Thankfully Uncle Harley interrupted Aunt Hen as she was beginning to speak. Aunt Hen is not a gifted storyteller. Actually, she wanders all around the story and it takes several questions to discover what she's trying to say. So it was something of a relief when she dashed off to be at Uncle Harley's side. "If you have time from your important matters to have tea, Lymond," I told him, "I'll be glad to tell you."

He laughed. "I told you I'd hear about that." I ignored him and he continued. "I always have time for tea with you, Roxanne. Where?"

We settled in the library, one of my favorite places, and I told Lymond about Miss Rowe's adventures as we drank tea. "All in all, Lymond," I said as I finished my story, "I was surprised at Miss Rowe's—Flora's—resourcefulness. I wouldn't have thought she would have the courage to defy her brother and set out on her own. I think this speaks quite well of her and will prove to great advantage on our Egyptian adventure."

"Uuumm." Lymond sipped his tea as he frowned. "Higgins. I've heard that name somewhere, Roxanne, and not in a flattering way. I can't remember where."

"Flora said he was completely odious, if that's any help."

Lymond shook his head. "I can't remember at all. Edward Higgins—I know the name and not in a good way. Miss Rowe is probably well rid of him." He put his cup down and smiled at me. "Perhaps I'll remember before I leave."

This was my opening. I put my cup down beside his. "You're leaving soon?" I asked casually.

"Tomorrow."

It was a good thing my cup was on the table. If it hadn't been, I think I would have dropped it. As it was, I had a terrible time hiding my astonishment at his precipitous departure. "You're wasting no time, Lymond."

"No." He leaned over and took my hand in his. "Roxanne, why go to Egypt? Why don't you go to France or rent a villa in Italy? The weather's wonderful there." His gaze was compelling. "I'll be in Italy soon and we could visit and see the sights."

I paused. Actually, I had been thinking of cutting my Egyptian visit short since I had heard the heat was intolerable, but something in Lymond's tone alerted me. Whenever he asked in this coaxing manner, it always meant that he knew something he was keeping from me. "Perhaps I will, Lymond," I said with a smile. "Italy would be nice, but after my trip to Egypt. I feel I owe it to Papa's memory to go to Cairo, visit with Mohammed, and reward him for assisting Papa to get the Cairo Cats. After all, if the cats hadn't come into our possession, we would have had no treasure. I think Papa would want Mohammed to share in our good fortune."

"Your father knew that treasure was in the cats. If he'd wanted Mohammed rewarded, he would have done it himself. And might have, for all you know. You told me yourself that he was always writing to Mohammed and receiving artifacts from him." He hesitated. "Egypt can be a dangerous place, Roxanne, especially for a female traveling alone."

"Only for a female, Lymond?" I felt my hackles rise. "Do I gather that you're going to be quite safe there?"

"Safer than you will be," he said bluntly, looking right into my eyes. He took a deep breath and licked his lips. "Please, Roxanne."

For a moment I wavered and glanced away. Whatever Lymond knew about traveling in Egypt must be serious since I couldn't remember him ever asking me in just that way. "My plans are all made, Lymond," I said firmly. "Flora and I have discussed it and we're committed. I assure you that I don't plan to travel about the country alone and get into scrapes of any kind. You can trust me on that."

Lymond leaned back and ran his fingers through his hair. "Roxanne, if I could believe that . . ." He stopped and took a deep breath. "Promise me that. I know you never break a promise."

"Promise what?"

"That you won't travel alone and get into scrapes. Promise me, Roxanne."

I started to promise, but then stopped. "Really, Lymond! I can see that you think I'm nothing but a green girl out on a lark. I assure you that I'm a responsible woman, as is Flora. Surely you can credit me with that much sense!" I rose, in a fine rage, and wheeled on him. "I'll probably rub along much better than you will. All in all, I'm sure it'll be nothing except a calm little jaunt to visit a friend."

Behind me, as I left the room, I heard Lymond muttering. "I certainly hope so, Roxanne. I certainly hope so."

Three

Imagine my surprise late that afternoon when I came into the front hall and discovered several cases and a trunk there. "Woodbury," I asked, surveying the pile, "do we have guests or does Mr. Lymond have someone visiting?"

"No, Miss Sydney." Woodbury looked positively funereal. "Mr. Lymond is leaving."

"Leaving! At this time of day?" At Woodbury's nod, I went off in search of Lymond. He had said he was leaving tomorrow. It took a while to find him, but Holmwood pointed me in the right direction. Lymond was sitting again on the garden bench, looking around at Holmwood's handiwork and enjoying a cigar. I walked up and sat beside him. He didn't throw away his cigar—by now Lymond knows that I rather like the smell of cigar smoke. Papa smoked them all the time and the odor, far from being unpleasant to me, brings back fond memories. Besides, I knew how much Lymond enjoyed a good smoke.

I wasted no time with pleasantries. "Why are you leaving now, Lymond? I had no idea you were going this afternoon. Isn't it rather late to leave? Why don't you wait until tomorrow morning? You could get an early start and probably get to London at about the same time. You are going to London, aren't you?"

Lymond laughed aloud. "Why don't you make a list for

me, Roxanne? Do you want me to answer in any particular order?"

I gave him an icy look. Lymond is always commenting on my questions. For some reason, my questions just seem to tumble out, although they seem perfectly logical to me. "No particular order," I said.

"Yes, it is late to leave, but I'm just going to Plymouth, so I hoped to make it halfway by nightfall, then leave before dawn tomorrow. Uncle Harley has booked passage for me on the *Mary Isabelle,* leaving Plymouth tomorrow morning."

I didn't wait for him to go on. "You're *sailing* tomorrow morning? Heavens, Lymond, I merely thought you were leaving Bellerophon tomorrow."

He nodded. "I need to be on board by eleven. You know Uncle Harley. Always impatient." He laughed and blew a cloud of cigar smoke. "He's dying to get to Egypt and hunt for that casket himself. I'd be willing to wager a good sum that he isn't able to stay in Italy above a few weeks. Aunt Hen will be doing splendidly if she detains him there a month."

"I think he'll stay. She's planning on three months, possibly more. I've promised to come see them after I visit Egypt."

Lymond looked at me and smiled. "Care to wager? After all, you can afford it now."

I looked at him and lifted an eyebrow. "All right, Lymond. I have faith in Aunt Hen. Name your terms."

He thought a moment while he smoked. "If he doesn't stay in Italy for five weeks or more, I get a reward. If he stays beyond five weeks, I'll give up my lease here at Bellerophon. The five weeks doesn't include sailing or travel time."

"Done." That lease had been a thorn in my flesh for too long now.

He grinned at me again. "You're committed. Don't you want to know what my reward is?"

"I can afford it, Lymond. Just name your price."

He regarded me for a long moment, then touched the side of my cheek with his finger. "A kiss," he said. "Not a peck on the cheek, mind you, but a kiss."

I felt myself blush. "Never! Do you know what you're saying, Lymond! A gentleman would never make such a suggestion."

"And when have I ever been accused of being a gentleman?" he observed, puffing on his cigar again.

"Never, but that reward is out of the question."

He shrugged. "All right. If I'm right, then you must extend my lease for another five years, price to be negotiated."

I hesitated. I could see Lymond at Bellerophon for years.

"Don't think Aunt Hen can do it?" he goaded.

"All right, Lymond. Done. Just don't come whining around when you lose your lease." I gave him what I hoped was a superior look. "In the meantime, do enjoy your stay in Egypt and I hope you're successful in doing all those very important things Uncle Harley has asked of you."

"I think I will be. I hope so, at any rate. Antiquities are devilish hard to track down, so I'm told." He stood up and looked at me. "I'm going to miss you, Roxanne. It's odd how one becomes accustomed to something. Rather like a briar in the foot—if it's there long enough, you get used to it." He touched my face with his fingertips, then tossed the remains of his cigar onto Holmwood's carefully tended grass. "You take care while I'm away, and if you need anything, you can reach me in Egypt either in care of Mohammed or at this address. This is the home of a friend of Debenham's. He's returned to London so I plan to stay there off and on. I probably won't be there, but you can leave a message for me." He pressed a small scrap of paper into my hand and turned to go.

"Take care of yourself, Lymond," I said, without thinking.

He turned a moment to look at me, and before I knew what he was doing, he caught me up and kissed me, right there in the garden. Worse, I found myself quite enjoying the process and proceeded to kiss him back. All too soon, he released me and looked at me a moment. "Goodbye, Roxanne," he said, turning and walking towards the front of the house. He didn't look back.

I stood there in shock for a moment until I heard a chuckle behind me. I wheeled around to see Holmwood leaning on his spade, clearly enjoying his role as voyeur. He was grinning from ear to ear. I should have given him a tongue-lashing right on the spot, but I was so confused that I did the only thing that seemed logical to me at the moment—I fled.

After my initial shock, I was angry with Lymond for taking such liberties. That, however, didn't deter me from going to the upstairs window so I could watch him leave. He rode his horse, The Bruce, and cut a fine figure. The carriage followed with his trunk and other baggage. I watched until the small procession went out of sight, then I turned back to sit down beside Bue with a sigh. Even though Lymond was maddening beyond endurance, when he wasn't at Bellerophon, the house seemed empty.

It took me a while to shake off the feeling of loneliness but I did, then I went to find Aunt Hen. She was all at sixes and sevens.

"Harley discovered that you had engaged Miss Rowe as a companion and he says there's no reason for us to delay our trip." She gave me a stricken look. "Roxanne, Harley wants to leave for Italy day after tomorrow," she gasped, holding on to a chair. I made her sit down and sent for tea and cakes. Aunt Hen always did better after restoratives.

"I'm sure you'll be ready then. I thought you were all packed and set to leave," I told her after she had drunk a cup of tea and had two pieces of fruitcake. "Didn't you tell me that all you had to do was put your things into a trunk?"

Aunt Hen nodded around bites. "Yes, but Roxanne, day after tomorrow! There's no possible way I could be ready. Just look!" She waved vaguely around the room. It was a mess. There were clothes and hats and turbans and feathers all over the place. If ever there was a project that called out for my attention, this was it. I flew into a frenzy of pressing, folding, and packing. By late that evening, everything was almost ready. Aunt Hen had also eaten all the fruitcake and drunk three pots of tea. I had made her sit and call out instructions to me which I largely ignored.

"There, Aunt Hen," I said, looking at the neatly packed trunks with satisfaction. "Everything's ready. You'll be able to take the coach to Plymouth and the ship for Italy from there." I turned and smiled at her. "I want you to have a wonderful time. You've wanted to visit Italy for years."

Aunt Hen was ready to cry. "And what about you, Roxanne? I can't bear the thoughts of you going off to that heathen land alone. It just isn't done. Why don't you take someone with you?"

"I'm taking Miss Rowe," I said.

She shook her head and got that stubborn expression on her face that I knew so well. I was beginning to question if Aunt Hen really wanted to go off to Italy and spend months there with Uncle Harley. "That won't do, Roxanne. You need a man to go along with you. You should have gone with dear Robert."

It was my turn to look shocked. "Aunt Hen! Whatever are you saying? What would society have made of that, I ask you?"

"I have it!" Aunt Hen jumped to her feet. "The very man to go along with you. He's experienced in dealing with all sorts of those heathens; he'll watch after your welfare in the same way I would. Furthermore, there will be no question of a breach of propriety."

"I am *not* going to take Uncle Harley along, Aunt Hen."

She looked at me, amazed. "Oh, dear me, no, Roxanne. I certainly didn't think Harley would be going with you. After all, if he did, then who would go with me? I was thinking of Woodbury."

"Woodbury!" I stared at her.

She nodded. "Yes, Woodbury has been in the Army, so he knows how to get things done. He would be excellent in arranging things for you. I've heard many of those men in Egypt refuse to talk to women, so that would be the very thing for you."

I sat down and looked at her. It hadn't occurred to me to take Woodbury along, but it certainly made sense. Once in a while, Aunt Hen comes up with a brilliant idea. I, too, had heard that many Egyptian men hesitate to make any kind of arrangements with a woman. It's something to do with their religion, I think.

"Aunt Hen, how perfect! If Woodbury will go, I'll be delighted to take him along."

"You *will?* It was her turn to be amazed. "I thought I would have a terrible time convincing you."

"No, a good idea merits consideration. After all, I do

plan to take Bue with me, so Woodbury would come in handy to take charge of him as well. Sometimes Bue can be a handful."

We wasted no time in sending for Woodbury and placing the proposal in front of him. I had expected some resistance, but to my surprise, he was delighted. In fact, he was so overcome that I thought he was going to cry right in front of us. "I was worried, Miss Sydney," he said. "I'm proud to be of service to you and my country."

"I don't think England will require any service, Woodbury," I told him, "but I'm sure your Army training will be of great help as we travel. I will, of course, take care of all expenses, and there will be extra funds available to you as well." It was time to mention Bue. Woodbury and Bue tolerated each other, but they were by no means the best of friends. "Woodbury, I plan to take Bue with me."

He paled. Before our conversation was over, he had convinced me to take along Jem, the stable boy, to watch after Bue. That was a total of five, one dog and four people: Bue, Flora, Woodbury, Jem, and me. If I didn't leave for Egypt soon, my entourage was going to number in the dozens.

The next morning I had chocolate in my room and worked on some letters dealing with Papa's estate, so I did not know until later that there was a letter waiting for me. When I finally got down to the small drawing room about noon, Uncle Harley and Aunt Hen were there waiting for me. "Send for her now," I heard Uncle Harley urging. "Now, dear," Aunt Hen was saying, "Roxanne needs her rest. After all, dear Robert's hasty leave-taking has been quite a shock to her." I immediately put on a smile and swept into the room. "Good morning," I said cheerily.

Uncle Harley glanced at the clock. "Morning by a minute or so." He picked up a dirty, tattered letter and handed it to me. "Why don't you open this now? It's addressed to you."

I took the letter gingerly in my fingers and knew immediately why Uncle Harley was so curious. The letter was from Mohammed in Cairo. It looked as if it had had a perilous time getting here, but the seal seemed to be intact. "How did this get here?" I asked. Woodbury had appeared behind me and, braving Uncle Harley's glare, reported that Jem had picked it up with the regular post some days ago but, unknown to the lad, the letter had been dropped on the way. It seemed that Bue had found it and had come wandering in with the letter in his mouth.

"That explains its condition, then," I said, placing the letter back on the salver Woodbury was holding.

Uncle Harley was having none of that. "Well, just don't stand there, girl," Uncle Harley growled. "Open the damned thing."

I thought for a moment about putting the letter in my pocket and opening it in the privacy of my room, but Uncle Harley looked as if he was going into apoplexy at any moment, so I was afraid to risk it. I broke the seal and read the letter, which wasn't easy to do. Mohammed's command of the English tongue was unique at best, but the letter had evidently gotten wet somewhere along the line before Bue, and the ink had smeared.

"Dammit, what is it? What does the damned thing say?" Uncle Harley bellowed.

"Now, dear, calm yourself," Aunt Hen said soothingly. "Would you like a nice pot of chamomile tea? A nap?"

"I just want to know what's in that damned letter," Uncle Harley said.

I handed him the letter. "It's merely a confirmation of my visit. I wrote him that I was coming and asked him to suggest some places to visit," I said. "Mohammed writes about the weather and the places it would be good to visit, but there doesn't seem to be anything else. He does inquire if I planned to pick up Papa's materials."

Uncle Harley took the letter over to the window and held it up. "No secret writing," he said in disgust. "It's just a letter." He spent several minutes looking at it then handed it back to me. "He tells you here that the weather might change and that you should hurry before it does. What does he mean by that?"

"I thought the sun always shone in Egypt," Aunt Hen said, "except when it rains. There are floods all over when it does that, I believe."

Uncle Harley pinned me with a look. "You're not going after the casket of papyri, are you? I wrote him I wanted it for my collection, but he said there was a previous inquiry from someone else. Was it you? Is that what he means by 'materials?' "

"Certainly not! I wrote Mohammed that I was coming to Egypt. He had collected some things for Papa a long time ago, but Papa never got to Egypt to get them. Mohammed had sent several things, but"—I paused and composed myself—"when Papa was killed, I neglected to notify Mohammed to stop collecting. As a result, he has several things he purchased especially for Papa. I felt I should get whatever he has and reimburse him. That's only the fair thing to do."

Uncle Harley relaxed. "Good." He eased himself down into a chair. "The man probably wants you to hurry so he can get his money quickly. Probably nothing."

I put the letter in my pocket and agreed. "Probably. I did send him some money for whatever he had purchased right after we discovered the treasure. I had no idea how much I owed him."

That would have settled Uncle Harley except Aunt Hen would not let it go. "But why would he worry about you getting to Egypt before the weather changed, Roxanne? I thought you weren't planning on any travel there except touring Cairo."

"My itinerary is flexible, Aunt Hen. I thought I'd wait until I get there. After all, after a trip of that length, one should see as much as possible." I rang for tea and fruit-cake, a sure way to distract Aunt Hen. "Don't you plan to do the same in Italy? Tell me, Aunt Hen, do you plan to go south of Rome? I have heard Naples is excessively hot."

"Could I borrow your letter for a few minutes?" Uncle Harley asked. "I'd like to take a look at it in the sun. Make sure I haven't missed anything."

With a sigh, I handed him the letter and he went out the door with it. He returned in half an hour or so, just the right length of time for him to do what we both knew he had done—make a copy. I was sure every word in the letter would be scrutinized for days. Perhaps he would even send the copy to Lymond in Egypt. Uncle Harley was notorious for seldom trusting anyone. He probably thought Mohammed and I were corresponding in code.

Aunt Hen and Uncle Harley set off the next day, somewhat later than they had planned. Uncle Harley, knowing full well how Aunt Hen's habits were, had told her they had to be in Plymouth a day before they actually had to be there. That way, he told me, they might actually get there on time. Aunt Hen was tearful. Now that the time had actually come for them to leave, she wavered. Only when Uncle Harley urged her to forget Italy and go straight to

Egypt did she become stubborn. Shortly, they were on the first leg of their journey to Rome.

As for myself, it took me longer than I expected to get off on my own journey. There were innumerable details. Flora proved invaluable during this time. I was surprised at her resourcefulness and diligence. She took care of dozens of minor details, leaving me free to make the final arrangements for passage, lodging, and so on. Every time I had mentioned that I intended to take my mastiff along, people paled. I finally began listing him as Beau Sydney and I paid full fare for him. I didn't see that anyone could object to that. However, the hotel in Cairo had demanded and got a rather large deposit in case of damages. I did make sure his collar was secure and well marked. Bue and I had been together for too many years for me to risk anything happening to him.

Finally, we were ready to leave. We were leaving from London, so my sister Cassie and her husband Owen came with us to the docks to bid us farewell.

"What in the world are you carrying?" Owen asked, looking at the box under my arm.

I explained about the book of sermons and was met with laughter. Actually Cassie chuckled while Owen guffawed. "The box may come in handy for souvenirs," he said. "I'm not too sure about the sermons."

"Oh, Roxanne, you'll be an aunt when you return," Cassie said to me, her eyes glowing. "I'll write to you."

I wavered, thinking I might stay until after her child was born, but then Owen put his arm around her shoulders. I wasn't really needed here at all. I put on a smile and bade them goodbye.

"Say hello to Lymond for me," Owen said.

"I doubt that I'll see him, Owen." I put my hand on Bue's

collar to quiet him. "I think Lymond was planning to tour the interior quite extensively while I was planning to stay close to Cairo. For all I know, the man may have even gone to Ethiopia by now."

Owen laughed. "I feel sure the two of you will run into each other. Say hello for me."

I started to give him an acerbic reply when I was almost accosted by a sailor. The man was unkempt and unwashed. He bumped right into me and I dropped the box containing the sermons. The man bent down and hastily picked it up. I thought for a moment that he was going to abscond with the book as he took a few steps away from me. Owen must have felt so as well, because he grabbed the man by the collar and turned him around. The sailor gave Owen a mean look and proffered the box back to me. "This's yours, miss," he said, odor emanating from him.

I stepped back a pace. "Yes, it is," I said stiffly. I noticed Owen had readied himself to take further care of the man if need be.

"Here 'tis." The man spat tobacco juice on the dock at my feet.

"Thank you." I took the box with my fingertips. The man just stood there. Owen reached into his pocket and handed him some money. The man nodded, thanked him, spat more tobacco juice, then pulled a greasy pouch from underneath his clothing and put the coins into it. With another nod and a glance at the box, he melted into the crowd.

"Evidently someone thinks you're carrying valuables in your box," Owen said.

I glanced down at the box of sermons. "They'd probably do him more good then they will me, although I doubt the man can read. He knocked the box from my hand, Owen, so why did you give him money?"

"You're going to have to learn, Roxanne," Owen said with a grin, "that everyone expects money. No matter how small the service or even if someone else has paid, everyone expects a reward. I believe in Egypt, they call it *baksheesh*."

Flora nodded. "Would you like me to see to that during our journey, Roxanne?"

I nodded at her. Flora was going to prove a priceless treasure. "You seem to be in good hands," Owen said to me with a smile. He turned to look at Flora. "I'm sorry I can't say the same for you, Miss Rowe. Try to keep an eye on Roxanne for us. We'd hate for anything to happen to her—we want our children to have the pleasure of an indulgent aunt."

I fought back a prickling behind my eyes, kissed both Owen and Cassie, and went on board. I had to come back to the docks to soothe Bue as Woodbury and Jem led him on board. Fortunately, I had remembered to bring a stock of Bue's favorite treat, heavily buttered bread. In just a trice, Bue was safely ensconced in my cabin and all seemed right with the world. Flora had the adjoining cabin. In what seemed like a very few minutes, we were off. I left Bue dozing and rushed to the deck. I could see Cassie and Owen waving to me and I waved back to them. Before long, they were dots on the shore, and then they disappeared from view. I was really on my way.

I returned to my cabin, somewhat depressed. I should have been excited—before me lay the travel I had always wanted, adventures in Egypt, sights to see, new things to learn—but I wasn't thrilled at all; instead I seemed to be getting a feeling of depression. I wandered around the cabin, picking up this and that, trying to shake the feeling until there was a discreet knock at the door.

Woodbury stepped in when I opened the door. "Mr. Lymond asked me to give this to you when you set sail," he said, handing me a letter. "I suppose that's now."

I thanked him and shut the door, then sat down on the edge of my bed and read the letter. Lymond was merely writing to wish me a safe trip and reminding me he would be in Cairo off and on and for me not to forget to call on him if need be. He repeated the address he had given me at Bellerophon. One thing in the letter disturbed me, however. Lymond tossed off a postscript asking me for a favor—if I didn't see him or hear from him, he asked that I send a message immediately to Debenham at the Home Office.

Curious, I thought to myself, refolding the letter and reaching for my reticule. That wasn't like Lymond at all. He usually went his own way, made up his own rules, and didn't care if anyone was ever notified about anything. Also, he was supposed to be on a trip for Uncle Harley and he didn't even mention that name or his search for the casket containing the papyri.

I'm not usually wrong—something was clearly afoot.

Four

To my complete surprise, Miss Rowe was an excellent sailor. Also to my complete surprise, I was not. I had not expected to have any difficulty, but we had been out no more than a short while when I began to get queasy. I was forced to take to my bed for most of the journey, a circumstance which greatly annoyed me. However, during the greater part of the voyage, I was too sick to care. Flora was magnificent. I couldn't have asked for a better nurse. I had to order her to take a turn around the deck twice a day just to get out of my cabin. Bue, too, was cooperative. He stayed with me most of the time, leaving me only when Woodbury took him out four times a day for his constitutionals. Only once did he cause any problem: while Woodbury and Flora were out on deck, my door opened quietly. I was in bed and turned my head when Bue growled. To my surprise, I recognized the sailor who had bumped into me on the dock as we left London. Before I could say anything, he sidled around the walls of the cabin, trying to avoid Bue, and came to my bedside. Just at the moment he put his hand on the box containing my book of sermons, I sat up in bed. At the same moment, Bue sprang, knocking the man right on top of me. For a few moments we were a screeching mass of sailor, me, and dog. I couldn't get Bue off of the screaming sailor, but the man's cries brought some crew members in to rescue him. The captain came in and demanded that I chain the dog, but I pointed out that the man had been creeping around my cabin uninvited. The captain said he had asked the sailor why he was in my room and the man had told him that he was worried about me and wanted to ask about my condition. When I mentioned the box, the sailor denied even seeing it. I would have laughed but my stomach was too sore, so I let it drop. However, I certainly didn't chain Bue.

My condition, as the sailor had put it, didn't improve at all. We were in some very stormy weather which exacerbated things. I went nowhere except from bed to chair. Worse, I kept reminding myself, unless I wanted to take a very risky overland route, I would have to endure the same thing on the return journey.

I had arranged to arrive in Alexandria because my father had been enchanted by the city and I wanted to see it as well. Queasy as I was, I went on deck to watch our entrance into the harbor, imagining the great lighthouse of Sostratus, its five hundred feet of white marble shining in the gleaming bay. It wasn't difficult to imagine myself in an ancient time, even on our journey through the city. There were unpaved streets and alleys filled with all sorts of people: women veiled in black from head to foot, men robed in white from the bottoms of their robes to the top of their turbans. Everywhere there were people, animals, and clutter on the streets. Everywhere were people, mostly children, with their hands out, evidently waiting for the baksheesh. I had been prepared for that. What I hadn't been prepared for were the dancing heat waves that made the buildings blur and for the incredible smells. It was a fetid, rotting odor and, to my eternal shame, I had to make the cart stop so I could dart into a cranny beside a building and cast up my accounts. I blamed it on my seasickness.

Flora insisted that we stay in the city for several days until I was well enough to travel to Cairo. On the map, it didn't look that distant, but it would be several days' journey. I took her advice and we spent a week in Alexandria before setting out for Cairo.

Everywhere on the trip to Cairo was water—the land was partially covered and there were pools and puddles everywhere else. Canals and irrigation ditches crisscrossed the land and everywhere I could see the Egyptians doing as they had probably done for thousands of years—dipping buckets attached to long poles into the water and irrigating their crops. It was a fertile country—at least, fertile where there was water.

The trip was more difficult than I had thought it would be, and by the time we got to Cairo, I was much thinner than I had been when we set out. I looked at myself in the mirror once we were settled in our hotel. I had wondered all my life what I would look like if I were thin and spare. Now I was and the effect wasn't what I had thought it would be. Instead of being elegant and slender, I looked gaunt. Even my blond hair, usually thick and shiny, had betrayed me. My hair was lackluster, my eyes hollow, my skin sallow, and my clothing hung from my shoulders. With bandages, I could have passed credibly for a recent mummy.

Flora looked at me in sympathy. "Do you wish me to alter some of your clothing?"

"No," I said with a sigh. "Perhaps this may be for the best after all. As loose as my garments are, I should be cool enough." I looked at her. The comparison was not flattering at all. The voyage—and the break from her overbearing brother—had altered her subtly. Her eyes, usually a nondescript blue, were glowing and her skin had acquired a touch of bronze during the voyage despite her best efforts. It was extremely fetching. Her hair, blond and usually pulled back into a severe knot at the back of her head, was slipping here and there into becoming ringlets around her face. They were small changes, but they had made Flora into a different person. She looked—there was no other word for it—almost beautiful.

I looked back into the mirror at my own image. I, on the other hand . . . In disgust, I turned away. "As soon as I'm feeling more the thing," I said to Flora, "I want to go visit the pyramids. We need to plan a campaign for our sightseeing." I sat down in the nearest chair, thoroughly weak. At the rate I was going, we'd be spending our entire stay in the hotel room. "Where's Bue?"

"Woodbury and Jem took him out. Woodbury thought both of them should go. He took him out alone this morning, and Bue was," there was a delicate pause, "somewhat unruly."

"I can imagine." I knew my dog well. He was lovable, but occasionally had a tendency to be willful, especially when he wished to explore. Cairo, I would think, would be a fascinating place for a curious animal.

We stayed inside the hotel for several days while I ate soup and got my strength back. While I chafed under the restraint, the time did give us the opportunity to make some plans for our travels. I also tried to read Livvy's book, but the results were the same as before. "The best thing about this book," I said to Flora in disgust as I closed the book for perhaps the hundredth time, "is the box. At least I can use that."

"It's a very handsome box," she agreed. "Did you ask one of the maids to take it down to clean it yesterday?"

I shook my head. "Certainly not. For one thing, it doesn't need cleaning. For another, I'd clean it myself if I had to. A little lemon oil is all that's necessary."

Flora frowned. "I stopped a maid at the door with your box in hand. She said she was going to clean it for you."

"Probably trying to be helpful." I shrugged. "It certainly isn't a valuable box. I've been keeping addresses in it." I pulled two slips of paper from the box. "I may drop a note to Lymond's address and tell him we're here. Not that I wish to see him, you understand." Flora nodded and I continued. "I also need to write Mohammed and tell him we're now in Cairo." I sat down to do both, but only managed to write Mohammed. I enclosed an invitation for him to come have supper with us as soon as possible. To my surprise, I received a prompt reply from him, delivered by some sort of street urchin. Mohammed wished to talk to me immediately, he wrote, but didn't wish to come to the hotel. Instead, he suggested, he would send someone to fetch me and we could meet, as he elegantly phrased it, at the house of his brother. I nodded to the urchin and, remembering Owen's dictum about payments, gave the child baksheesh. "Tell Mohammed that I'll be delighted to meet him and I'll be downstairs by the front door at four o'clock tomorrow afternoon."

I had not expected servility, but I did expect good manners; however, the urchin merely looked at me, bit into my coins to see if they were real, and shrugged. He started towards the door just as Jem and Woodbury came in with Bue. Rather, Bue came in dragging them behind him. The sights and smells of the street had brought out the unruliness in him again.

The urchin took one look at Bue, made a horrified sound, tossed my coins back at me, and ran out the door, his bare feet pounding on the floor. "Whatever brought that on?" I asked, picking up the coins. "I only hope he remembers to deliver my message."

Woodbury didn't answer me—he collapsed into a chair and reached for something to drink. Woodbury and the heat weren't getting along. To tell the truth, it was bothering me as well, but I refused to give in. I hadn't had a choice about giving in to seasickness, but this time was different. I could contend with the heat and I resolved to get the better of it.

I asked Woodbury if Bue had been unruly. He merely looked at me and moaned, making a vague gesture with his hand towards Bue, who was now lying comfortably on the floor, looking up and me and grinning. Most dogs do not grin, but Bue has a very fetching grin when he chooses to use it. I knew that look well, so I handed Woodbury a glass and a bottle of whiskey. Woodbury, ever conscious of what he considered the proper thing, gratefully accepted them and tottered off towards his own quarters.

The next day, I dressed as coolly as possible and went downstairs. Woodbury and Jem insisted on accompanying me, so I left Flora with Bucephalus and instructions not to open the door. It was strange, but in Egypt, the usual proprieties didn't seem to apply. I felt as if I could go anywhere I wished and do anything I wanted—almost, at any rate. Among strangers, the social conventions could be relaxed.

Woodbury, Jem, and I waited for almost an hour. The day was getting late, and I had just suggested that we go back upstairs when a young man appeared out of nowhere. He handed me a note of identification from Mohammed and, in almost perfect English, asked that I accompany him. He was surprised that Woodbury and Jem were planning to accompany me, and told me it wasn't necessary—he would guard me with his life, if necessary. However, Woodbury was having none of that. Actually, I was quite glad Woodbury was so protective—even if the usual proprieties didn't apply, I certainly didn't want to be walking the streets of Cairo in the evening with a total stranger. After one of those peculiar staring matches men have between themselves when they take each other's measure, Woodbury seemed to approve of the stranger. The young man, who told me he had been in England for several years and had attended school there, motioned us towards the door and we set off. The young man asked us to please call him Henry. All his English friends called him Henry, he explained, as his Egyptian name seemed to be difficult for Englishmen—and English ladies he said, with a nod at me—to pronounce.

It was my first time in the streets since our arrival and I could understand Bue's excitement. Every inch of the town seemed to be alive with people or animals. There were people selling things, people buying things, people going from one place to another, and animals almost everywhere. The sight was almost as overwhelming as the noise. Everyone seemed to be talking. Even more noticeable was the smell. It was a mix of dust and heat, animals, food cooking, and unwashed bodies. I had never smelled anything quite like it.

Henry was a marvel. He threaded along streets that twisted and turned in a dozen directions. I hoped sincerely that he was going to guide us back to the hotel because I lost all idea of direction. The further we went, the quieter the surroundings became. Finally, we came to a nondescript house on a small street. Everything was quiet and the house appeared uninhabited. There was no sign of life at all from the street. Henry knocked discreetly and the front door swung open. We walked inside and into a different world.

If the house belonged to Mohammed's brother or, as I

suspected, to Mohammed himself, he had done very well indeed. We walked through a small room and into a court-yard that was a small gem. In the corner of it was a small fountain and some carefully tended plants. There was also a small pool with lotus blossoms floating on the water. I thought we would stop there, but we went on into a cool, dim room. It took my eyes a few moments to adjust to the darkness and I realized that there were several people in the room. I seemed to be the only woman. I felt a strange sensation in my stomach and it took me a moment to iden-tify it as I hadn't felt it in years. It was intimidation.

There were four men there. One was a vigorous, mid-dle-aged man, dressed rather richly. He was sitting at the center. Two other men flanked him. Off to one side, there was an older man who was dressed in one of those striped, loose garments most of the Egyptians seemed to favor. He was wearing a headdress and appeared to be small, al-though not at all frail. I looked at the man at the center of the group and forced myself to shake off the strange feeling of inferiority. I squared my shoulders and stepped briskly forward. "Mohammed, I believe," I said, stopping in front of the man. "It's good to see you at last. I feel we know each other from our correspondence."

The man nodded and said something in Egyptian to Henry. In a split second, Henry was at my side, showing me a seat. "Mohammed said he is delighted to see you, the daughter of his old friend, George Sydney," Henry translated, sitting on the floor beside me. "He said you resemble your esteemed father very much." Woodbury and Jem were motioned to the fringes of the group, but stub-bornly came to stand right behind me. Jem moved to stand slightly to one side. Actually, it was rather comforting to me to know they were there.

Mohammed said something else and Henry translated. "Mohammed wishes to know if you had a safe journey. He understands you were ill and wants to know if . . ." Henry paused delicately and began again. "He wondered what your illness might have been."

I smiled. "A touch of seasickness only." Henry translated and Mohammed nodded. "Why does he ask?" I asked Henry. "At any rate, I thought Mohammed could speak English. My father didn't mention that he couldn't. And what about all those letters? Did Mohammed need to have someone write them for him? I've thought for years that he wrote his own letters."

Henry translated, only a few words. "Mohammed asks about your illness because he was worried when he heard of it. He thought you might have eaten something that caused it."

I shook my head and looked at Mohammed thoughtfully. I felt a nudge in my back from Woodbury standing behind me. Evidently he was having some of the same thoughts as I. "Henry," I said slowly and distinctly, "tell Mohammed that my father was delighted with the eagles he took from Cairo. They have been a source of much delight. I'm sure Mohammed knew they were not valuable, but my father prized them greatly."

There was a murmur of approval from Woodbury as Henry translated. Mohammed answered and Henry smiled at me. "He is happy that your father was very pleased with his acquisition. The eagles were a special gift."

I stood up. "Come on, Woodbury," I said with a bravado I certainly didn't feel. I kept a wary eye on the two men flanking Mohammed. They might have knives on their persons for all I knew. "Henry, tell Mohammed that my father never purchased any eagles. He bought two cat statuettes

which have proven very valuable indeed. I wrote Mohammed and told him as much."

The older man in the corner stood up. "It is good to
know my friend George lives yet in his daughter," he said
with a smile. He came towards me, surprisingly quick on
his feet to be older. "I apologize for testing you, but one
must be wary in the world today. I deal in many valuable
antiquities, and there are those who would like access to
my house for base reasons. I can never be too careful." He
bowed his head slightly at me. "I am your father's friend,
Miss Sydney." He cast a quick glance at Henry who nodded.

"That is the correct form of address," Henry murmured.

I concentrated on the older man before me. "My apologies as well," I said to him, "I should have been able to
recognize you. However, under the circumstances, I feel I
too must require some sort of identification from you."

He smiled. "Of course. I expected as much." He reached
down to a small side table and handed me a packet of papers. One was a letter from Papa, two others were letters
from me, and the last was a letter from Lymond. I hesitated
a moment, opened the letter from Papa and glanced at it,
then looked at the letter from Lymond. To my surprise, it
was addressed to me and I read it slowly. Lymond had
written that he was going up the Nile and probably wouldn't
be in Cairo when I was, but Mohammed would be glad to
take care of whatever I needed. Lymond also asked me to
send a message to Uncle Harley that all was going well.
Then he finished his letter with a suggestion that I return
to England as soon as possible. It seemed, Lymond wrote,
that Egypt was not a particularly safe place to visit and he
would feel much better if I were back home in Brighton. I

read it again, felt myself get angry all over again, then looked at Mohammed. "May I keep this letter?"

"Certainly. It is yours; I have not read it." He made a small gesture with his fingers, so small that I only saw it by chance. In a second, Henry was at my side. "Will you sit with us and eat? I, being familiar with English customs, have made the arrangements myself." He spoke with more than a bit of pride. Woodbury jabbed me in the side with his finger and I jumped as Henry looked at me strangely. "Of course," I said politely. "We'd be delighted."

Henry led us to a small room that had been appointed with a table and chairs. A chair was quickly brought for Woodbury and we—Woodbury, Mohammed, Henry, and I—all sat down. Jem took a seat directly behind me. I felt as if I were living a scene from the *Arabian Nights*. From nowhere a figure dressed completely in black appeared carrying bowls of steaming food. I judged it was a woman, but I really didn't know. The only feature visible was the eyes. She silently placed the food on the table before us. Woodbury took a look at his and jabbed me in the side with his finger again, apparently worried we were about to be poisoned. I glared at him— after all, we were guests. I picked up my spoon and sipped delicately at the thick mixture in the bowl. Woodbury stirred his vigorously. Henry and Mohammed ate heartily, spooning down the spicy mixture with gusto. All the while, they chatted about inconsequential things such as the weather, the appearance of the moon, and so on. I ate only a few bites.

"Is your food not good?" Henry asked me.

"It's excellent," I replied, tasting another spoonful. "However, since my illness on the boat, I've had to be careful when I eat."

Henry and Mohammed nodded as they finished their bowls. The veiled figure appeared again from nowhere and brought a platter of flat bread and some kind of meat and vegetables on a platter. It smelled quite good. For the first time since I left England, I wished to eat, but another jab from Woodbury ended that. I nibbled on a small portion, and enjoyed some fruit that was brought. A rather thick, sweet tea finished our meal. Mohammed looked curiously at me and it took me a while to realize that this was probably the first meal he had eaten with a woman seated at a table in his life. It was quite a courtesy he extended to me.

After the meal, Mohammed leaned across the table towards me. "I would have given my life for George Sydney," he said, looking right into my eyes. "He was a true friend. I feel the same way about his daughter." He paused. "You must go home," he said softly.

I was incredulous. "Home?" I said blankly before I could stop myself. "Certainly not. After all, I've planned this trip for months and we've exchanged a great deal of correspondence about it." I paused and looked at him shrewdly. "Has Lymond put you up to this?"

There was only the faintest flicker in his eyes, but it was enough to tell me that my guess had hit home. "Mr. Lymond?" he asked innocently. "I have met the man only twice, although I must confess that I was greatly impressed. Mr. Lymond is a shrewd man."

Shrewd was hardly the word I would use to describe Lymond. Right now the leading candidates were *sly, cunning, and subversive.* "Just why is Lymond here, Mohammed?" I asked. "He isn't in Egypt to enjoy the weather."

Mohammed laughed and shook his head. "He is, I believe, enjoying a trip along the river and searching for a valuable antiquity. There has been much talk of this casket of papyri, and I have sent him to a village where it was last seen. I believe he said he was searching for the casket on behalf of his uncle." Mohammed dismissed Lymond with a wave of his hand. "But you, Miss Sydney—"

"I am not returning home. I wrote you that I wished to come to Egypt to speak to my father's old friends and perhaps retrace some of his travels. I intend to do so."

Mohammed sighed. "Mr. Lymond told me you were a woman of strong opinions, much like your father." He looked at me and smiled. "Have you made the acquaintance of anyone while you've been here?"

"No. As you know, I was ill on the voyage here, so I've been in the hotel recovering for several days. I hope to be out and about by tomorrow."

Mohammed beckoned to Henry, just a small movement, but Henry was standing beside us in an instant. "May I offer the services of my nephew? He would be more than glad to show you around the city and the country. After all, your father is the one who arranged for Henry to travel to England for his education—"

I looked at Henry in surprise. "That's strange. Papa usually kept me apprised of his affairs and I never recall him mentioning Henry. Papa was the kind of man who would have invited Henry to Bellerophon for holidays."

"He did," Henry replied, looking right at me, "but I preferred not to intrude. I had my studies and was learning about the political system. That was all I wished." He smiled broadly at me. "My English is fair, as you know, and I would be delighted to show you around."

"An honest guide might be a good thing," Woodbury murmured in my ear. "Lots of scoundrels about here."

I hesitated, then put aside my reservations as churlish. After all, my father had vouched for Mohammed on more than one occasion. Then too, if my few days here had brought home one point, it was that Egyptian was not a language I was going to learn easily. Henry's English would be a Godsend. I smiled back at him. "Thank you so much. Since none of us know anything about the city, we'd be delighted to have a guide. I hope we won't be taking you away from your work."

Henry relaxed noticeably and gave a slight bow. "I am yours until you leave," he said solemnly.

Mohammed told me he had stored the artifacts he had collected for Papa and we made arrangements to have them shipped to London. Then, shrewd businessman that he was, he mentioned that he was on the track of artifacts that he knew Papa would have wanted. I told him I really wasn't interested in artifacts; I preferred to tour the country and absorb the culture. All I really wanted from Mohammed were some stories about my father. Then I added, "Perhaps, you might approach Mr. Lymond with the artifacts. I'm sure his uncle would want to have them." Mohammed nodded. I suspected the wily old man had already made his pitch to Lymond and was seeing if I might be interested as a way to get some competitive bidding going. Papa had told me of such things.

That settled, we said our goodbyes to Mohammed and left, promising to meet again very soon. As we were leaving, I caught a glimpse of a figure veiled in black watching us from behind a doorway. It vanished as quickly as I glimpsed it as though the person didn't wish to be seen at all. I decided I would quiz Henry about the figure and the way of life for women here as soon as it was convenient.

The attack on us occurred not too far from our hotel, just as we were rounding a corner. Suddenly there were two brigands on Henry. One seemed to be older and the leader, as he was shouting the commands to the other. They quickly knocked Henry down and I saw the flash of a knife as Henry rolled and twisted, trying to elude them. The older one shoved him aside and turned to grab me, but Woodbury rushed in between us. Evidently our attackers hadn't counted on Woodbury and Jem being as stalwart as they proved to be. Woodbury looked rather old and worn, but he was still an Army man to the core. He set upon one of the ruffians and yelled for Jem. Just as the second brigand was ready to hit Woodbury from behind, Jem jumped onto his back. At that point, I started hitting the man about the head with my reticule. With what sounded like a curse, he flung Jem from his back and turned to me, striking me full in the face. I staggered back, surprised, as Jem scrambled to his feet and attacked again. By this time, Henry was getting up and he joined in the fray as best he could. Blood was dripping from his fingers.

I looked around for something to use as a weapon, but saw nothing. I tried my reticule again, shouting all the while for Woodbury. From the corner of my eye, I saw a flash of white as someone else came around the corner of the building and walked into the fray. All I noticed was that there were two of them. The odds would be impossible for us with four attackers. I wheeled to try to stop the newcomers and flailed my reticule at one of them. He caught it easily in one hand and the strings broke. "What the . . . ?" he asked. My heart lifted as the sound of my native language.

"Help us!" I cried, turning back to use my fists to beat on the back of one assailant who was choking Woodbury. Rough hands seized my waist and I thought for a moment that I had been wrong, but then realized that the man had merely shoved me aside so he could pull the man from Woodbury. The attacker turned to fight, looked at the man, and yelled something in a language I did not understand.

The other attacker leaped up from where he had been pummeling Henry and Jem and both ruffians ran. In a second, they had disappeared and the street ahead looked as tranquil as any dusty street in early dusk.

Dazed, I slid down along the wall until I was sitting on the street, propped against the building. My illness had evidently left me weaker than I thought. One of the gentlemen who assisted us came over to me and squatted down to eye level. "Are you all right?" he asked, touching my face. "That's going to be a nasty bruise."

I felt my face but it was numb. "I'm fine." I looked past his shoulder. "Woodbury?" There was no answer. Woodbury lay sprawled on the street, face down. "Woodbury!" I tried to rise.

The gentleman put a hand on my shoulder. "I'll see to him. You stay here." I sat there while our two saviors attended to Henry, Jem, and Woodbury. "He's all right," the gentleman said, running his hands along Woodbury's limbs. "He'll be stiff and sore for a few days, but I don't think there's any real damage." He returned to me. "What about you?"

"I'm fine." I tried to stand but just didn't have the strength in my legs. "Just give me a moment." I heard Woodbury stir and call my name. "I'm here, Woodbury," I called out. "Everything's all right."

"Miss Sydney?" the man said. Evidently it was time for introductions.

"Yes, Miss Roxanne Sydney of Brighton," I said as coolly as possible under the circumstances. For some reason, my heart was pounding in my chest. "And you, sir? I would like to attach a name to my sincerest thanks."

He chuckled. "No thanks needed. If ever I saw a damsel in distress, it was you." He glanced back at the other man, obviously a relative as there was a strong resemblance. "I'm Orlando Nash and this is my younger brother, Edward."

"Nash?" I mentally raced through the names in my mind. I had heard that name somewhere before. "Lord Brydges?"

"You have me," he said with a laugh.

Edward glanced at him. "Orlando fancies himself a democrat, Miss Sydney. He tries—unsuccessfully, I might add—to leave his style at home, but it seems to follow him everywhere." Edward grinned at his brother. Obviously they were quite fond of each other.

"As well it should," I replied. "I want to thank both of you sincerely. If you hadn't come along, who knows what might have happened?" Involuntarily I shuddered.

Brydges smiled at me as he helped Woodbury stand. Woodbury was somewhat worse for the wear and wobbled a bit. Brydges sat him down beside me. "I'm delighted to assist, as is Edward. After all," he said, as he smiled again, "how often do we have the opportunity to rescue beautiful English ladies here?" Although I knew his comment was pure fustian—I had looked in the mirror before I left the hotel—I still blushed and found myself smiling back at him. I probably would have made some simpering comment back to him but was saved from the embarrassment by Edward calling him over to look at Henry.

"Is he hurt badly?" I asked in alarm as the two men bent over Henry.

"I'm not sure," Brydges said, not turning around to me. I thought I saw the flash of a knife, although I wasn't sure, and I leaped to my feet. I was by Henry's side in a second and saw a knife in Edward's hand. "What's that for?" I asked in alarm. It occurred to me that I really didn't know anything about the two Englishmen. They could be scoundrels posing as the perfectly respectable Brydges brothers for all I knew. Mohammed had been right—one must be wary in the world today.

Edward looked up at me blandly. "I was just cutting this from his neck because it was twisted and knotted. I thought it might be choking him." He handed me a small leather pouch on a leather string. "Would you like to keep it for him?"

Embarrassed, I took the pouch and sat down on the street. Between my illness and my exertions, my legs didn't want to hold me upright. "We'll have to take Henry back to the hotel," I told them. "I have no idea how to get him back to his home. For that matter," I added, "I have no idea where his home might be."

"We could take him with us," Brydges said to his brother. He turned to me with a smile. "I'm not sure there'll be room in the hotel to get a room for him on short notice."

"He would probably be uncomfortable there at any rate," Edward said.

Again my suspicions were aroused. "I don't think he should . . ." I began, then realized I didn't know what to say next. "He can stay in my room until I can reach his family," I said. "I'll stay with my companion."

"It will be no trouble for us," Brydges said, helping Henry to his feet. Henry looked at me, dazed, blood running down the side of his head, but began taking a few steps. After a moment or two, he seemed to be more sure of himself. "I think it would be much the best thing for you to stay with us, Henry," Edward continued. "I'm sure Robert won't mind at all. He's going back in a day or two anyway."

"Robert? You have another brother?" I asked as Woodbury fell into step beside me, Brydges on the other side. Jem followed us.

Edward laughed and put his arm around Henry to steady him. "No, Robert's a friend of ours. He's been here doing some work for . . . doing some work that's been taking him out of the city. However, he's been using a friend's house as a base while he was here. We've been at camp in the valley, and needed to come into Cairo. Rather than stay in a hotel, Robert invited us to stay with him while we're here. It won't be long; we're getting some supplies for our excavation."

"Your excavation?" I seemed to be able to speak only in fragments.

"Yes," Brydges said enthusiastically. "We're doing some digging up in the valley to find some treasures in the tombs and temples. I really think we're on to something. I told Elgin—"

His brother interrupted him. "Elgin would sell his soul for what we think we're going to discover. It'll put those marbles of his in the shade."

"Hardly," Brydges said, evidently forgetting the rest of us. "Those marbles are magnificent! There's nothing like them. However, our discoveries will probably open all of Egypt up." He turned back to me. "I thought we had enough supplies, but we ran out. I've already purchased enough to see us through and had them shipped ahead. Edward and I decided to stay over another day or two since we've been at the camp for several weeks. That was where we first met Robert."

"But in the meantime," Edward continued as our hotel came into view and I breathed a sigh of relief, "while we're here in the city, please allow us to show you around Cairo. It's a fascinating city. Even Robert agrees that it's interesting, and he's not easily impressed."

We were back to Robert again as we walked into the

hotel. I had a question about this. Just how many Roberts could there be in Cairo? Still, I didn't wish to pry openly. "Has your friend Robert been here long?" I asked.

Brydges shook his head. "No, just a short while. He's one of those people who seem to assimilate and become familiar with everyone and everything almost immediately."

Edward nodded as he helped Henry sit and called for a cloth. "I suppose that's why he's so interesting. He's been traveling about looking for—"

With a warning nudge, Brydges cut him off. "Still, as an Englishman, he was easy for us to recognize. There aren't too many of us here." He laughed.

Now I knew something was afoot. Brydges' obvious attempt to cut short his brother's comment was like a flag. "Perhaps I've met the gentleman. What did you say his name was?"

Brydges looked at me, puzzled, obviously thinking he had already given me this information. "Lymond," he said, "Robert Lymond."

I caught my breath, my suspicions confirmed. Woodbury evidently had no such inkling. "Mr. Lymond!" he said with joy. "He's here in this heathen city?"

Brydges looked at us with interest. "Do you know Robert?"

Woodbury answered before I had the opportunity. "Quite well, my lord. He's almost a part of our family."

"We knew he was in Egypt and I have his address here, of course," I said, "but I thought he was traveling up the Nile somewhere, looking for valuables."

"Well, he was," Brydges said cheerfully, "but he had to return for a few days. Something about 'a fly in the ointment,' he said. I have no idea what he was talking about and didn't ask."

I didn't have to ask. I knew exactly what—or who—Lymond's fly in the ointment was. It was I. That was the reason for the letter in my reticule suggesting I go back home; that was the reason for Mohammed suggesting the same thing.

The only factor I couldn't explain was the attack. Lymond might do many things, but he would never stoop to harming another person. There was no way I could see him as the instigator of the attack on us.

I turned to Brydges as he took his leave of us. "I would like very much to see Lymond again, if that were possible. Would you and your brother like to have supper with us and bring Mr. Lymond with you?" I smiled what I hoped was a cordial smile. "After all, we do owe you a debt of gratitude and need to begin paying it."

Brydges and his brother promised to eat with us the next evening and bring Lymond if he were free. In the meantime, they asked if they might arrange a short excursion for us to view the pyramids. As that was the first thing on my list of things to see, I gratefully said yes. With that, they left.

I turned to make sure Henry had been attended to and was relieved to see that he was up and about, the wound to his head superficial. There had been more bleeding than wound and I deemed he would be fine by morning. He was feeling much better and told us that he preferred to return to his own lodgings. I tried to dissuade him, but he did seem to be feeling much better. I have learned that it is no use to try to persuade a man once his mind is made up, so I told Henry to take care, and he went on his way.

As soon as Henry left, I went up to our suite, still fuming about Lymond. By the time I reached the door, my anger knew no bounds. I flung the door open and stalked inside. "Flora, you'll never believe what happened!" I shouted, tossing my ruined reticule aside without even looking for her. "Lymond's here in Cairo and has the nerve to send me a message urging me to go home! He must be on the track of something Uncle Harley wants very much. I wouldn't be surprised if he had staged the attack on us! The nerve of the man. I'd love to get my hands on him!"

There was a chuckle to my left. I whirled around to face Lymond standing there, a drink in his hand. "Hell hath no fury," he said with a laugh, holding both hands out. "And you'd like to get your hands on me. Ah, how I've longed to hear you say those words, Roxanne. Here I am—just put your hands anywhere you wish."

I threw my book of sermons at him.

Five

It took the better part of fifteen minutes for me to calm myself. I thought about apologizing to Lymond for throwing my book at him, but decided he deserved it. If anything deserved the apology, it was the book. On second thought, it didn't either. The thing was execrable.

Lymond poured both of us a small brandy while I picked up my book and tried to stuff it into its box. Unfortunately, the box now had so many scraps of paper in it that the book wouldn't fit so I put it on the top instead. Lymond watched me with an amused smile, then handed me my brandy and insisted I drink it immediately. It did have a calming effect. Lymond moved his chair closer to mine and sat beside me. "Just what were you saying about an attack, Roxanne?" he asked.

I told him about the attack on our party by the two ruffians, watching his face all the while for signs of complicity. To my surprise, he seemed worried. "Would you recognize the men who attacked you if you saw them again?" he asked.

"Of course not, Lymond," I said, draining my brandy and putting the glass on the table. Lymond refilled it. "All I remember is that they appeared to be natives. There was a great deal of rolling and tumbling on the ground with those loose garments flying everywhere. Henry might be able to identify them." I paused. "Or your friend, Brydges. He and his brother came to our rescue."

This did seem to surprise him. "Oh, you've met Brydges. I knew he was wandering around the city and I'm glad he came to your rescue." He sipped his brandy and got out a cigar, devoting his attention to making sure the end was just right. I was more than ever convinced that something was afoot. Lymond just didn't act this way unless he was trying to obscure something.

"Yes. He came by at a most opportune moment. I think the ruffians might have overcome us if he and his brother hadn't fended them off." There was a pause. "Brydges tells me that he's staying at your lodgings for a few days."

Lymond nodded. "I'm staying at his camp in the valley off and on, so I felt the only thing I could do was offer him my rooms when he came to Cairo. He was determined to live like an Egyptian and had nothing but the meanest of hovels on the outskirts of the city. Every time they left home, thieves cleaned them out." Lymond chuckled. "Brydges and his brother are quite involved in discovering antiquities, although they seem to be more involved in financing the expedition than really doing any searching themselves. They've hired a professional for that. Of course, they've also hired a professional to see to the day to day workings of the camp."

"Is that where you're based? At Brydges' excavations?"

Lymond looked at me and smiled affably. "As I said, I'm there off and on. You might call it my base since I've been using it as something of a home point while I'm tracking down that dratted casket and papyri Uncle Harley wants. I'm away from there more often than I'm present, but the last rumor Mohammed gave me put the casket and papyri at the village near the camp, so I expect I'll be there more often now. How is Uncle Harley, by the way?"

"Fine, as far as I know. Don't try to change the subject, Lymond. I want to know what you're up to."

He gave me his smile—the one calculated to melt feminine hearts everywhere. It had little effect on mine, although I own it was a wonderful, warm smile. "Up to? Good Heavens, Roxanne, I thought you were the stickler for grammar." He smiled but I said nothing. He went back to his cigar for a moment but I still said nothing. Finally he stood and began pacing the floor in front of me—a sure sign that something was afoot. "Roxanne, will you stop this nonsense! You know why I'm here. Uncle Harley wants me to track down that blasted papyri for him. Not just any papyri, mind you, but the papyri in a metal casket. The papyri dealing with tribute to Rameses. Do you have any idea how difficult that is? I've heard a thousand rumors and investigated half of them. This whole town abounds in rumor."

"So you're only working for Uncle Harley?"

He shrugged. "I'm doing this more as a favor to him than anything else. This is a damned uncomfortable country. If it isn't heat, it's insects or filth. I'd much rather be at Bellerophon going for a ride with you." He smiled again, looked at me carefully, and frowned. "The country doesn't seem to be agreeing with you at all, Roxanne."

I sighed and touched my hair. I knew full well how I looked without any hints from Lymond. "I have discovered," I said woodenly, "that I am not a sailor." To my chagrin, Lymond laughed aloud and touched my shoulder. "At last—something you're unable to control. Tell me, was it that bad?"

I glanced down at my loose dress and sallow skin. "It was worse than bad, Lymond."

He sat down beside me and put his fingers on my hand. "Poor Roxie," he began, but stopped and moved back as a door shut behind us.

"Oh, I'm sorry," Flora said, putting her hand to her mouth.

"You're just in good time, Flora," I told her, standing and moving to a chair. Lymond occasionally had a strange effect on me and I felt the need for space and air. "Do come join us."

Flora came and we sent for tea. In just a moment, I was myself again, but I was unable to get any further information from Lymond. He did charm Flora thoroughly and exerted his usual effect on Woodbury and Jem. Since Jem had known Lymond, he practically worshipped the man and, for his part, Lymond was more than kind to the boy. Jem smiled for joy when he saw Lymond and even forgot himself to the point of clasping Lymond's hand and shaking it vigorously. Jem had a bruised face from our altercation and Lymond tweaked him about it. He did mention to Jem that he wanted to speak to him later and I knew that he would extract every scrap of information the boy possessed. What Lymond didn't know was that Jem didn't know any more than I did.

For his part, Woodbury almost fell at his feet in relief when he saw Lymond. Woodbury's assessment of Egypt was much the same as Lymond's. "Indeed, this is not a place for Englishmen," he told Lymond, nodding sagely. "We're bred for the green countryside and God's own rainfall."

Lymond agreed and I refrained from mentioning that God also watched over the Egyptian weather. Woodbury's feelings are easily hurt.

The next day, there were messages from both Lymond

and Brydges. Lymond's, which I opened first, merely said he would be over around eleven and would like to discuss some things. Brydges' was much more congenial, asking after my health and well being, then asking if I felt up to touring some of the city during the late afternoon when things were cooler. After checking with Flora, I penned a note to Brydges accepting his kind offer. By that time, it was almost eleven.

By half past noon I had decided Lymond wasn't coming and, frankly, I was glad. I went to my room and stripped off my gown, then stood there dribbling tepid water on myself trying to cool off. I had never been so hot in my life. The water was only a temporary reprieve and I collapsed on the bed in my shuttered room wearing nothing but my thinnest shift. The heat was suffocating. Perhaps, I thought to myself, Lymond had roasted on his way over. The thought was not unwelcome.

Flora had opted for a nap during the hot part of the day. The heat didn't seem to bother her as much as it did me, another cause for annoyance. Although I had never traveled, I had always imagined myself a good traveler. Papa was always telling me about the pleasures of travel in Greece, Turkey, and Egypt. I don't think he ever mentioned the heat.

I put down my fan and checked the glass of lemonade by my bedside. It was empty. I stood and pulled my sticky, wet shift away from my body and went into the other room where I had left the pitcher of lemonade. As I was standing there in my damp shift, I heard the door open behind me. I whirled around to face Lymond, one hand holding my glass and the other spread ineffectually over my bosom to cover myself. "How did you get in here?" I gasped, backing toward my bedroom door.

Lymond looked at me strangely, licked his lips, and turned casually away. He held up a key as he picked up the lemonade pitcher. "The hotel thinks I'm one of your party," he said, pocketing the key and pouring himself a glass of the sweet lemonade. His back was to me and, after a moment, I decided the only thing for me to do was go get a dressing gown. In a few moments, more suitably attired, although hotter, I came back in and sat down across from Lymond.

"I'll inform the manager that the only ones in our group are Woodbury, Jem, Miss Rowe, and me." My voice was the coldest thing in the room.

Rather than be embarrassed, Lymond grinned at me. "Don't forget the dog. Bue always has considered himself a Sydney."

"As he is."

I waited for some sort of explanation, but there was none. Lymond merely sat there sipping his lemonade, regarding me over the rim of his glass. "Egypt just doesn't agree with you, Roxanne," he said, putting the glass down on the table. "You don't seem to be recovering from your seasickness."

"I'm well aware how I look, Lymond. I assure you that Egypt agrees with me as well as England does." This certainly wasn't true, but I wasn't about to admit to Lymond that I longed for the cool greenness and the salt tang of the air at home.

Lymond had the grace to look abashed. "I didn't mean your appearance, Roxanne." He flashed his smile at me. "As far as I'm concerned, nothing could have looked better than you did when I came in. You should wear that more often."

"Lymond! You forget yourself."

"I wish I could," he said, as he turned away from me.

"Roxanne, is there any possibility that you would return to England if I asked you to?"

"None whatsoever, Lymond."

He sighed and turned back to me. "I was afraid of that. Roxanne . . ." He ran his fingers through his hair while he searched for words. "Roxanne, this is not a good place for you to be."

"I thought we covered that already, Lymond." I looked at him steadily as I felt sweat trickle down my back and wished I could pack my bags and go back home. "I have no intention of leaving Egypt. I came here to see the sights and look at some of the things my father told me about. I'm quite looking forward to it." I had to restrain the urge to fan myself.

Lymond sat down across from me, so close that our knees were almost touching. "Roxanne, I think you should go home. After all, this weather clearly doesn't agree with you. You could even go to Greece. I think your father was much more interested in Greece than Egypt."

I stared at him. "Why are you trying to get rid of me, Lymond? Is Uncle Harley afraid that I'm going to spend all my time buying up antiquities? If that's the case, I assure you that you can rest comfortably at night. I have all the antiquities I want or need. More than I need." This was true—Papa had left enough artifacts to stock an entire wing of a museum. It would take years to go through them.

"It isn't that, Roxanne." He hesitated again. "You were attacked yesterday. This place isn't safe for you—for a woman. It could very well happen again and Brydges or someone else won't be around to rescue you."

I was almost convinced as I looked at him and remembered my fear of the day before. Then Lymond ruined it and brought back all my suspicions. He smiled that melting smile at me. "I would be devastated if anything happened to you."

"Stop trying your tricks on me, Lymond," I said, on guard again. I recognized that persuasive tone he used when he wanted something. "I intend to stay. And I plan to be careful. Your friend Brydges has offered to show me around the city and I have every intention of being the tourist. However, you are right on one point—I realize that the ordinary rules of law and order do not apply here."

"An understatement," Lymond said.

I ignored him. "From this moment on, you may style me 'Careful Roxanne.' "

"Good God, what an oxymoron!" He jumped to his feet. "Roxanne, do you have any idea what's out there? People have disappeared here and never been heard from again. People have been murdered in their beds."

"I realize that, Lymond. That's why I've purchased pistols for my butler and me."

Lymond sat back down and put his head in his hands. "That's even worse. You're likely to blow your own foot off." He looked up at me for a moment, then bounded up again and began pacing the floor. "Christ, Roxanne, why can't you be reasonable? This is no place for you and you know it. Look at yourself—you're sick and worn out before you even begin to tour the country. Hell, it's time for you to go home and think about getting married like your sisters."

Cold fury swept over me as I sat there, trying to decide which of his ridiculous statements to answer first. They all jumbled together in my mind. I jumped to my feet to face him. "You're just like every other man in the universe, Lymond!" I screeched. "Adventures are for men while women are good for nothing except staying home and having children!" Before I thought, I picked up the lemonade pitcher and threw the remainder of the contents right in his face.

Lymond stood very still and I realized he was trying to control himself. "I'm leaving, Roxanne. I'll come back later and try to talk some sense into that head of yours. I don't think it's possible to do it, but I feel I owe it to you to try." With that, he walked out the door, closing it softly behind him. It was almost a very effective exit—I would have been most impressed, except the slice of lemon dangling from his hair over his ear detracted from the effect.

By the time I had refreshed myself with a tepid bath, the cooler part of the day had begun to arrive. It was cooler only relative to the heat of the day—it still felt unbearable to me. I dressed as lightly as possible and awaited Brydges. I did wear my sturdy shoes as I assumed our visit to the Pyramids would entail a great deal of walking. I felt a rising tide of excitement; I had always wanted to view the Pyramids up close.

I was to be disappointed. Brydges and his brother were late—in fact, I had, with much muttering, given them up and had settled down once again with those infernal sermons to while away the evening. It was still early, but the evening stretched before me. By the time Brydges and his brother arrived, it was such a relief to see them and know that I didn't have to spend the evening alone with my book of sermons that I said nothing about their tardiness. Brydges apologized profusely.

"We were on an errand that took longer than expected," he explained. His brother Edward failed miserably in his attempt to nudge Brydges unobtrusively in the ribs. "We, uh, had to attend to some, uh, some . . ."

"Visiting," Edward said. "It's difficult to get in all one's social obligations when one is out of the city most of the time."

"Visiting friends of the family," Brydges said. "As late as it is, do you mind leaving early for the Pyramids tomorrow? That way, we'll have the entire day. I'll have the cook pack a luncheon for all of us."

That settled, we sent down for supper and spent the rest of the evening eating and playing cards with Flora as a fourth. I tried a dozen times to get something from Brydges about Lymond, but I was unsuccessful. Both he and Edward kept wanting to discuss their excavations. It turned out that the two of them were hoping to bring to light an exciting discovery—anything would do as long as it was magnificent. They had been told that the place they were excavating was rich in artifacts. Imagine my surprise when I discovered that Mohammed was the one who pointed them in the right direction and had even provided a nephew of his to be their guide to the village. The man must have a monopoly on Englishmen who came to Egypt.

"I think we'll find quite a treasure," Brydges said as we put away the cards and just settled down to talk. "We've hired a capable man in Atherton and Mohammed knows what's located in this country."

"Obviously." I sat near him as Flora engaged Edward in conversation across the room. "Tell me, Brydges, does Lymond place as much reliance in Mohammed as you do?"

"Of course. Everyone does. If you want to know anything, ask Mohammed. How did you hear of him, by the way?"

I told him of Papa's interest in antiquities and collections. Brydges was suitably impressed, especially with the Greek descriptions. Papa's Egyptian collection was not nearly as good as his Greek antiquities. "I daresay that he was working with Mohammed on his Egyptian collection when he, um, expired," Brydges noted.

"Yes. I thought of going to Greece simply because I know more about it, but I wanted to find out something more about Mohammed and some statuettes of cats he had gotten for Papa." There was a pause and I couldn't think of anything else to say.

"I know just the thing to do," Brydges said with excitement, "if you want to see the country and really get into Egyptian antiquities." He leaned toward me. "Come with us to our camp and join us."

I was startled. "I really couldn't do that! Our intent was to tour Cairo and the surrounding area. We really aren't prepared to go out into the country."

Brydges shook his head. "You won't need a thing. We have everything necessary for comfort there. All we have to do is pitch another tent for you and you'll be all set. If you prefer, you can stay on our boat. We have a *dahabeah* tied up on the shore and an excellent cook. Or rather, we will have when we get back—we came here in the *dahabeah*. It's slower, but a much more comfortable way to travel. I think you'd enjoy it."

I shuddered slightly. In my mind, I could picture myself in a tent in the middle of a burning, baking desert, sweat dripping from my brow. The picture wasn't pleasant. The houseboat sounded better, but not much. "Thank you for your kind offer, but no," I said with a smile.

"Well, if you change your mind, do join us. Or, if you decide to come on later, that'll be all right, too. We have plenty of supplies. You won't even have to bring a tent and a bed along since I made sure to lay in extras."

I smiled again and shook my head. The very idea was preposterous.

* * *

Our trip to the pyramids at Gizah was uneventful. As we approached the pyramids, it seemed to me that they were very small. "I can't believe they're no larger than this," I said to Brydges. He laughed at me. "Just wait until we get closer," he said. It was true—the closer we got, the larger they loomed, until they seemed to fill the entire sky above me. Nothing quite prepares one for the sheer grandeur of the pyramids. No wonder that the millennia have been awed by the spectacle. I felt as if I could turn and see Herodotus standing there, taking notes for his book. Thousands of years seemed to fall away and I could imagine myself back in the time of the pharaohs. Strangely, I was more unsettled by the Sphinx. Up close, there seemed to be an untamed, brutal quality about it that never comes through in drawings. It was as if I almost expected it to turn and spring. Herodotus doesn't mention the Sphinx at all—he may have been as overcome as I.

Other things that are never in drawings are the dirt and the masses of Arab souvenir sellers around the base of the pyramids. However, I do confess to playing the tourist and buying some trinkets to take back with me. As we left, I turned away to look back over my shoulder at the monuments. I was unprepared for the magnificence of the sight as the last rays of the sun caught the tip of the larger pyramid. I gasped and was almost speechless; Woodbury and Jem were clearly overawed. Brydges was quite pleased with our reactions, as he told me the next day.

"I knew you'd stand there with your mouth open," he said with a chuckle as we sat in the coolness of the afternoon. "Everyone does the first time. Even Lymond. That was where I saw him the first time."

"Oh, and what was he doing?"

"Same as you—playing the tourist. Everyone who comes through Egypt has to take a trip to the pyramids. I think somewhere it's written down as obligatory." He chuckled. "It's a good thing that one never tires of the pyramids." He looked at me and smiled sunnily. "Have you thought any more about going to the camp with us? I think you'd enjoy it. We could always use more assistance, particularly a secretary."

There it was—I had thought he wanted me along for the company or at least for my personality, but they needed a secretary. "Absolutely not," I said. "Miss Rowe doesn't take kindly to heat and sand." This wasn't exactly true, but would suffice.

He looked at me and put on a sad expression. "I told Lymond you weren't coming, and he bet me a pony that you would."

"Mr. Lymond loses again," I said, pouring glasses of lemonade for us. "Tell me, where is he? I haven't seen him for a day or two."

Brydges shrugged. "I haven't seen him myself since yesterday. He's always off and about somewhere. I think he said he was going somewhere with Woodbury and Jem today. Was I mistaken?"

"Oh, no. I had merely forgotten." In fact, Woodbury, the sly dog, hadn't mentioned his destination at all. He merely asked if he could have the day and take Jem along. This meant that Flora and I must stay in all day to watch Bucephalus, but after our visit to the pyramids, a lazy day inside was appealing. I had told Woodbury by all means to take the day. The reprobate hadn't said a thing about going somewhere with Lymond. I recollected myself and looked at Brydges. "Woodbury often takes jaunts." I tried to appear casual. "Do you know where they were going?"

Brydges shrugged. "I have no idea. I seldom know where Lymond is going or what he's doing."

"That seems to be quite common," I said before I thought. Brydges looked at me inquisitively and I realized it was time to change the subject. "Tell me, Brydges, how is your quest for antiquities coming along?" I knew this was an excellent topic for diversion.

"We're doing all right, but not as well as I had hoped. We haven't discovered any gold or jewelry yet. Still, Atherton tells me that he's sure it's there, so I can hardly wait to return. I didn't want to leave at all, but I did want to make sure we had plenty of supplies. For some reason, our foodstuffs keep disappearing."

"The workers—and their families—are quite well fed now," Edward added dryly.

We all laughed. "They are living quite well," Brydges acknowledged. "I don't mind—the rewards should greatly outweigh the expense."

Edward clapped his brother on the back. "Besides, your friend Elgin will be jealous beyond words when we find our tomb. Cairo is interesting, but nothing can match the excitement of finding something in a tomb, even is it's only a potsherd. Just think to actually touch something thousands of years old!"

Brydges looked at me and smiled. "For the most part, Edward, I would agree. However, this time, I might challenge that statement. Cairo has its charms." He leaned towards me. "Miss Sydney, you've made Cairo worth visiting. I wish you'd reconsider and come with us. Your presence would certainly enliven our camp."

"As a secretary?" I couldn't help myself.

"Dash it, no. I'm always saying the wrong thing, Miss Sydney. We don't really need a secretary. I just thought that might be an excuse. I just wish you'd come along because I like your company." He blushed slightly as Edward chuckled.

I laughed. "Much better, Brydges, but the answer is still no."

He sighed. "Perhaps I might visit you when we get back to England. We're going back to the camp tomorrow and I hate to think this will be good-bye." He pulled a scrap of paper from his pocket and scribbled on it. "If you change your mind and decide to join us, here's our direction. You could get Henry to bring you—I'm sure Mohammed would let him go."

"I won't change my mind, I assure you," I said firmly, "but perhaps we may meet again in London." I folded the scrap and put it in my box.

"I certainly hope so, Miss Sydney," He said as he signaled to his brother to leave. "Remember, you're welcome to visit us," he repeated as they went out the door.

I smiled as I closed the door behind them. The man was certainly persistent. "No sweltering in the desert for us, Flora," I said to my companion. "We'll enjoy the peace and quiet of the hotel for a while, then wend our way back home."

Peace and quiet were not to be ours for long. Just before midnight, Bue began to howl. He was on one side of my bed and tried to leap over me. Instead, he became tangled in the bedcoverings and wound up practically crushing me. I came out of a sound sleep trying to fight him while he was yowling. "Be quiet, Bue. Quiet!" If he caused any more problems, I could see the management of the hotel putting us out on the streets in the dead of night. "Quiet!"

I said more sternly. He stopped howling but didn't move, so I was pinned to the middle of the bed. There was no way to reach a light or a weapon. My pistol, unfortunately, was in a drawer on the other side of the room. I heard the door open and Bue started howling again. "Quiet, Bue!" I said again.

"Shut up, you damned idiot!" Woodbury said, stumbling against the bed. "Sorry, Miss Sydney, I didn't mean you at all." Bue quieted at the sound of a familiar voice and I could hear Woodbury searching for a way to light the candle by my bedside. In the darkness, my other senses came into play, and I smelled the strong odor of spirits. Woodbury had been drinking again.

When he got the candle lit, Bue jumped from the bed, tail wagging and almost knocked him down. I sat up in bed and struggled into my dressing gown. It was then that I saw Woodbury's condition for the first time.

"Woodbury, what happened!"

Woodbury wiped blood from his face. "We were set upon. Mr. Lymond . . ." He gestured towards the other room.

I leaped to my feet. "Is he hurt badly?" When Woodbury didn't answer me immediately, I seized his shirt front. "Answer me, Woodbury, is he hurt?" A horrible thought assailed me and I stepped back a pace and put my hand to my chest as I felt the blood drain from my face. "He isn't . . . isn't . . . *dead,* is he, Woodbury?"

Woodbury said nothing, but his head made movements. I couldn't tell if he was shaking his head no or nodding yes. In desperation, I began to run into the other room. Close to the door, I fell right over Bue. The last thing I remember was a flash of light as my head hit the door.

I heard Lymond before I saw him. When I opened my

eyes, his face was close to mine. "Here, drink this," he said, putting his hand under my head and lifting me slightly. "You're going to have the devil of a headache."

"Are you dead, Lymond?" I asked in my confusion.

"Yes," he answered, forcing some brandy down my throat. I reached up to grab him and feel for myself—he looked alive enough to me—and wound up knocking the brandy glass right into his face. His face was covered with blood and now, brandy. Lymond, as he often does in such situations, began cursing fluently. He was definitely alive.

"You don't have to use profanity, Lymond," I said mildly as I sat up and turned around on the couch so I was sitting beside him. Bue came up and began lapping at his hands and coat front; Bue has an unfortunate weakness for spirits. Lymond tried to push him away and, if possible, became even more fluent. Lymond has an extensive vocabulary in that area, possibly from consorting with Army types.

I took the moment to look carefully at Lymond. My own head was aching abominably, but however bad I felt, Lymond had to feel worse. There was a cut on his head that was bleeding and his coat was torn. There was a gash on his arm that looked suspiciously as if it had been made by a knife. I looked at Flora and asked her for clean, wet towels and she promptly handed me one. "Shut up, Lymond," I directed as I mopped at the head wound with the towel.

"Dammit, Roxanne, be gentle! You're not digging in the dirt, you know."

"I *am* being gentle, Lymond. If you'd be still, this would go better. I'm not a bad nurse, you know." I glanced up to see Woodbury, a large cut under his eye and a suspiciously swollen nose, looking at us. "Flora, would you mind tending to Woodbury?" I looked back at Lymond. "Where's Jem? Surely he isn't hurt, too."

Lymond glanced at Woodbury. "Jem's fine," Woodbury said. "He was quick enough to dodge without more than a bruise or two."

"I don't believe you," I said, standing. My head spun and I reached for a chair back to steady myself.

"I'll show you," Woodbury said. I thought he was going to fetch Jem, but he simply yelled at the top of his lungs for Jem to come here.

"Good God!" Lymond hissed, "don't wake the entire city. We had enough trouble getting into the hotel without being seen. I'd hate to have to explain our appearance at this hour."

Jem came running in. "Did they follow us?" he asked with wide eyes—or rather wide eye. The other one was black and beginning to swell.

"No," Lymond said wearily. "Why don't we just put an announcement of our activities in the newspapers?"

I sat down beside him and jerked the towel away from his head. It looked much better now—there had been more blood than cut, although his face was bruised. Whoever attacked him had evidently tried to pummel his head. The gash on his arm was much worse. "You're going to have to get that bound up," I said, cutting away his shirt sleeve.

"My good shirt," he moaned. "My arm will be fine. Just put some bascilicum powder on it and bind it tightly. I heal quickly."

I did as he wished, all the while urging him to go to a doctor. As soon as I had finished binding the arm, I tossed the bloody towels in a basin and stood to face Lymond and Woodbury. "No more nonsense," I said sternly. "I want to know what's going on here."

"I don't know," Lymond said wearily, leaning back and closing his eyes.

I didn't believe this for a moment. "Why did you take Woodbury and Jem away this evening? Who set upon all three of you? What happened? There has to be an explanation, Lymond."

"Thieves," he said. I would have believed him except for the stunned expression on Woodbury's face. It was there for only an instant, but it was there—I was sure of it. "That's right," Woodbury agreed. "It had to be thieves. We were traveling late and they must have known we were unarmed."

"Where had you been?" I asked again.

"Just looking at the city," Lymond said innocently.

"That's right. We were just looking around," Woodbury said. Jem nodded his head vigorously. I saw that I wasn't going to get any explanation from them at all.

"Perhaps Jem should go on to bed," I suggested gently. "It isn't good for boys his age to be up so late." I knew something strange was afoot when he practically dashed out of the room and Woodbury stood up. He twitched his nose as the sticking plaster on his face pulled a little, then thanked Flora for her nursing. "I believe I'll turn in myself. It's been a long day." He yawned theatrically and I got another strong sniff of whiskey. "Walking around the city can be tiring."

"So can being set upon by brigands," I replied tartly. "Very well, Woodbury, good night. Do try to sleep in tomorrow morning and rest."

Flora glanced at me and I nodded at her. Without another word except a goodnight, she went on to bed as well. As I said, the proprieties that would have existed in England seemed to have no significance here. I could just imagine Aunt Hen's reaction to my sitting here after midnight in my dressing gown with Lymond at my side.

Lymond saw no problem in the situation. He reached down and removed his boots. "Roxanne, I've got to stay here tonight. I don't mind going to my lodgings, but I'm in no shape to fend off another attacker, should one decide to set upon me." He put his feet behind me, almost bumping me off the sofa, and stretched out.

"Another? Is someone after you for some reason, Lymond?"

"Don't be ridiculous," he said, twisting to try to get comfortable. He was longer than the sofa. It wasn't particularly comfortable at the best of times, even for sitting. I looked down at his bruised face. The bruises seemed even more livid because he was drained of color—I had never seen his skin so pale. He had his hands wrapped around his arms and the scars where he had been burned were visible. Without thinking, I reached out and touched his hand.

"Lymond," I began.

"Please, Roxie," he mumbled. "I'm too tired to talk. I'll talk to you in the morning." He twisted again, a grimace flitting across his face as he hit his arm.

I stood and shook him. "Get up, Lymond. You can't stay here on this sofa all night. You'll be in worse shape than you are now if you do. You take my bed and I'll sleep with Flora tonight."

He rolled over and looked at me, the trace of a smile on his lips. There were circles of fatigue under his eyes. "Would you do that for me, Roxie?"

"I'd do it for any wretch in the same shape," I said firmly, taking his hand and helping him to his feet. "Come on. Do you need help in undressing?"

He paused and grinned down at me, an impish spark in his eyes. "Is that an offer?"

"Of course not. I merely wanted to know if I needed to

go get Woodbury." I went into the room with him and spread up the bed a little. I had thrown the covers all over the place in my tussle with Bue. "There you are, Lymond," I said, glancing down at the table beside the bed. "There's my book of sermons for your general instruction. You may benefit from reading one or two."

He laughed. "I'm sure I could find other things I'd benefit from much more." His hand slipped up my arm and I felt a tingle that ran all the way down to my toes.

It was time for a retreat. "Good-night, Lymond," I said, picking up my hairbrush. "I'll see you in the morning." I turned to Bucephalus. "Come on, Bue."

In answer, Bue flopped down beside the bed and looked up at me, his nose between his paws. "You seem to have acquired a protector, Lymond," I said as I closed the door behind me. I could hear Lymond muttering something about a damned mutt as I made my way to Flora's room.

We all slept in late the next morning. I got up and walked into the sitting room, wearing my dressing gown and carrying my hairbrush, and was surprised to see Lymond sitting there. "How did you sleep?" I asked, pulling the bell to send for coffee and rolls.

"How can anyone sleep with that dam . . . that dog? I woke up twice to find it stretched out on the bed beside me. I got it off the bed once, but the second time, I decided the struggle just wasn't worth it." He paused. "The dog snores."

"I know. I do, however, forbid him to sleep on the bed." I paused not knowing whether to stay and keep an eye on Lymond or to go get dressed. I wanted to discover more about his activities. There was a discreet knock on the door and Lymond leaped to his feet. "That'll be breakfast, Roxanne," he said, vanishing into my room. "You get it. I don't want anyone to know I'm here."

Coffee and rolls had been sent up, along with fresh fruit and little pastries. There was enough to feed four or five, and Lymond did justice to the tray. When we finished, there was hardly a scrap left. Lymond felt the stubble on his chin, ran his fingers through his hair, and drew out a cigar. "I believe I may survive," he said through a cloud of smoke. I breathed the cigar smoke in deeply, enjoying it almost as much as Lymond did.

"Good," I said, pouring water into my coffee. I had discovered quickly that Egyptian coffee and English coffee are two different brews. "Now tell me exactly what's going on."

Lymond looked at me blankly. "Whatever do you mean, Roxanne? Nothing's going on except that this city is full of petty thieves. You saw a good example of that yourself when you were set upon." He paused. "I told you it wasn't safe here."

I was having no part of this. "I know that look of yours, Lymond," I said. "You're involved in something nefarious and I want to know about it. Does it have anything to do with the recent upheavals in government here? Or perhaps you've stumbled onto something valuable that others are trying to get as well? Have you perhaps found the casket?"

"I don't know what you're talking about, Roxanne. I'm probably the least nefarious person you know." He put his cigar into a small bowl and reached for his coat on the back of the sofa. "How long are you going to be in Cairo?"

"A few days. Flora and I thought we'd see the city and then perhaps begin our trip back home. We may take a boat to Crete and then on to Greece. I haven't really made up my mind."

I could almost feel relief emanating from Lymond. "I think that's a good idea. There isn't much here. I think Mohammed is planning to have Henry show you around the city. Be sure to take a short boat trip on the Nile. It's a fascinating river."

"I'll do that, Lymond." I leaned back casually. Two can play at this game. "And how about you? How long do you intend to stay here?"

"Not long. In answer to your previous question, no, I haven't found the casket. However, as I told you, I may have a good lead as to its whereabouts. It seems to be in or near the village near Brydges' camp. I've got to meet a man there and see what he has to offer. If it's the casket and papyri, then I should be ready to leave soon." He stood up and smiled sunnily down at me. "I'm glad you've decided to visit some other places, Roxanne. As I said, this country can be dangerous."

"I've noticed," I said dryly as I stood beside him. "Will you be in London when you return? If you are, leave a message with Cassie. I'll do the same when I get there."

"I'll do that." He looked down at Bue who had draped himself over Lymond's feet, sidestepped to get out of the way, and muttered, "Damned dog," under his breath. I walked to the door with him. "Good-bye, Lymond," I said with a cheerful smile.

He leaned against the door and put his hands on my shoulders. "It'll be so good to know you're safe at home," he said, his finger tracing a line along my jaw and chin. I met his eyes and suddenly felt dizzy. Lymond must have felt strange as well as he paused and licked his lips as he looked at me. "Roxie," he said in a husky voice and leaned toward me, his hands tightening on my shoulders.

The door opened right on his injured arm and he jumped

back and yelped in pain. It was Woodbury. He stood there and gawked at us. I suppose being in my dressing gown with Lymond at midnight was one thing; being in my dressing gown having breakfast with him was entirely another. "Do come in, Woodbury," I said, closing the door behind him. "We'll have to send for more breakfast for you."

Woodbury looked decidedly green. "I don't wish any breakfast," he said. "Nothing."

"Miss Sydney has just told me that she doesn't plan to stay in Cairo much longer," Lymond said, "and I'm leaving the city immediately, so I'll be saying goodbye to you and Jem, Woodbury. Take care."

Woodbury looked at me strangely as this was the first he had heard of this plan. However, Army to the end, he always adapted. "Goodbye, Mr. Lymond," he said with a nod.

Lymond looked at me again and smiled that wonderful smile. "I'll see you as soon as possible, Roxanne." With that, he was out the door, shutting it softly behind him.

"Sooner than you think, Lymond," I said to the door. I turned around to face Woodbury. "Go begin packing, Woodbury." I went over to the desk and pulled out paper and ink. "We're going digging for artifacts."

Woodbury sat down heavily on the sofa. "What? We're going home to dig for artifacts?"

"Of course not." I glanced at him. "Woodbury, I know Robert Lymond. When he acts this way, something is afoot. I owe it to Uncle Harley and Aunt Hen to keep an eye on him and keep him out of harm's way. We're going to accept Brydges' kind invitation to spend a while at his dig. If Lymond's in any danger, we'll be there to protect him." I sanded and sealed the note, then pinned Woodbury with a look. "He *is* in danger, isn't he, Woodbury?"

"Is he?" Woodbury looked confused. "How do you know?"

"I know," I said, ringing for someone to deliver my acceptance to Brydges. "Don't forget, Woodbury, that I'm a shrewd judge of character. I always know when Lymond is prevaricating." There was a small noise as Woodbury downed a cup of syrupy Egyptian coffee down at one gulp. "He's prevaricating now, Woodbury," I continued, "and I intend to get to the bottom of it. Sometimes," I said as I went into my room to pack, "Lymond needs someone to save him from himself."

I heard Woodbury moan as he poured himself another cup of coffee.

Six

Brydges postponed his departure on the dahabeah for two days so we could get ourselves packed and ready. I also wanted to purchase a few items of clothing, including some sturdy boots. I had difficulty finding them, but Henry finally located a pair for me. They were men's boots, but small, so they fit me reasonably well. Flora purchased some sketchpads, pencils, and colors to use for drawing the sights we would see.

The afternoon before our journey, I determined to go pay a goodbye visit to Mohammed. Woodbury and Jem insisted on accompanying me although both of them were still bruised from the effects of their evening with Lymond. I probed Woodbury to try to discover what had happened, but he wasn't saying. Jem was next on my list at the earliest opportunity, but I would have to get him away from Woodbury.

Today, however, they stuck on either side of me like two battered warriors as I went to say my good-bye to Mohammed. He was all graciousness and we spent a delightful afternoon—he told me stories about Papa and their adventures in Egypt. I had not realized that my father was so adventurous, especially since I got the impression that Mohammed was being careful to delete the worst aspects of his tales. At the close of the afternoon, I informed him that

I was traveling upriver to visit Brydges's camp and spend a week or so there. To my surprise, Mohammed didn't attempt to dissuade me; rather he nodded and told me that I was my father's daughter, a comment which pleased me immensely. He did warn me of the heat, the sand, the wind, and other inconveniences of the trip. I brushed these all aside, telling him that I was prepared for such hardships. Mohammed nodded, but then insisted that I take Henry with me. "It will be good," he said, "to have someone with you who speaks the language." That had been a worry, so I accepted Henry's services with gratitude. "It is a pleasure to do a favor for my friend, George," Mohammed had assured me.

"Have you talked to Mr. Lymond recently?" I asked casually as I was preparing to leave. I had hoped Lymond's name would arise in our conversation, and, although I had mentioned him once or twice, Mohammed hadn't risen to the bait. I hated to ask so baldly, but I didn't know any other way to introduce the subject.

Mohammed nodded again, looking at me in a strange way. "An excellent man. I have seldom met an Englishman of such honor—not since your father."

"Lymond's looking for a casket containing some papyri for my uncle and is looking in the general area of Brydges' camp," I told him. "He told me you have told him to search there." There was silence as I cast around for something else to pry some information from Mohammed, but was singularly unsuccessful. I couldn't think of a thing. "I hope his search is bearing fruit," I said.

"I would hope so," Mohammed said. The man was as inscrutable as the Sphinx. "As I said, he is an intelligent man. You would be wise to rely on his advice."

"Which is?"

Mohammed nodded sagely and spoke slowly. I had noticed he did that and, at first, thought it an affectation, but now I had decided that he was translating his thoughts into English in his head. I was impressed with his command of English. "He tells me he has advised you to return home as the country here may not agree with you. Also, it is dangerous for a . . . a female to travel alone here." He nodded some more. "Returning is an excellent idea."

I brushed dust from my gown and prepared to leave. "I do intend to follow his advice—just as soon as I return from my stay at Brydges' camp. I want to see a real Egyptian tomb—it's a trip my father would have loved."

"There are people here you do not understand."

"Just what is going on, Mohammed?" I demanded. "Not only were Henry and I attacked, Lymond was as well. What is the mystery here?"

Mohammed shrugged. "Cairo is a city of rumors—most of them false, but occasionally one is true. There is a rumor about you. A sailor in Alexandria began the tale as best as I can discover. He said you carry a priceless box which contains the instructions for finding a cache of gold that was given as tribute to a pharoah. I have heard that several attempts have already been made to steal the box." He paused and looked at me. "I don't know if the attacks on you and on Mr. Lymond are related."

I thought a moment. "Woodbury and Jem were with Lymond when he was attacked. Perhaps they were the real targets."

"It is possible." There was another pause. "Do you carry such a casket or box?"

I laughed aloud. "Good heavens, no! Papa had many artifacts, but, as you know, the only really valuable things he had were the cat statuettes. I've never seen any kind of a casket. I can't even imagine how such a rumor began."

Mohammed shook his head and grimaced slightly. "There is often no basis at all. That is why they are called rumors rather than facts. The sad part is that many people regard rumor as fact." He looked at me again. "Take care, daughter of my friend. You know and I know that this story is false, but there are those who don't." He appeared worried. "I have tried to quell the rumors, but to no avail." He looked at me sadly. "That is why Egypt is not safe for you—thieves think you are carrying a great secret."

"That's ridiculous!" I began to pace the floor. "Anyone with common sense would know better."

"Greed has no common sense." Mohammed paused. "Do you know you have been followed?"

I caught my breath. "Followed? Is that why you've insisted on Henry accompanying me?" I resumed my pacing. "Surely people know better. I'm here to see you and to visit Egypt."

Mohammed gazed at me solemnly. "You know that; I know that. However, others do not. I am doing my best to dispel the rumors, but . . ." He spread his hands in a gesture of futility. "I don't think you will take an old man's suggestion—your father wouldn't have—but I think it would be wise if you took Mr. Lymond's advice."

I looked at him steadily. "I trust your judgment, Mohammed, so I will take his—and your—advice, just as soon as I get back from visiting Brydge's camp. Surely no one could believe I was going there for any reason other than sightseeing."

Little did I know.

* * *

Lymond had been correct—the trip up the Nile was spectacular. Brydges' dahabeah was luxurious with ample room and comfortable furnishings and, as he had promised, a wonderful cook. I had been worried about my seasickness, but it did not return, perhaps because of the slow pace of the boat.

As for the Nile valley, I had never seen anything like it. All in all, I had the best time of my journey; the scenery was spectacular, the company entertaining, and the heat bearable. I was very glad I was taking the trip. I could just imagine Lymond's expression when he saw us coming into Brydges' camp. The thought almost made me wish I were good at sketching. Perhaps Flora would capture it for me on the pages of her sketchpad.

The camp was farther up the Nile than I had expected. I had thought it would be a matter of a few hours, but it was much longer than that. However, the scenery was so wonderful that I really didn't mind. I enjoyed seeing everything, amazed that this thin strip of green could have produced one of the world's great civilizations. The eastern slopes were particularly fascinating.

Brydges insisted on mooring the boat whenever something interesting came into our sight. He was an excellent guide, and I also had my copy of Herodotus with me which helped greatly. In addition, I realized that I was going to have to pack away some of my clothing and wear only things with long sleeves. Every time we stopped, I was amazed at the heat, the sand, and the wind. There were times when my skin was almost abraded by the wind scouring it with sand. The Egyptians, I told Brydges, paid a price for living in beauty and plenty.

Another reason the trip upriver lengthened was because at night Brydges had the boat moored in a safe place so he and his brother could sleep on shore. As a result, we wound up stopping at midafternoon, pitching a tent, and setting up a camp. It also took a while in the morning to break camp and get started again. I appreciated his concern for our reputations, but I was chafing to get to the camp. However, Brydges seemed in no hurry at all. Rather he, as he told me, wanted to show me all of Egypt and relive the excitement of someone seeing it for the first time. To his delight, I was suitably impressed. 'Overawed' might be a better word. Throughout the trip, Flora proved to be an excellent companion. She was as excited as I to see the sights and was an excellent source of information. When she had discovered we were traveling to Egypt, she explained, she had read several history and guide books. She also put to excellent use her other talent—she was an exceptional artist, able to capture the essence of a scene in just a few strokes. The night before we arrived at the camp, I asked her if she would sketch Lymond for me when we arrived in camp.

She looked at me in surprise. We were preparing for bed in Brydges' rather luxurious quarters. "Mr. Lymond is a very handsome man," she said.

"Balderdash." I spoke calmly as I stepped over Bue. Bue, for some reason, had been quite unruly; it had been necessary to tie him to the bed. There were crocodiles in the water and he kept wanting to leap into the Nile and fetch one of them to me. Large as he was, Bue was no match for a crocodile. I patted him absently as I answered Flora. "Lymond may be many things, but he isn't exceptionally handsome."

"But he is," Flora continued. "And I've noticed he seems very taken with you." She paused. "It would be a good match."

I turned to stare at her. "Flora, you've turned into my Aunt Hen. There is no possibility, *none,* of a match between Lymond and me. I know the man too well. He's deceitful, fond of prevaricating, lying . . ." I paused while I searched for more suitable words.

"And handsome," Flora supplied, quite unperturbed. "I'd be delighted to sketch him for you, Roxanne."

"It isn't for that reason," I protested. "I merely want to see the expression on his face when we show up unexpectedly. It should be worth saving on paper. Be sure to capture it exactly and I'll have it framed and put on the wall in the drawing room at Bellerophon." I chuckled as I crawled into bed. Lymond would be beside himself.

My plans were for naught—Lymond wasn't at the camp when we arrived. I did, however, make a casual comment or two about him and elicited the information that he would be returning within a few days. He had taken a guide from the village and gone inland on a search for the casket and papyri, I was told.

The camp wasn't what I expected although Brydges was excited beyond all measure. A tomb had been found during his absence, he informed me. We all dashed up the hill to look at it and I tried to hide my disappointment. There was no real tomb—just the beginnings of a hole in the ground where some rough steps seemed to be. The workers were digging sand and carrying it away in baskets. It appeared to me that they weren't making much headway; sand kept falling back into the hole. Brydges had the hole guarded day and night to keep villagers and thieves from taking artifacts. It was difficult, he told me, to find a man to guard at night because the natives were convinced that the night air was alive with demons and ghosts—afreets, he called them. Looking around at the stark landscape, I could see how such a belief originated.

The camp itself was larger than I had anticipated. There were tents for the men Brydges had brought with him, a tent for Edward and Brydges, some tents for storage and cataloguing any finds, and a mess tent for eating. The cooking seemed to be done over a fire outside. There were boxes and boxes of supplies. It seemed a camp wasn't a particularly glamorous place and the work wasn't at all exotic; it was a backbreaking and tedious process if it were done properly. At least that's what the man in charge of digging told me. He also added that a camp was no place for women and suggested ever so nicely that we might wish to return from whence we had come, the sooner the better. Perversely, I resolved to stay as long as I could.

Brydges introduced us all around. The man in charge was a no-nonsense Scot named Alexander Harris. He seemed to take me into instant dislike, more so because I was a woman. He thought Flora might be useful because she could draw, although I could see that he gave us that scrap only to be polite. It was quite obvious that he was wishing both of us in Hades. His assistant was much nicer. He was Anwar LeSepp, a part-Egyptian, part-French young man who had been educated in France. His English was good, although with that peculiar accent all Frenchmen give it. Brydges told me that he was lucky to have hired Anwar as the young man was a brilliant scholar.

"Has he been infected with Napoleon's ideas?" I asked, looking at him working at a distance. He was quite handsome, very dark, with a touch of French dash.

Brydges shrugged. "I would term him pro-Egyptian rather than pro-French. He seems to have resented Napoleon's plundering of the country and feels Egypt should belong to and be governed by Egyptians."

"Reasonable," I said. "I was afraid from his background and education that he was an admirer of the Corsican."

"No, if anything, he's an admirer of Robespierre. However, we don't discuss politics here to any extent. Anwar was born in the small village near here. His mother raised the boy alone after Anwar's father abandoned the family. His potential was discovered by a local missionary who intended to send him to England, but he met a Frenchman who offered to sponsor the boy in France. He spent several years there, I understand. Strange he should come back to such a small village in the hinterlands."

"Possibly he still has family there."

Brydges nodded. "He does. Actually, I think everyone in the village is related to everyone else. At any rate, Anwar doesn't stay here; he prefers to stay in the village. I can't complain; he's an excellent worker and scholar."

I smiled at Brydges. "That's what's important, isn't it?"

Brydges offered Flora and me the use of the dahabeah as our quarters, but we deemed it too far from the camp. The boat was anchored on the river, but so far away as to disappear into the horizon. True, it was luxurious and comfortable, but I wanted to be *in medias res*. We opted for tents, and Brydges had them pitched not far from his. There was a striped tent for Flora and one for me. I was surprised—I had thought we would be sharing quarters and said as much to Brydges.

He smiled at me broadly. "I wanted you to be comfortable so you would stay as long as possible. You'll be perfectly safe here—I'll be right over here and that tent not far behind you is the one Lymond uses. I'll put Henry on the other side of Flora. That should afford you protection and privacy."

"You think of everything, Brydges."

We were interrupted by a shout from the hills above the dig. I looked up, shaded my eyes, but could see nothing except the interminable sun and sand. Brydges, however, began waving. "Colonel Atherton," he explained as a figure came into view." He's been my agent in Egypt since I first came here. He handles all the local permits, conversations with the neighboring villages, and so on. He also seems to know every inch of the valley and speaks the language like a native."

Atherton drew close to us. He was a large man with rather long, gingery hair and a large moustache that was a shade or two darker. His face was leathery from being out in the sun for many years. He was dressed in loose clothing with an Arabian headdress on his head. I could see the practicality of it—it covered his head and protected his neck from the sun. I resolved to find something similar for me. Atherton put on a smile when he got close to us, and the smile never wavered or faded. He held out his hand as he approached. "Well, Brydges, I see Harris was correct—you've brought us some delightful company," he said jovially.

"I'm surprised Harris would use the word 'delightful,' " I said with a laugh, extending my hand. Atherton took it, but instead of merely shaking hands, kissed the back, not once, but twice.

"He didn't exactly use the word, but I'm sure that was what he meant." He turned to Brydges, the smile still on his face. "We've made some headway, but I think the villagers are holding out on us. Either that or one of them has discovered a tomb we don't know about." He pulled a shard from his pocket. "I found this in the village. If this was there, then you can be sure that more is. I'll get to the bottom of it soon."

"Do you think it's our people?" Brydges asked, turning the shard over and over in his fingers. "This doesn't look like much."

"To be sure," Atherton said, with a dismissing wave of his hand, "but this is only what I managed to get my hands on. These sneaky villagers have hidden anything and everything of value. The name of the game is cash—has been for a thousand years."

Brydges handed the shard back to him. "Do you think our men are involved?"

"Of course." Atherton shrugged. "They'd sell their mothers to the highest bidder. I'm just worried that they've found a tomb with some real valuables in it that they're concealing."

Brydges frowned. "Perhaps Anwar could find out. He has friends and relatives in the village. I'll speak to him." He looked back at the camp. "I haven't had a chance to talk to Harris yet. Will we uncover the doorway to the tomb soon?"

Atherton paused significantly. "There's one thing I'd like to speak to you about. If you have a few moments privately . . ."

If there's one thing I can do, it's take a hint, especially one that bold. "If you'll excuse me," I said, "I'll go inspect my tent."

Breeding will tell. Brydges wheeled about and clasped my arm. "There's no need for you to go," he said. Then he turned to Atherton. "Is this something of a nature that cannot be discussed in front of Miss Sydney? Remember, as

I told everyone the first day we assembled, we have no secrets here."

Atherton flushed pink under his tan. "It isn't secret at all. I merely wanted to discuss the possibility of replacing Harris on this project. I didn't wish to discuss it in front of a . . . a . . ."

"A stranger," I prompted. "I quite understand Colonel Atherton." I turned to Brydges. "It has been a long day thus far and I would like to go to my tent and do some things." I walked away and left them alone.

I bumped into Harris as I was approaching my tent. He was hurrying to the largest tent there, the one that held the tables and boxes full of items unearthed from the digging. "Have you found something new?" I asked conversationally.

He stopped, turned, and looked at me. "Nothing that would interest you at all," he said. He paused as if making up his mind, then put his hands on his hips and spoke. "You strike me as another like Atherton—just here for what you can get to sell or place on a shelf in your drawing room. The true purpose of archaeology, Miss Sydney, should be to advance knowledge, not to enrich the participants."

"I quite agree." I reined in a sharp retort and forced myself to be pleasant. After all, the man's future was being discussed not a thousand feet away.

"If you agree then, Miss Sydney, perhaps you would care to assist in the search. There are dozens of things you could do around here, things that would free another man to get in the trenches and dig."

"Pay my own way, as it were, Mr. Harris." I was still calm and collected, although it was becoming an effort. "I would like to inform you that I am not one of those missish society women to whom a success means dressing better than any other woman at a ball. I happen to know more about the ancient world than most people." Some demon possessed me suddenly and I said more than I intended. "Actually, Mr. Harris, I would love to do some work here. After all, this is something of training for me—I plan to organize and finance my own expedition to search for antiquities."

Harris wasn't impressed. Instead, he shoved a broken pot at me. "Good. Take this to the tent and have Anwar show you what to do with it. He's in there cataloguing and reassembling some pots. You could do that." He turned to leave. "Tell him to join me as soon as he shows you what to do. I could use him." With that, he was off, leaving me standing there, holding the broken pot in both hands. I probably would have thrown it at him except it was ancient and would have splintered against his head. I admit I had to fight against the impulse.

Henry stepped up beside me and took the pot from my hands. "The man is in need of—how do you say it—tact?"

"Definitely in need of tact," I said, walking with him towards the tent Harris had pointed out. "However, he has done one thing—I am resolved to stay here and prove myself useful." I paused to look around at the hills surrounding us, reaching like broken red fingers into the sky. "I would like to find something, Henry. I could have my own expedition like this. Who knows what lies beneath the sands?"

Henry chuckled. "The fever has you, has it?" He looked around. "Untold numbers of things have been unearthed and shipped away. Most of the easy things have been stripped which is why the Englishmen are having to dig for treasure. Perhaps you should stay and see just how dull and boring an expedition like this can be."

"I'm accustomed to dull and boring, Henry," I said

briskly, going into the tent. Anwar looked up from his work, surprised. "We've come to assist you, Anwar," I told him. He looked at me dubiously.

I ignored his look and sat down beside him. He was brushing a pot with a tiny paintbrush, meticulously removing every grain of sand. All about me were implements that would do any doctor proud—tiny knives and scrapers, a variety of brushes, small and large screens, plaster, various glues, and enough paper to catalogue a museum. Brydges evidently didn't stint on supplies. "This will give you a chance to get out of the tent and work," I told him. "Of course, you'll have to spend a few days showing me exactly what to do. I'll also volunteer Miss Rowe's services. She's an accomplished artist."

To my surprise, Anwar didn't seem as enthusiastic as I had thought he would be. "It's very tedious work," he said. "Very exacting."

"Fine. I'm excellent with that sort of thing." I wasn't bragging. I had worked for years with Papa's artifacts and his manuscripts. Both involved great amounts of research and careful work.

Anwar gave me a doubtful look and proceeded to try to show me I couldn't do it. I proceeded to show him I could. He seemed amazed that a woman could do the work, although I suppose the general attitude of Egyptian males would engender such a feeling. He was even confident enough to leave me alone with the pots for a while. I sent Henry for Flora and she was delighted to be able to put her talents to use. She was as meticulous as I, measuring each thing multiple ways and drawing the pot to scale in every particular.

By the end of the day, I wished I could be doing something else, but certainly couldn't admit that. My neck ached, my fingers cramped, and I was, in general, miserable. Still, when I leaned back and looked at my work, it gave me a great deal of satisfaction. Even Harris, who came in just before supper to inspect our afternoon's output, gave grudging praise. "A good start for an amateur," he said, glancing at my work. He actually picked up Flora's sketch-pad and walked outside with her drawing. "Perfect," he breathed, noting her notations about the measurements, "absolutely perfect." He gave the drawing back to her. "Miss Rowe, you're going to be a real asset to us. How long will you be able to stay?"

Flora blushed. "Until Miss Sydney decides to leave," she replied.

Harris looked my way and frowned. "Oh, yes." I could see that this wasn't pleasing to him, but his need for Flora's drawings outweighed his brusqueness towards me. "Perhaps that will be a while," he muttered as he turned and left. I thought it quite a concession on his part.

Supper was more elaborate than I had anticipated, given the cooking conditions. Atherton leaned towards me as we ate. "I see Brydges has decided to bring us some real food for a change, no doubt because you came along. On behalf of the camp, I thank you, Miss Sydney."

"What do you mean?" I looked down at my plate. Everything looked ordinary.

Atherton laughed. "When Brydges first came, he decided it would be excellent for us to live, think, act, and, needless to say, eat like ancient Egyptians. The dress wasn't practical, of course, but the food was as authentic as he could make it. All we ate for weeks was bread, radishes, onions, and beer." He looked down at his plate. "Food at last. We were all sneaking continually over to the village to the local marketplace. Onions and radishes do wear on one."

I laughed and asked Atherton about the village. He entertained me with stories of the villagers and of his various adventures in Egypt. He had heard of my father, but never met him.

After supper, I sat down beside Brydges for some quiet conversation while the others mingled or talked. I caught Atherton looking at Harris several times. No matter that Harris was brusque, I felt he had the best interests of the expedition at heart. I truly hoped Brydges didn't decide to replace him. Harris might have no tact, but he was an engineer at heart and the excavation was run like a well-oiled machine. Even a newcomer such as I could see that.

Atherton took Brydges off to talk as it was getting dusk, and I decided to explore. I set out on my own, only to have Henry come flying after me. "You'll get lost," he explained, his headdress flapping as he ran towards me. "The desert can be deceptive." He looked all around him in the gathering dusk. "Besides, there are things in the night."

"Nonsense, Henry," I said. "I certainly don't believe in such tales. Also, I have Bue with me. He can find his way back and get help if need be." I had taken Bue out on a leash. Or rather, he had me on a leash. He seemed to be pulling me along as he ran, sniffing and snuffling in the sand. We rounded a group of rocks and were suddenly out of sight of the camp. Abruptly the desert appeared more menacing and the darkness seemed to fall like a blanket; I had not realized how comforting the presence of others had been. "Very well, Henry," I said, "I'll trust your judgment. I understand there's a village nearby and I'd like to go there tomorrow. Perhaps we can leave during the late afternoon when it's cool enough to walk."

Henry nodded and we returned to camp. I had thought that I wouldn't sleep well in a strange place, but I was so exhausted that I fell into a deep, dreamless slumber.

The next day was a learning experience for me. I spent the day in the collection tent, learning how to brush sand from pottery, how to clean pottery, how to glue pottery back together, and how to pack pottery so it would be protected. Harris was a stickler for getting things right. His favorite word seemed to be *systematically*. Everything had to have a system. The man should have been in science. I saw more potsherds that I ever wanted to again, but, if I was going to be helpful, it was necessary to learn about them. However, a strange thing began to happen: the more I learned about them, the more interesting they became. By the end of the day, I was looking forward to tomorrow. Flora, too, had a productive day. She sketched and measured all day, numbering each piece and its corresponding drawing. She, too, seemed to become more and more infected with enthusiasm as the day went along. Harris came in often, and, at the end of the day, went so far as to compliment both of us, although I own he was more effusive with Flora.

Right after supper, I hunted up Henry and reminded him that I wanted to take Bue and walk to the neighboring village. Henry wasn't enthusiastic, but I insisted as Atherton had told me it wasn't far. If we hurried, we could get there and back before dark. We left, following the path that led up around the hills and down into another small valley. Bue spent all his time sniffing the ground and trying to run to the side to investigate whatever scent had caught his fancy. There were so many smells that I was amazed that he could sort out any one of them. Henry was surefooted on the path, assisting me at intervals with Bue's leash. Bue was being particularly difficult this evening. Aside from trying to sniff everything, he wanted to run free, but I knew it might be weeks, if ever, before I saw him again if I let him go.

As we threaded our way through the rocks along a footpath, we came upon Anwar and several of the village men. There were some women at the rear of the group, all of them crying in distress. "Has someone died?" I asked Henry under my breath. To tell the truth, I had very little breath, as Bue was straining at the leash trying to get to the villagers and it was all the two of us could do to restrain him. I hoped his leash was strong enough.

Henry pulled the leash around a convenient rock and listened for a moment. He and Anwar spoke briefly in their native tongue, then Henry turned to me. "A small boy is missing. He's been gone most of the day, but was only discovered an hour or so ago. His mother thought he was with his grandfather, and the grandfather thought the boy was with his mother. They're afraid he might have met with disaster."

I nodded. "How old was the boy?"

Henry and Anwar spoke again, although Anwar could understand me perfectly. "Two," Henry told me. "Just big enough to wander away." He paused and looked up the mountain at the rocks. "It gets cold here at night. The boy isn't heavily dressed." He made a face as he looked up into the heavens. "Then too, there are the afreets that walk in the night."

I thought about calling him to task about such heathenish beliefs, but we had already gone over that ground, so I merely nodded and stood by Bue as the procession of villagers passed us, searching the rocks as they went. One man in particular seemed to be searching frantically. "The boy's grandfather," Henry said. "He feels responsible."

"No more responsible than the boy's mother," I said. "Do you think we should assist them?"

Henry looked at the villagers, then up the mountain. It was drawing on to nightfall and the sky was becoming dusky. "Why don't I assist them, and you go on back to the camp? I'll be glad to go walking with you to the village tomorrow."

"All right," I sighed, dragging Bue after me. Henry went on ahead, calling out to Anwar in their own language. I supposed he was offering his services.

It took forever to get Bue back to camp. He literally dug in his feet and refused to budge. A mastiff is not an easy animal to move when he's determined not to move. Finally, however, I got him back to the edge of the camp as darkness fell. I turned to look at the mountain behind me and stopped, enchanted. "Bue," I told him, "I understand why Egyptians love their land." It was beautiful—the moon was hanging over the mountain, lighting the top with an incandescent glow. Dark shadows furrowed the sides and the rock formations almost had a life of their own. It should have been sinister, but it wasn't. It was absolutely beautiful. Off to my far left, I could hear the faint cries of the villagers looking for the lost child and the sounds and the sight transported my imagination back a thousand years. In that instant, I understood my father's fascination with Egypt and I knew that I would be returning again and again. "It's beautiful, isn't it, Bue?" I asked softly, relaxing my grip on his collar.

Bue was not impressed by the scenery. What did impress him was that I wasn't dragging him along, and he seized the moment. He bolted towards the mountain, yowling in full cry. I thought for a moment about using some of Lymond's vocabulary, but didn't really have the time to articulate my feelings. Instead, I ran after Bue. I tried to call his name, but couldn't catch my breath enough to make noises. I sprinted across the rocky sand, panting. I still had him in sight, but he was getting farther and farther away.

To my surprise, Bue stopped at a bend in the pathway and began scrambling up the path. His leash caught between two rocks and he was stopped. In frustration, he began clawing at the rock. "That will do you no good, Bucephalus," I said severely, catching up with him and seizing his leash. I collapsed onto the rock and tried to catch my breath. My side hurt abominably and I took in great gulps of air. Bue looked at me, then started scrabbling up the path. I wrapped his leash around my arm twice and pulled, but he was stronger than I so I found myself being dragged up the side of the mountain at no slow clip. I stumbled and fell against a rocky outcropping. Bue, however, didn't slow down and dragged me across the rock. I could feel my skin scraping against the sharp edges. "Stop!" I shrieked at him.

To my surprise, he stopped and looked back at me. I could see him in the moonlight and his eyes reflected the light like two glowing coals. If I hadn't known this was my pet, I would have been terrified. Still, for a moment, I wondered if he had been possessed. The stories about afreets, demons, and ghosts suddenly seemed very real.

I shook off the feeling and forced myself to speak calmly. "Bue, come here," I said, feeling blood begin to ooze from the scrapes on the side of my head. "Come here now."

He looked at me, then turned his head and made a whining noise. Then there was silence followed by another noise. I listened carefully but all I heard was the faint echoes of the villagers searching for the boy. Bue woofed and there was an answering snuffle from the rocks to our left. Bue started across the rocks and I had no choice but to follow. I worried about what was there: it could be a lion, it could be anything.

It was the little boy: Bue stopped and licked the child's face to allay his fears and I reached for him. He had fallen between two rocks and was wedged. I tried to get him, but couldn't. From the rock on which I lay, it was all I could do to reach him at all. The poor little thing was almost past crying and was terrified. I smoothed his hair and tried to speak to him, but he spoke no English. He kept trying to say words in his native tongue, and I had no idea what he was saying. "It'll be fine," I answered, trying to soothe him. He answered with dry, heaving sobs.

I was afraid to leave him for two reasons. One, I hated for him to be alone in the night desert. After all, if I left him, I wouldn't be able to explain why I was leaving him and he wouldn't know I was trying to rescue him by going for help. Two, even if I could go get help, I was afraid I might not be able to find my way back. After pondering for a few minutes, and noting how the sounds of the villagers and the people in our camp carried on the night air, I took the only course I deemed viable at the moment. I stood up on top of a rock, out in full view of the camp, and screamed at the top of my lungs.

Seven

My voice was beginning to give out when Bue took up the cry. He yowled for all the world like a spirit lost on the River Styx. Between the shadows on the rocks, the scudding clouds over the moon, and Bue's lost wailing, I felt a frisson of fear go up my spine. "Quiet!" I squawked hoarsely at him. "You'll send everyone in the other direction with that infernal noise." Bue, to my surprise, quieted and began lapping again at the boy's face. It seemed to calm them both. I looked around and clambered up onto another rock, this one higher and more prominent. Perhaps someone in the camp could see me and would come to our rescue. As I looked around, I had more than ever the feeling of being transported into another world and an ancient time. I could almost imagine myself hearing the chink of hammers as the workers prepared the tomb to receive the royal body.

I froze. I had heard something and it wasn't a hammer. It was a falling rock, followed by a stealthy footstep. I looked into the darkness, but could see nothing where the moon illuminated the path. An unexpected fear gripped my heart and I scrambled down from the rock as quietly as I could, picking up a small rock on my way down. It wasn't much as a weapon, but it was better than nothing. The footsteps were getting closer and closer and every ghost story

I had ever heard came flooding into my memory. I had to force myself to be calm, reminding myself that footsteps are made by humans, not ghosts. To my annoyance, Bue began woofing and wagging his tail as though someone were petting him. I thought about telling the boy not to touch him, but realized the child wouldn't understand my language. Besides, if I spoke, whoever was coming would hear me. Instead, I backed into the rock as much as I could and raised my weapon as the footsteps crunched ever closer. The person paused and then I heard him coming stealthily around to my hiding place. I crashed down as hard as I could with my rock.

"What the . . . ?"

I was forcibly grabbed and pulled around to face my attacker. "Roxanne, are you insane?" Lymond demanded. "You could have killed me."

"Oh, good God," I moaned, looking at the blood on his head. "I've hurt you."

He shook his head as if to clear it and touched the bloody spot with his fingers. "No, but I think you reopened my wound." He touched his head gingerly again, this time with his handkerchief. "It was almost healed, too." He looked at me in the moonlight and pushed me up against the rock. His very nearness almost took my breath away as I caught a whiff of the scent that always reminded me of Lymond—a trace of soap, a trace of cigar smoke, and a heavy measure of something else that was indefinable.

Lymond pressed close to me. "I thought that was you standing on that rock silhouetted against the moon," he said, his face only inches from mine.

"Did you hear me calling?" I said, trying to speak. Whenever I was this close to Lymond, I always found speech difficult.

His voice was husky. "Yes, but it was your silhouette against the moon that—"

I pushed him back so I could speak. "The boy. Bue found him. They're over there."

"What boy?"

I explained about the lost boy and Lymond said he had seen the villagers searching and wondered what they were doing out so late. "Bue found the child," I said, "but I couldn't get him out. He's wedged between two rocks. I think he must have fallen." I stepped back to catch my breath. Lymond still had his hand on my arm, holding me tightly.

Lymond sighed and stepped back as well, releasing me. "Oh, well, I might as well get to the matter at hand," he said, walking over towards Bue. Bue bounded away from the boy and hit Lymond in the chest, almost knocking him down. Then Bue lapped Lymond right through the middle of the face. "Damned dog," Lymond muttered as he shoved Bue aside and knelt beside the boy.

"You shouldn't use profanity in front of the child," I told him.

"He can't understand me anyway," Lymond said, sliding down the rock so that he was closer to the child. He spoke something in a language I couldn't understand and evidently the child couldn't either because Lymond had to repeat himself slowly. This time, the child answered him and held up his arms to reach for Lymond. Lymond tugged, but couldn't move the boy. Lymond edged his way closer and reached down to grab the boy's waist. There were more guttural instructions as the boy put his arms around Lymond's neck. With a grunt from Lymond and a cry from the boy, Lymond managed to shift the child sideways, and, in just a moment or two, he had the boy out. "Here," he said, holding the child up so I could get him. "I can't get out while I've got him."

I took the child and he put his arms around my neck. To my amazement, I, who had never cared to be around children, was suffused with the most maternal of feelings. He seemed so very small and frightened. I patted him on the back and made soothing noises. The child patted me back.

"Let's take him to camp," Lymond said. "You can watch after him while I go get his family. I know they're at wit's end." Lymond took the child in his arms. "You manage the damn . . . the dog, Roxanne, and I'll carry him."

"Bue happens to be a hero, Lymond," I said, trying to walk beside him on the path. The path was too narrow, and I wound up following several paces behind like some ancient Egyptian woman honoring her mate. I didn't like it at all.

Back in camp, Lymond deposited the child in my tent with me and left to find the family. The child and I stared at each other for a while, and I offered him some sweets I had brought along. I wouldn't eat them as they had melted in the heat, but the child took a tentative nibble, then gobbled them down. I gave him some water which he drank thirstily. I was at wit's end what to do with him when Flora came in.

"You've found him!" she cried, falling to her knees in front of the child. "We must send for his family!"

"Lymond has gone to fetch them here," I said. "Flora, do you know anything about children? I gave him some sweets and water, now what do I do?"

She took the child in her arms and began washing his face with a cloth. In a moment, he began wriggling, hopped from her lap, and jumped into mine. "Now what?" I asked, looking down at the tiny being.

"Just hold him until his family arrives," Flora said with a smile. "It seems you've made a friend."

Bue came over and draped himself across my feet as the child stuck his thumb in his mouth and went to sleep. This was how Lymond found us when he returned. "The very picture of domesticity, Roxanne," he said, coming into my tent, followed by an old man whose eyes lit up when he saw the boy. "He's come to get the child," Lymond said unnecessarily.

I glanced down at the sleeping child, still with his thumb in his mouth, and again experienced a rush of strange, thoroughly maternal, feelings. The boy looked so peaceful, trusting, and innocent as he slept against my shoulder. He looked so *dependent*. True, my sisters had been dependent on me in years past, but this was different. Carefully, I moved the small body so I could hold him out to his grandfather. The grandfather came towards me and bowed at my feet, saying something I could not understand. Not knowing what else to do, I smiled, nodded, and handed the child to him. He bowed again, said something else, and went out.

Lymond walked over and sat on my camp bed. "It seems you're a heroine, Roxanne," he said. As best as I could understand, the grandfather says the boy owes his life to you, therefore, the grandfather owes you beyond repayment. Whatever you wish of him, you have but to command."

"Bue was the hero, not I." I shrugged. "After all, anyone would rescue a lost child. I'm just happy that we found him unhurt." I turned and looked slowly at Lymond. "I believe I should attend to your head. Your wound is trying to bleed again. Flora, will you hand me a cloth?" I stood and looked at his head, then poured some water on a cloth and washed it gently as Flora fetched some ointment. Uncharacteristically, Lymond sat still and didn't say a word. "There. That should make you feel better," I said as I finished. I had put a bandage on it, and it stood out starkly against Lymond's dark skin. Flora looked at Lymond and at me, then resumed her seat. "Are you enjoying your visit to these parts, Mr. Lymond?" she asked politely.

"Yes, except for the wind, sand, flies, and heat." He smiled. "I would probably enjoy it more if I knew you and Roxanne were on your way back to England."

"Too bad, Lymond." I sat down across from him where I could see his face clearly. "As a matter of fact, I intend to stay here for a while and learn about the excavation. In the short time I've been here, I have, as Henry says, been infected by the fever and fallen in love with Egypt. I've decided to finance my own expedition next year."

"Oh, God," Lymond groaned. "I should have known."

"It's a fascinating experience," I went on. "Even Flora is enjoying her work."

"Yes," Flora said eagerly, "Mr. Harris has put me to work sketching the objects unearthed. He had planned for his sister to do it as soon as she arrived here, but he says I'm a much better artist." She blushed rosily in the lamplight. "Not that I am. I'm sure he's only being polite."

"Not at all," I assured her. "His sister? I can't imagine a man as overbearing as Harris having a family, much less a sister. The poor thing must be quite cowed."

"She's a widow, he tells me," Flora said, "and he really doesn't want her here as he thinks a camp is no place for a woman like that—those are the words he used, 'like that'—but evidently she has nowhere else to go. Her husband died almost a year ago, I understand."

"That's all we need here," Lymond growled. "Another distraction."

"I suppose you're including Flora and me in that category," I said. "Tell me, Lymond, just what are we distracting you from?"

"And I thought you were the perfectionist about grammar," Lymond said with a smile. "You're slipping sadly, Roxanne." He paused, apparently finished, but I prompted him again. "I'm merely here looking for Uncle Harley's casket full of papyri," he said, all innocence. "The word I have is that the papyri were discovered stored in a jeweled casket which was in turn in a large pot. The whole package is supposed to be hidden somewhere around here, either in the hills or in the village." He looked at me and raised an eyebrow. "The place is rife with rumor. There's also some crazy talk of someone who knows the whereabouts of a cache of gold that was a tribute to some Pharoah, so both rumors are probably incorrect. I may have to go home empty-handed." He grinned. "Do you think Uncle Harley would like that?" He swallowed and wiped sand from his face. "Do you have anything to drink around here?"

"Water?" Flora asked.

Lymond looked rather horrified.

"I believe Lymond has something else in mind," I said, getting up and rummaging through my trunk. I pulled a bottle of very good brandy from its depths. "For medicinal purposes only, Lymond." I handed him the bottle.

"I can always depend on you, Roxanne." He didn't waste time on a glass, but rather tipped the bottle up and drank straight from it. "For medicinal purposes," he said with a wicked smile as he handed the bottle back to me. "Be sure to save it for me."

"I'll do that, Lymond." I hid the bottle back in my trunk. "Tell me, if the papyri are around here, why did you go off to parts unknown?"

"One of the villagers, a very well paid one, by the way, insisted that the papyri had been sold upriver. I went haring off after them, only to discover the tale was completely false. I should have known." He gave me a sheepish grin. "He went with me part of the way, then left me, saying he had to return to the village. I came back to extract my money from the rogue, but he's disappeared."

"I'm not surprised, but unless it was a great deal of money, there's no harm done. After all, Lymond, Uncle Harley can afford it." We shared a smile, both of us fully aware of Uncle Harley's clutch-fisted ways.

"Perhaps you can find the casket and papyri in the village and be on your way," I suggested. "The village is small, so I hear, therefore the casket shouldn't be hard to find."

"Nothing is hard to find if you know where to look," Lymond said. "What's difficult is getting the truth of the matter. Some of the people in this country don't think Egyptian antiquities should be going to collectors and museums in other countries."

"At least they're carefully preserved that way." I thought a moment about Lymond's problem. "Perhaps, Anwar could help you. He visits the village regularly and has relations living there."

Flora nodded. "Mr. Harris tells me that Anwar is extremely intelligent. He would probably know about any papyri."

Lymond gave us both a blank look. I knew that look from old—it meant that he knew something he wasn't telling. "You're using this merely as a ruse; there are no papyri here. Isn't that correct, Lymond?"

He gave me a surprised look. "I certainly hope the papyri are here, Roxanne. I'd hate to make any more trips out into the desert." He leaned back and extracted a cigar from his waistcoat. After a questioning look at Flora, he lit it and puffed contentedly for a moment. "I understand the fascination with this place, but I think it amazing that such a great civilization could spring up here. The place is a damn . . . sorry, Miss Rowe—a furnace and has very few redeeming features." He grinned at me. "I'd much rather be in Brighton."

"And I'm sure you had rather I were in Brighton as well."

He stood and smiled at me. "That goes without saying, Roxanne." He pulled his watch from his pocket. "It's late and Harris likes to begin at daylight before the heat becomes oppressive. When I'm here, I usually help with the work, so I'll bid you ladies goodnight." With that, he was gone, leaving behind that scent I always associated with Lymond. He also left behind about a dozen unanswered questions.

"Something's afoot, Flora," I said, watching the tent flap settle back into place. "I'd stake my reputation on it."

I felt I had been asleep only minutes when I was awakened by a shout from outside my tent. "Wake up, Roxanne!" It took me a few moments to realize that Lymond was outside shouting at me. Groggily I sat up, sore all over. After that first night, my body had decided that it and the camp bed were not compatible at all. "Go to Hades, Lymond," I shouted back. I was answered with a chuckle.

The noise had awakened Bue, who woke in fine fettle, ready to go out for his morning constitutional. I had to get dressed to go out and search for Jem to take him for a walk. By that time, I was up and about and ready for breakfast. To my surprise, Flora was already at breakfast, sitting beside Mr. Harris, who seemed to be outlining the day's work to her. Lymond was sitting at a small table with them and, since there was an extra place there, I sat down with them.

Flora turned to me, her cheeks rosy. She looked as refreshed as if she had spent a week vacationing in the Lake Country. "Roxanne, do you have any idea how long you plan to stay here? Mr. Harris needs me to sketch some things until his sister arrives. I wasn't sure of our—your itinerary."

I glanced from Harris to Lymond and took a shuddering sip of strong Egyptian coffee. "I plan to stay for a while. Brydges extended his invitation for as long as we wished." I turned to Harris. "I'm delighted we can be of service."

He grunted and rose. "I'll see you shortly," he said to Flora as he stalked off.

"Your charms are wasted there, Roxanne," Lymond said with a grin. He was dressed only in boots, breeches, and a shirt. The shirt was open at the neck and his sleeves were rolled up. I felt a strange feeling in the pit of my stomach as I looked at him. For some reason, Lymond *en dishabille* always does that to me. I forced myself to look at Flora. "I do hope you'll be able to stay around Harris without hitting him with something. He's unbelievably lacking in manners."

"He's quite nice when you get to know him," Flora said, rising. "I must get my sketchbook and get to work. I believe Mr. Harris is quite behind in sketching and cataloguing the items found. He's not expecting his sister for a week or so."

"I'm surprised anyone would allow a sister to come stay here," Lymond observed.

"I don't think Mr. Harris had much choice in the matter," Flora said. "He told me his sister wrote him that she was coming here and he needed to arrange for transportation to the camp for her." Flora paused. "The poor dear. She's a widow, you know, and probably is still distraught. From Mr. Harris's description, she's a plain little thing." Flora brightened. "Perhaps she'll meet an eligible *parti* here." She turned as she left. "Roxanne, do you need me to help you catalogue? I'll be sketching there in the tent, so just let me know." She waltzed away, humming to herself.

"Such a subtle hint," Lymond said with a grin. "I think that translates into 'Get to work, Roxanne.' "

"I don't mind working on the artifacts; in fact, I rather enjoy it."

Lymond gave me a strange look. "Is that why you're staying? Or is it Brydges?"

"What do you mean, Lymond?"

He looked steadily at me. "I didn't think I'd have to spell it out for you, Roxanne, but here it is: Is Brydges the reason you're staying in Egypt?"

I couldn't believe my ears. Between Lymond's tone and his scowl, I could almost believe he was jealous. I smiled at him sweetly and a horrible impulse came over me to goad him. I'm sorry to say that I gave in. "How clever of you to notice, Lymond. Brydges would be quite a catch, wouldn't he? Lady Brydges has such a ring to it." There was an unreadable expression on his face before he carefully made his countenance a complete blank. Immediately I was overcome with guilt. "I'm sorry, Lymond, I really didn't mean that. I'm staying because I enjoy the work. As I told you, I may finance an expedition myself." I stood and tossed Bue a crust of buttered bread. "And what of you, Lymond? Do you work for your keep as well? Or are you the dilettante of the group?"

"Hardly. As I told you, I always work when I'm here." He stood beside me and I was intensely aware of the scent of him. "I like working here. There's something about honest physical labor that helps one to sleep at night."

I moved away from him. "I'm sure that's a novel experience for you."

He chuckled as I walked out. "Sleeping at night or physical labor?" he asked.

I didn't answer him.

The tent where Flora and I worked was hot. Not just hot, but *hot*. Poor Bue was too hot to move and spent the day at my feet. In fact, he spent part of the time on my feet, no matter what I did to discourage him. I certainly didn't want pounds and pounds of hot, panting dog on my feet, but had little choice in the matter. Still, the morning went quickly. I got caught up in the meticulous work involved in measuring, making notations, and cataloguing each piece. It was exciting to think that each thing I picked up had been last touched by someone thousands of years ago. I, who had always disdained antiquities, was enchanted. I could almost imagine Papa up in heaven looking down and laughing.

Flora left for luncheon before I did. I had one last batch of shards to catalogue and I wanted to finish them. I was writing carefully in the large index book when I was aware of a familiar scent. I turned around to discover Lymond looking over my shoulder. His nearness took my breath away—that, and the fact that he was, as was I, soaked in sweat. His shirt clung to his body in a suggestive way and I had to force myself to look elsewhere.

"I've brought you a visitor," he said, stepping aside. There was the young boy, his entire family, and the grandfather. The grandfather bowed ceremoniously. "I've brought Henry to translate for you," Lymond said, motion-

ing Henry to the front to stand beside me. "I have a smat-
tering of the language, but not enough to do more than ask
about the necessities." He nodded at the grandfather and
the man stepped forward and spoke briefly.

"The boy's family is in your debt," Henry translated.
"They wish to express their gratitude to you. It seems the
child's father is dead, and the child is the only one left to
carry on the name." The grandfather nodded and spoke
again. "They have nothing to give you that is worthy of
expressing their gratitude, but they do wish you would take
this trifling present as a token of their feelings."

"I don't really want . . ." I began, but Lymond nudged
me in the ribs. "Don't offend them," he whispered, his lips
barely moving. The family was looking at me anxiously as
if they were afraid I would be insulted by their gift.

"Tell them I am greatly honored," I said to Henry.

Henry translated and a look of relief washed over the
faces in front of me. The grandfather bowed and held out
a package in both hands. He spoke and smiled. "He says
it is not enough," Henry translated, "but he also wants you
to know that his life is yours. Whatever you need, you have
merely to ask. His name is Abdullah."

"Tell Abdullah and his family that I am pleased beyond
measure." I reached out and took the package with a smile.
"Tell him as well that I am happy I could be of service to
his family and look forward to knowing them for many
years. I hope we will meet again before I leave."

Henry translated my words and Abdullah bowed again.
The family bowed as well and began to back out the door.
In just a trice, they were gone. "Good, Roxanne," Lymond
said. "For a moment there, I thought you were going to
insult the old man. Unintentionally, of course."

I glanced down at the package in my hands. "I certainly

didn't intend to do that, Lymond, but I do hate to take anything from them. They look as if they don't have very much."

"They are quite well thought of in the village," Henry said. "The old man is one of their leaders."

"What's in the package?" Lymond asked, reaching for it.

"I don't know, but intend to find out right now." I sat down at the table and put the package on it, opening it carefully. The wrappings were many: the outer layer was a piece of striped cloth, inside that was some kind of linen, then a layer of old, heavy papyrus. I moved the papyrus away and looked down at the item. "What is it?" We all looked at it carefully. "I have no idea," Henry said, handing it to Lymond. It was oval on top and had a handle; it looked rather like a large spatula. I was just rewrapping the item when Harris walked in looking for Flora. "Roxanne's been given a present by one of the villagers," Lymond told him, "but we can't figure out what it is."

I unwrapped the object and held it up. Harris looked at it and took it from my fingers. "It's a mirror," he said slowly, "and, as best as I can see without cleaning it, a very fine one at that."

"A mirror? Where did the glass go? I didn't know Egyptians had mirrors. It doesn't have glass." I took the object back and looked at the oval part.

Harris leaned over and turned the mirror in my hand. "Here's the handle. You'll note that the whole thing was made of brass. The front side of this was highly polished to make a reflective surface, here." He pointed to a blackened, tarnished flat area. "The back is decorated, although I really can't make out the design until it's cleaned thoroughly. I can tell you that it's a very fine piece." He stroked it with his fingers "An excellent find." He leaned against the table and frowned. "Did your benefactor say where this was found? Did he offer any particulars at all?"

I shook my head. "He just gave it to me. I'll ask him if you wish."

"Would you do that? I'd say that this probably came from a royal tomb, or else from the tomb of a high born woman. If he knows its origin, we might be able to go right to it." He stood and started to leave. "If there's anything left, that is. These villagers take anything that's loose." He paused. "I suppose I don't blame them. If I lived here and could get my hands on anything to sell, I'd do it, too."

Lymond and I watched him walk over to the mess tent. "I can't figure Harris," I said, rewrapping my mirror. "I think he knows what he's about, but he really has no sense of how to get along with people."

"He's excellent, but doesn't take kindly to anyone being lazy on the job," Lymond said. "Roxanne, I think you should lock that mirror up in a safe place. It may be more valuable than you think."

I looked down at the package in my hand. "I'll do that immediately, Lymond." I started for my tent, only to find Lymond in step with me. "I assure you, Lymond, that I'm fully capable of unlocking and relocking my trunk." Lymond's manner had been rather distant with me since I had goaded him, so I smiled. "I appreciate your interest, however."

He grinned. "Just making sure, Roxanne. It may be a good thing if more than one person knows where this is." He stood right beside me while I unlocked the trunk, carefully put the mirror inside, and relocked it. I began to put the key in presentation box, but Lymond stopped me. "Better make it a safer place," he said, taking the key from my fingers. He looked around my tent and finally picked up a small miniature I had of Papa. Quickly he stripped off the back and inserted the key, then replaced the back into the frame. "That's better," he said. "After all, there may be—" He was interrupted by a terrible uproar outside. Someone was bellowing at the top of his lungs—someone who sounded very familiar. Bue had joined in the uproar, barking continuously. Lymond and I dashed from my tent to the clearing in front of the mess tent. There we recognized it—the sound that froze the blood in our veins.

"God help us," Lymond gasped, "it's Uncle Harley!"

Eight

It was not only Uncle Harley, but Aunt Hen as well, and she was not taking the trip well at all. Lymond and I helped her into my tent where she collapsed into a heap on my small camp bed. "I can't bear it," she sobbed. "I told Harley I didn't want to come here, but nothing would do him except come on. After he met Mrs. Drummond and discovered she was coming here, nothing could have kept him from sailing for Egypt. Not even those lovely Florentine churches!"

"You actually got Uncle Harley into a church?" Lymond was amazed.

I, however, had another question. "Who is Mrs. Drummond?" I asked Aunt Hen.

"Harley ran into her in Florence. She's the widow of the son of an old acquaintance of Harley's. I didn't know either one—the son or the father. Harley was at school with the father, I believe—a Mr. Drummond."

"That stands to reason," Lymond said with a chuckle and I shot him an evil look. "Why was Mrs. Drummond coming to Egypt?" I asked. "Surely the trip was grueling for her as well. How old is she?"

Aunt Hen paused. "She must be six-or-seven-and-twenty. Perhaps a year or two either way. Her brother is here, I believe."

Lymond and I looked at each other and nodded. "Harris's sister," I murmured.

"Yes, and a viper in my bosom!" Aunt Hen cried.

Lymond and I both raised eyebrows at this. "Aunt Hen, you're distraught," I said, proffering her some of the medicinal brandy. "Mr. Harris assures us that his sister is the quietest, meekest of women. He even described her as plain."

Aunt Hen downed the brandy in one gulp. "She's a viper, I tell you, Roxanne. If you could have seen her with Harley! Such a flirt! She appealed to Harley's good nature by telling him how alone in the world she was and how she had nowhere to go since the death of her husband. The hussy!"

"Really, Aunt Hen," I murmured, looking around the tent to see if anyone had overheard.

"It's true, Roxanne. Nothing would do Harley but to offer her his protection. Of course, he was looking for an excuse to come to Egypt anyway. Harley and I had a terrible argument in Florence . . ." She stopped to weep into a sodden handkerchief. "I told him to go to Egypt with Mrs. Drummond and they could both go to Hades. He told me not to be ridiculous." She looked up at the two of us. "So here I am. I knew if anyone could talk sense into Harley, it would be the two of you."

It took two more glasses of brandy before Aunt Hen rested and went to sleep on my bed. I looked down at her—the trip had taken its toll on her. She looked fatigued beyond words and seemed to have aged in the weeks since I had seen her. I said as much to Lymond.

"This heat, wind, and sand takes it toll on everyone, particularly ladies of Aunt Hen's stripe." He peered down into the brandy bottle. "I'm going to have to replenish your medicine the next time I go to Cairo. I think this experience is going to call for several bottles."

"Will you be serious, Lymond?"

"I am. There's enough for two glasses in here. Do you want one?"

I paused and thought about spending time here with Uncle Harley and Aunt Hen. "Definitely," I told him.

Lymond sipped his brandy slowly. "There's no point in dawdling around and putting off the inevitable," I said to him. "You're going to have to go talk to Uncle Harley and find out what's going on."

He sighed and put down his empty glass. "I know. I suppose you want a full report on whatever I discover."

"Of course." I smiled up at him as he stood and he smiled back, that slightly crooked smile that everyone found so charming. I shook my head as the tent flap closed behind him. I must be getting sentimental I thought to myself—Lymond's smile was beginning to have its effect on me. Still, I was delighted that Lymond's cool demeanor had changed—he seemed very much his old self.

Flora came into the tent shortly. The heat trapped inside the canvas was stifling and I had her open the flaps and tie them back. She offered to sit with Aunt Hen and I accepted her offer gladly. Lymond hadn't returned, and I was consumed with curiosity. I made my way outside and paused while I located the source of conversation in the camp. It seemed to be coming from the mess tent, so I went over there and started inside. I stopped suddenly, looking at the scene before me. There was a ravishing young woman, surrounded by most of the men in the camp. Lymond was right up there beside her, Brydges was on her other side. She was laughing and smiling up into Lymond's face.

I glanced down at my dress, sweat-stained and filthy

from handling all the pots I had measured and packed. My hands were dirty as well, the nails chipped and dirty, and I could feel my hair plastered to my face and neck in sweaty wisps. On the other hand, Cecilia Drummond looked as if she were attending a garden party. Her blond hair was artfully arranged with tendrils of curls framing a lovely face. She was dressed in pink and white stripes, and looked as fresh as if she had just stepped from a pattern card. Lymond looked down at her and smiled. In turn, she batted her eyelashes at him and gave him a flirtatious look. None of the men was aware of my presence.

Exasperated by the fawning clods the men were proving to be, I went outside. Harris was there, looking glum. "I knew everything would come to a complete halt whenever Cecilia got here," he said in disgust. "It always does." He threw a rock down into the sand with great force. "Hell and damnation! Women!" He turned and bit his bottom lip. "I'm sorry, Miss Sydney. I forgot myself."

"I've been in that tent," I told him, "so I understand exactly what you mean." I paused. "Why did you tell Flora that your sister was plain? She's quite a beauty."

"Do you think so? I've never thought Cecilia was particularly pretty, but then, perhaps I know her too well." He paused. "I'm going back to the tomb. Perhaps I'll get some work done today."

I wanted to ask him what he meant by knowing Cecilia 'too well,' but he seemed upset enough by her presence. I certainly didn't want to add to his distress. So I did what English ladies have done since time immemorial—I changed the subject. "I measured and cleaned the pots on the shelf on the left and Flora sketched everything," I told him, hoping to make him feel better. "Do you want me to get Jem to help me pack everything and move the boxes to the other tent?"

"I'd be most grateful. The boxes are in the supply tent and, if you don't mind, put plenty of packing around each piece. We don't want to risk breaking anything." He took a few steps and turned around to face me. "I apologize, Miss Sydney."

"For what, Mr. Harris?"

"For the way I acted when you and Miss Rowe arrived. You see, I've always been accustomed to women acting like Cecilia and my mother. They were always expecting someone to be at their beck and call, never taking on their share of the work." He paused and a bitter look flashed across his face. "I thought you and Miss Rowe would be the same. I realize that I was mistaken and I apologize. The two of you have already proven invaluable to the project."

I smiled at him. "Apology accepted, Mr. Harris. I do admit I came here with no clear idea of the amount of work involved. Will you consider both Miss Rowe and me in training? We want to learn and be of help to you. As I mentioned, I hope to finance an expedition of my own."

"I'd be honored to help you." He smiled at me and I was surprised at the way the smile altered his features. As he strode off towards the workmen standing around the excavation, I realized that Lymond had been right—the man had responsibility for the whole expedition. Brydges and his brother were financing it, Atherton, from what I could see, primarily kept the supplies and workers flowing, but the three of them did little work. Everything was on Harris. I resolved to be nicer to him in the future and to try to help him. I said as much to Flora when I went back into my tent. I shared Harris's apology with her since she was involved as well. To my surprise, there was a tell-tale blush on her cheeks when I mentioned his name.

I dragooned Woodbury into sitting with Aunt Hen as she slept so Flora, Jem, and I could go to the pottery tent to continue with our sketching, and packing. We worked hard all afternoon. Bue even cooperated by hollowing out a spot under a shelf and claiming it as his own. He was enervated by the heat. In a while he got up and was gone. When he returned, he had evidently made the rather long trip to the river and had gone for a swim. He was wet all over and, of course, flopped right down on my feet to go to sleep. He, like Aunt Hen, slept all afternoon.

By that evening, all the men had erected a tent for Mrs. Drummond, but the tent for Uncle Harley and Aunt Hen had not been put up. Lymond decided, after much agonizing, that he would invite Uncle Harley into his tent, and I could keep Aunt Hen. Aunt Hen didn't wish to join the others for supper, so I carried a tray into my tent for us. After supper, Uncle Harley came to see about her. Evidently he had no idea that his behavior toward Mrs. Drummond had distressed Aunt Hen. He had Lymond in tow, and they sat down on rugs like Oriental pashas. "Hotter than Hades," Uncle Harley said, mopping at his face. "This is the first time we've been alone, Robert," he said to Lymond without further preamble. "Have you found the casket and papyri?"

"Not yet, but I think I'm close. The last rumor I had placed the casket in the village. I'm still asking and looking. This seems to be the best information I've received about it."

"Rumors, hrrumph. I never know whether or not to take credence in rumors." Uncle Harley looked at me. "Roxanne, are you aware that there is a very strong rumor in

Cairo that you and Robert here have discovered some kind of treasure or valuable antiquity here? I heard it from two acquaintances I looked up, so I stopped in Cairo long enough to talk to Mohammed and he told me that there had been attacks on both of you. You're supposed to have a golden box containing a map leading to a Pharoah's cache. What secrets are you keeping?"

Lymond and I looked at each other in shock and Lymond gave me a small shake of his head. "Whatever are you talking about, Uncle Harley?" I asked. "I don't know anything about a Pharoah's map; the only antiquities I've seen have been a bunch of broken pots. Do you know anything, Lymond?"

Lymond shook his head. "No, of course not." He laughed. "I'm not surprised at what you've heard. This place almost has London beaten for rumor and gossip. Notice I said *almost.*"

"Nothing but rumor." Uncle Harley frowned. "I had my hopes up, but I was afraid it was all a hum. By the way, Robert, I received your letter about your expenses. What have you been doing?"

Lymond gave him an injured look. "I've been chasing all over the Nile Valley after those papyri you wanted. Uncle Harley, you don't realize how much papyrus is here. There are scraps of papyrus all over the Nile Valley, but nothing in a casket. Especially a casket of filigreed metal studded with jewels. I'm beginning to doubt its existence." He sighed. "Even if it were here, I'd have the devil's own time tracking it. The political situation here is so explosive that it's difficult to talk to many people."

Uncle Harley nodded. "Yes, I read all about the defeat of the Mamelukes some time back and the chaos that was prevalent. The Frenchies didn't help a thing either—Napoleon thought he was another Pharoah or some such. What do you think will happen now?"

"I don't know." Lymond ran his fingers through his hair. "There's a very strong nationalist movement—Egypt for the Egyptians and all that sort of thing. In a way, I hope that's the way things go. After all these years of exploitation, it's time the Egyptians controlled their own county and destiny."

Uncle Harley stared at him. "Never would have figured you for a revolutionary, Robert. What these people need is a good governor."

Lymond grinned. "And a chance to pledge allegiance to the Prince of Wales? It's not going to happen, Uncle Harley."

"I know, but it should. What kind of papyri have you found for me? Anything else of note turned up? Mohammed told me that all types of antiquities could be found here—that's one of the reasons I came."

"And to escort Mrs. Drummond," Aunt Hen put in.

"Dammit, Henrietta, no man can let a woman travel alone in a country like this. I told you in Florence that we needed to assist her. The poor woman would still be in Italy looking for a way to come to her brother if we hadn't stepped in." Uncle Harley pulled out a cigar and lit it. "Besides, I'd seen enough." He turned to Lymond. "If you've seen one church, you've seen them all. Italy must have ten thousand churches. Have you heard of any golden objects, Robert? Are your sure the two of you aren't hiding something from me? The rumor from Cairo about the map you two have was specific. Are you sure you know nothing about it?"

"How ridiculous," I said. "If I had such a map, I'd be

on my way to look for the cache. How did such a silly rumor begin, anyway?"

"How do rumors always start?" Lymond shrugged his shoulders. "I've been trying to convince Roxanne to return to England because of the attack on her. It might have been random, but I don't think so. It had to be tied to the rumor."

"And the attack on you, Woodbury, and Jem?"

"The same, I'd say." Lymond frowned. "If the rumor has penetrated to here, you may not be safe, Roxanne. You really should go home."

Aunt Hen nodded vigorously. "That's an excellent idea. We should all go home."

"You need to convince Roxanne, not me," Lymond said, getting to his feet. "I'm ready as soon as I either find the casket or discover it's all a hoax." He looked from Aunt Hen to Uncle Harley to me. "Don't you need to walk the dog?" he asked.

"No." I was puzzled. The last thing Lymond ever wanted to do was be around Bue.

"I think you need to walk the dog, Roxanne. I'll go with you." He looked again from Uncle Harley to Aunt Hen.

I finally caught his drift as he looked from Uncle Harley to Aunt Hen and back again. "You're right, Lymond. Uncle Harley, will you stay here with Aunt Hen until I get back? We have to take Bue out regularly." I got his leash, fastened it to his collar, and gave it to Lymond. He took it with distaste as we went out of the tent. "Let's tie the dog to a stake somewhere," he muttered as soon as we were out of earshot. "We'll probably have to sit out here for half an hour or so."

"We're going to take the dog for a walk, Lymond," I said firmly, taking Bue's collar and pulling him. Bue was be-tween us, and as soon as he realized he was out for his constitutional, he began to run towards the excavated tomb door, dragging Lymond along behind him.

As we approached the hole in the ground, a white wraith suddenly appeared. "Lymond!" I squawked, releasing Bue's collar and grabbing Lymond around the neck. Lymond was taken off guard, dropped Bue's leash, and staggered sideways under my weight. He stumbled and caught himself with his hands. "What the—what's wrong, Roxanne?"

"Didn't you see it?" I demanded as I stood upright and looked at the excavations. "A ghost." I stopped and got my thoughts in order. "It can't be a ghost, can it? There are no such things."

"I'm glad you realize that," Lymond said, picking himself up and dusting his clothes. "Bucephalus seems to have headed for parts unknown." He looked towards the excavation. "Which way?"

I took a tentative step towards the excavation. "Let's see if anything is here, then we can look for Bue. I don't worry too much about him—he's big enough to take care of himself."

"Unless someone else takes care of him," Lymond said. I could see a worried frown on his face in the moonlight. "That damned dog has caused me more . . . I feel responsible for the stupid thing. Do you remember when he stood between me and a bullet?"

"I know." I tugged at his sleeve. "This will just take a minute. I know I saw something. Something white and moving. If it isn't a ghost, there must be a perfectly logical explanation, and I want to know what it is."

Lymond sighed. "Probably just Mustapha. I think he's standing guard tonight. Since we uncovered some steps going into what we think may be a royal burial site, Atherton and Harris were worried that someone might try to break into the tomb tonight."

"Mustapha. The crew leader? Isn't he afraid of all the afreets and ghosts and demons that all the other villagers seem to fear?"

"Of course he is. That's why Brydges is paying him triple for tonight." Lymond moved up towards the hole in the ground and called out.

"If it isn't Mustapha, " I whispered, "then you've frightened away whoever it might be."

"If it was Mustapha, which I think likely, he's armed with two pistols and a musket. I don't want to risk *not* identifying myself." Lymond called out again and was answered this time. Mustapha came out of the shadows, garbed in some sort of striped stuff. Our wraith must have been someone else. I didn't have time to reflect on it, however, as Mustapha had his pistol at the ready and was pointing it at us. Lymond quickly gave his name and mine. Mustapha didn't drop the pistol and I own I found it quite unnerving. A pistol looks so much larger when one is looking at it head on.

Lymond spoke to the man and assured him we were merely out walking the dog. Mustapha looked around for the dog and didn't see him, so the pistol came up again. "Atherton told him not to trust anyone," Lymond muttered. "He certainly took his instructions to heart."

We bade Mustapha goodnight and went off to search for Bue. Rather we backed off while Mustapha kept his pistol pointed our way. Lymond held on to my arm as we backed up. "Never turn your back on a pistol, Roxanne," he said between his teeth. "All sorts of unpleasant things can happen."

Mustapha stood there until we were well away from the

excavation, then he disappeared down the steps, dropping out of sight by degrees. After the excavation was quiet again, Lymond and I veered off towards the mountains to search for Bue. We looked for the better part of two hours and didn't discover him. Lymond was becoming more and more irritated as well as more and more fluent with his curses. I made no move to stop him; if I had not been brought up strictly, I would have indulged in the same vocabulary. Bue was proving something of a trial.

Finally, Lymond sat down on a rock near the path to the village. "Let's give it up for tonight. I can't see much in these shadows where the moon doesn't hit, and Bue's not answering our calls. We'll begin tomorrow morning early before it gets too hot."

I sat down beside him, thoroughly discouraged. "I agree, Lymond. If I only knew that Bue wasn't hurt somewhere, then I wouldn't mind abandoning the search. What if he's gotten his collar caught and is hanging somewhere?"

"I think he'd make some kind of noise if that happened." Lymond looked around some more. "Sound travels far here, and we could hear him if he was in trouble, so he's probably all right. One thing I've noticed about Bue: he has amazing powers of survival."

"You're right, I know, but I still worry." I glanced back at the camp. "Do you think Aunt Hen and Uncle Harley have made up their differences? Aunt Hen was furious with him because he'd been paying attention to Mrs. Drummond."

"Aunt Hen? Jealous?" Lymond chuckled. "To think, the family has paid me at times to take Uncle Harley off their hands, and here Aunt Hen is afraid Mrs. Drummond will snatch him. I don't believe there's any worry."

"I noticed you were quite entranced with Mrs. Drummond yourself." I could have bitten off my tongue, but the words just slipped out.

Lymond turned and looked at me in surprise. *"Et tu,* Roxanne? I can't believe it!"

"There's nothing to believe, Lymond. I was merely commenting that you, as well as every other male in the camp except Harris, were making total fools of yourselves over Cecilia Drummond. Aunt Hen says that she uses people."

"Don't most women?"

I jumped to my feet. "No, most women don't. You're completely impossible, Lymond!" I wheeled and began walking back to camp.

Lymond stood and began following me, chuckling all the while. "You're just saying that, Roxanne, because I won the bet."

I turned. "What bet?" The second I said the words I remembered. "Oh, good God!"

He laughed. "That's right, Roxanne. I bet you that Uncle Harley would have Aunt Hen in Egypt. Here they are and my lease is extended for another five years." He sauntered up beside me and began counting on his fingers. "Let's see—that's one, two, three, four . . ." I left him and stalked off to my tent as he stood in the middle of the sand and counted.

The man was *impossible.*

Aunt Hen was alone when I got back inside my tent. Evidently the time alone had not healed the breach. She was sitting in my camp bed, sniffling. "I'm glad you're back, Roxanne," she said, waving her vinaigrette. "I don't think I'm going to be able to sleep." She slid down into bed.

I looked around. There was no place for me to sleep except on a rug on the sand. There was nothing to use for padding under me except the rug. With a sigh, I opened my trunk and piled some of my clothes on the floor, making a lumpy mattress. Between worry about Bue, annoyance at Lymond, and the lumps in my mattress, I scarcely slept. Aunt Hen, on the other hand, snored gently all night—in my bed.

As the first streaks of dawn broke across the sky, I awoke cold and stiff. The temperature had dropped drastically during the night. Grabbing a shawl, I crawled out of the tent and tried to straighten my body. I felt as if I had been beaten with a stick. I heard a moan off to the side and turned, catching Lymond doing the same as I. We looked at each other and didn't even have to speak to know how the other felt. Lymond limped over to me. "Was your night as good as mine?"

"As good or better," I replied. "Do you think we could get a cup of tea or coffee and then look around for Bue?"

We set out for the mess tent and discovered that we were the first there, except for the cook. His tea was execrable, but the coffee was even worse. The coffee was almost a dark brown syrup. Both Lymond and I opted for tea.

We were just finishing our tea when Harris came into the tent, rubbing sleep from his eyes. He sat down with us and had a cup of coffee, drinking it down without even tasting it. That was probably a good thing.

"Are you as eager to get started as I am?" he asked. "I think our tomb has been opened before, so we may find something, but more probably we may find nothing. Still, I want to go slowly. Brydges is all for blasting the door open, but I'd rather not." He paused. "Atherton told Brydges the tomb was still sealed, but what does he know? The man's no scholar at all—he's merely interested in what he can sell and for how much. I took a very careful look and told Brydges the seals on the door had been broken, but probably a thousand years ago. He's hoping that nothing was disturbed inside."

"What are the odds on that?" Lymond asked.

"Slim to none." Harris frowned into his cup. "Still, even if nothing is left but the wall decorations or a few mundane items, we might be able to learn something about the burial or the name of the person in the tomb."

I nodded in approval. "You remind me of Papa," I told him. "He was always interested in preserving artifacts and finding out about the people who had made them."

Harris gave me a quick look. "Unfortunately, we're in the minority." He rose. "Do you want to go with me?" His gaze settled on Lymond, but I pretended I was included. When Lymond rose, I got up as well. Harris gave me a brief look and smiled at me. "I suppose you and Miss Rowe have earned the right to be at any discoveries we might make. Come along."

"Strange," Harris said as we approached the excavation. "Mustapha should be here."

"He was last night," I told him. When he looked at me curiously, I told him I had been out hunting for Bue and had seen Mustapha. I didn't mention that I had been with Lymond. I didn't want Harris to get the wrong idea.

Still, there was no trace of Mustapha at the entrance to the hole in the ground. Harris went down the steps alone while Lymond and I stood at the top. In a moment, I heard Harris taking the Lord's name in vain. He wasn't as fluent as Lymond, but was louder. He came bounding up the steps two at a time. "Someone's been in there! The door's been forced!"

"Has anything been taken?" I asked before I thought.

"I don't know." He shook his head and began sprinting

towards the camp. Lymond and I debated about going inside the tomb, but decided to wait for Harris to return. In just a few moments we saw him sprinting across the sand toward us with Brydges and his brother in tow, both of them still in the process of pulling on their clothing.

I left the men to search the tomb, since there seemed to be few comments made that didn't include profanity, and I went back to the camp. I was worried about Bue and gathered up Woodbury and Jem to help me search for him. They were not happy to do so, but had little choice in the matter. "As large as he is, Woodbury," I said anxiously scanning the horizon, "he won't last long without water." Although I wouldn't say so to Lymond or anyone outside the family, Bucephalus wasn't the most intelligent dog on the planet. He could be halfway to Ethiopia by now.

"He probably went towards the river for another swim," Jem said.

I shuddered, remembering the crocodiles we had seen. "The river must be two miles or so away," I said. "Let's look there first, then we'll start on the hills and work our way back to the village." I thought of the grandfather and his pledge. "If all else fails, Woodbury, I'll go see Abdullah and his family and see if they will help us search. Finding Bue would be more than any other repayment he could ever give me."

We saw no trace of Bue at the river, although Jem was kind enough to point out that if Bue had been devoured by a crocodile, there would be no trace. With a heavy heart, I led them back to the camp and we began searching the rocks at the base of the hills. There were so many, and so many places where Bue could have been trapped. We called and called, to no avail.

After several hours, Woodbury sat down on a rock and

mopped at his face. We were all worse for the wear—the sand flung about by the wind felt as if it had scoured the very skin from my flesh; the sun was so bright as to be almost blinding; and the heat drained the life from my body. Woodbury looked as if he were in worse shape than I. "I can't go on, Miss Sydney," he gasped. His face was beet red; I didn't know if from exertion or from sunburn. "I can't go on."

I sighed and sat down beside him, calling to Jem. "I know, Woodbury. Let's go back to camp and perhaps after the sun cools this evening, we can resume our search." I looked at him. "I must find him, Woodbury. Or some trace."

Woodbury understood. After all, he knew that Bucephalus had been a gift from Papa and meant more to me than most dogs mean to their owners. He offered to persist in the search, but I knew he couldn't go on. Woodbury meant a great deal to me as well.

We were in the hills among the rocks, traveling on the path that led from the village to the camp. Suddenly Jem shouted and pointed his finger skyward. "Bue!" he shouted.

I shielded my eyes with my hand and looked up. Sure enough, there was Bue standing on a rock, something in his mouth. I shouted his name, as did Woodbury and Jem, and he bounded down towards us, the object falling from his mouth. At that second, a shot rang out, the bullet ricocheting off the rocks around us, sending flying chips of rock into our midst. Woodbury fell on top of me, knocking me to the ground. We crawled behind a rock and waited, but there were no further shots. In the meantime, Bue had reached us and was happily lapping at our faces with his rough tongue. He, I think, was happier to see us than we were to see him.

After a few moments, we risked sitting up and I hugged Bue and petted him. He wagged his tail furiously, then bounded off again. I started to run after him, but Woodbury restrained me. "I must get him, Woodbury," I said. "He'll get lost." I eluded Woodbury's grasp and ran out onto the path. Bue was returning to me, the object in his mouth again. "He's merely gone to retrieve whatever he dropped, Woodbury," I said, smiling at Bue and making little noises at him. Bue ran up to me, tail wagging, and dropped the object at my feet.

It was a pistol.

Nine

I picked up the pistol and smelled it. It had recently been discharged and there was still some heat on the barrel. "It must have gone off when Bue dropped it," I said to Wood-bury and Jem. "There's no danger to us." I handed the pistol to Jem and grabbed Bue's collar as he had lost his leash somewhere in his travels during the night. Bue seemed as eager to get back to camp as we did, and we got to my tent in just a short while. As we came into camp, I saw Brydges, Anwar, and Lymond talking. I sent Bue on with Jem and Woodbury and went to see them, the pistol still in my hand.

"Ready for battle?" Lymond asked as I approached.

I raised an eyebrow. "Hardly, but there are some who might benefit from this. If it's of any concern to you, Bue has returned."

"I knew he would," Lymond said. "He's not going to find any buttered bread out in this country."

I ignored his attempt at humor; he knew how much Bue meant to me. Instead, I turned to Brydges and waved the pistol towards him. He leaped backwards into Anwar. "Don't worry," I reassured him, "I know how to handle a pistol." I heard Lymond chuckle behind me. "Bue was car-rying this in his mouth and dropped it against a rock. I suppose you heard the noise when it discharged."

Brydges took the pistol from my fingers. "So that was what that was! We were just discussing it and wondering if we needed to send a party out to investigate. As you know, Mustapha is missing." He held the pistol up and looked at it carefully. "Look, Lymond, this is one of ours. I had my initials engraved on each one of them so I'd be able to recognize it." He pointed to some small initials on the bottom of the barrel. "It's number eleven. Anwar, do you know which number Mustapha had?"

Anwar nodded. "Eleven."

The three men exchanged glances. "Perhaps you should organize a search party after all," I suggested.

"Yes," Brydges agreed. "He may have merely lost it in his flight, but there might be a more sinister meaning. Where did the dog find it?"

Here I was lost. Knowing Bue, he might have carried the thing in his mouth for an hour or so. After all, he had been gone all night.

"Perhaps," Brydges suggested, "we can take the dog and see if he will lead us to anything. We might find a trail or . . ."

This was easier said than done. Harris didn't want to release any men to spend time searching for a defector, as he termed Mustapha and Atherton ridiculed the idea as a waste of time. However, Brydges showed a stubborn streak and insisted, making up a search party of himself, Lymond, Woodbury, and Jem. Bue, however, had other ideas and wanted no part of a search. He sat down next to Lymond's feet and refused to budge. Lymond began walking along the trail to the village, and Bue merely looked at him, curled up, and proceeded to close his eyes. There was no moving him at all.

I watched the whole proceeding from the entrance to my tent. The wind was up today, and the hot sand seemed to scour my skin, so I had no wish to go outside. With a chuckle at Jem's and Lymond's attempts to get Bue to his feet, I went into my tent.

"I see very little reason to smile in this place," Aunt Hen said. She was, as usual, reclining on my camp bed, propped up by pillows, with her vinaigrette and fan in her hand. "The heat, the sand, the people coming in unexpectedly . . ."

"Such as?" I put a pillow on the floor and sat down.

"Such as the man who slipped right into the tent while you were gone. I roused up and gave him a good tongue-lashing, I can tell you."

I sat bolt upright. "What man, Aunt Hen? Was he looking for anything in particular? Did he say who he was?"

"I don't know his name." Aunt Hen waved a hand in the general direction of the rest of the camp. "All these workers look alike to me. No doubt the man was Egyptian although I couldn't see his face at all under that headdress. He was all in white—some kind of native costume."

"A galabeah? Hardly costume, Aunt Hen," I said. "It's what they wear every day."

"Whatever." She waved her hand vaguely. "He had to be a native because as soon as I began screeching at him, he said something in their language and backed out the door. I thought perhaps you had sent him to fetch something."

I shook my head. "No."

"Then perhaps he blundered into the wrong tent. All the tents look alike, I'm sure."

"Mine is striped."

"Don't go finding mysteries, Roxanne?" Aunt Hen waved her vinaigrette under her nose. "Have you seen Harley? More importantly, have you seen Mrs. Drummond?"

"No to both," I said, just as my name was called from the entrance to my tent. In just a second, Brydges entered, paused, then squatted down beside me.

"Is there any way I could prevail on you to go with us and lead your dog?" he asked. "He doesn't seem to be succumbing to any of our blandishments."

I laughed, knowing Bue as well as I did. When he didn't want to do something, he didn't do it. "We need to find Mustapha—he may have left as Harris thinks, but he may be injured," Brydges said. I hadn't considered that possibility. Thinking of an injured man out in the heat and sand pricked my conscience, so I agreed and got a scarf to wrap around my head and face. "You'll roast," Aunt Hen said ominously, fanning herself.

I didn't. The headgear was only slightly warmer than nothing, and actually seemed to catch a little of the breeze. Best of all, it kept the sand away from most of my face. If I only had something to cover my eyes, I might be able to get about in this land.

When I reached Bue, I knelt and petted him, gave him the pistol to sniff and lick, then tugged on his leash. I had expected rebellion, but he was on his feet instantly and almost dragged me up the path. It was as if he knew what he was supposed to do.

We traveled towards the village a while, then turned up into the rocks. There, Bue stopped and sat down, looking at me expectantly. I realized he was expecting a reward of buttered bread, but I had neglected to bring any. "I'm not sure about this place," I explained to Brydges. "You might look around."

Brydges fell to his hands and knees in a small clearing in the rocks. "It looks as if the dog has been here and perhaps picked something up." He pointed to an indentation in some sand caught between the rocks. "Perhaps we should look up there." He looked up at the mountain and the rocks over our heads and began climbing while Bue and I sat down in the shade of a rock. Bue, needless to say, was petulant and kept snuffling around for his bread and butter.

I was becoming restless myself after half an hour or so. I had work to do with some faience rings and some pots Harris had brought me and simply didn't have time to waste sitting around waiting on some men to wander around the rocks. I looked up at the men, shielded my eyes, and called to them that I was returning to camp. Brydges turned to say something to me, then pointed down and motioned to the other men. He began waving in an agitated way and pointing off to my left. I peered over that way, but saw nothing. Brydges was scrambling down the rocks, Lymond right after him. Before they reached the place I was standing, however, they veered off to the left, above my head. In a second, Brydges peered over the edge of the rock. "It's Mustapha," he said, white and shaken. "He must have dropped the pistol from here."

I started up the side of the rock, Bue's leash still in my hand. Brydges reached down and touched my shoulder before I could see. "Don't look," he said hoarsely. "It isn't pretty."

"Death seldom is," I said.

Lymond looked down at me. "You'd better stay there. His throat's been cut and he's bled to death," he said shortly. "We'd better go get some men to help us move him to camp."

Brydges jumped down from the rocks to stand beside me. He leaned back against a rock and took a deep breath.

"At the risk of seeming heartless, this is going to cause problems."

"It seems it already has, especially for Mustapha," I said.

Brydges took my arm and we began the descent down towards the camp. "I didn't mean that. God knows I feel sorry for the fellow, but I'm sure many of the workers will regard his death as some kind of divine retribution. I had enough trouble getting him to stand guard all night."

"Surely no one in his right mind will think that a demon or ghost carries a knife around to slit throats," I said. "One might be scared to death, but hardly knifed to death."

Brydges shook his head. "They have all kinds of strange superstitions. Sometimes I think the whole country runs on superstition. I won't be able to get a native to stand guard again. We'll have to take turns."

"Do you think that was why Mustapha was killed? I don't think we can entertain the idea that he might have fallen on a knife—this was deliberate murder. Do you think his standing guard was the reason he was killed?"

"I don't know. If he was, why was he killed up in the rocks? Why wasn't he killed right there at the tomb?" Brydges unconsciously increased the pressure of his hand on my arm as he talked. "Why was he killed? Mustapha certainly knew nothing of what we had discovered."

"Have you discovered something important?"

"No, that's what puzzles me. Oh, Harris says there's some chairs and other pieces, but nothing really valuable—no gold or so on. I don't know why anyone would kill him."

"Perhaps," I said as we walked into the edge of the camp, "if you answer the *why* question, you'll find out *who* killed him."

* * *

Brydges had been correct about one thing: the announcement of Mustapha's murder sent the entire camp into a frenzy. The workers stopped what they were doing and rushed up to the rocks to see for themselves. When the body was brought down, there was a great deal of discussion about what to do with it. Anwar pointed out Mustapha's connections in the village, and suggested that we turn the body over to the village elders for the proper ceremonies and burial. I thought we should wait on the authorities, but Brydges pointed out that it might take the authorities several days or even weeks to get here, and by that time, between the heat and what naturally happens to bodies . . . I saw his point immediately and hastily agreed with Anwar.

That evening, the camp had quieted. We all met for supper in the mess tent and I noticed the conversation was somewhat subdued. Harris was talking to Flora, and I could see from the intensity of his expression that he was discussing the effect of the event on the excavation. Uncle Harley and Aunt Hen seemed to have made up or were at least speaking to each other. Edward and Colonel Atherton were discussing anything and everything: the political situation, supplies, the possibility of the authorities in Cairo interfering, and how much money it would take in bribes and baksheesh. Atherton soon monopolized the conversation with his favorite theme—the villagers were stealing everyone blind. I had concluded through close observation that the villagers might pilfer a thing or two, but by no means did they engage in wholesale thievery. Atherton was quite prejudiced against the natives, and I said as much to my dinner partner, Brydges.

"I agree," he said perfunctorily, leaning towards me slightly. "Enough of life here," he said with a smile. "Tell me, Miss Sydney, something of your life. Why haven't I seen you around London? I would have thought we might have met at some soiree or the other."

"I don't get out into London society," I answered. "I prefer to spend my time at Brighton. My father left an extensive library and hundreds of artifacts. It takes most of my time to sort and catalogue his things. I doubt I'll ever finish."

Brydges laughed softly. "I wondered where you acquired your amazing skills. Perhaps you can help us when we discover our treasure trove and take it back to London." He chuckled and a strange expression crossed his face. I knew that look: I had seen the same expression on Uncle Harley's face when he was greedily discussing an acquisition.

"You plan to take everything you find back with you?"

"Only the valuable things. The rest can stay here."

I shook my head. "Who's to say what is valuable and what isn't? Just because something is made of a precious metal—"

"Gold, you mean."

"Correct. Just because something is made of gold doesn't make it valuable in the historical sense. My Papa taught me that."

"True. Look at Elgin's marbles. Not a touch of precious metal and yet beyond price as a feast for the eyes."

I nodded approvingly. "I'm glad you see reason. I think you should perhaps consider leaving as many things as possible here for others to come study in their native surroundings."

Brydges laughed. "You sound exactly like Harris and Anwar. The process of learning is the thing. In my opinion, it may be better to take antiquities from here in the wilds and display them in museums of cities where many people can see them."

"True, but most of the antiquities I've seen or heard about have been in private collections, far removed from the average person in the city."

"Granted." He changed the subject. "Tell me, have you heard anything interesting from London? I haven't heard any on-dits in a while."

I filled him in as best as I could, pointing out that I had little to do with either society or gossip. "If you really wish to know anything, perhaps you should ask Mrs. Drummond," I said in conclusion, casting a glance at the beauty and Lymond eating at a table across the room. "I'm sure she would know about such things."

Brydges followed my gaze. "She certainly seems to have entranced Robert. I'm rather surprised at that."

I followed his gaze in time to see Lymond look deep into Mrs. Drummond's lovely eyes and smile at her. She smiled back, and I did have to own that there seemed to be a link there, rather like John Donne's poem about lovers with eyes strung upon a double thread. Worse, Lymond put his hand over her smaller one briefly. The touch was short, but it was there. "It appears you are right," I said to Brydges, forcing my eyes back to more pleasant matters.

"A love match in the wilderness," Brydges mused. "I admit I would never have thought of it."

"It does rather sound like the plot for one of those novels published by the Minerva Press." I shifted my chair so I didn't have to look at Mrs. Drummond and Lymond. I hadn't noticed them before, but now I couldn't seem to focus my eyes anywhere else. I moved to face Brydges. "There's a draft," I explained. We spent the rest of our meal discussing the expedition and I learned a great deal that would be of use when I began my own project. I did have an animated discussion with Brydges over his obviously biased remark that he doubted that Egyptians would work for a woman. Very matter-of-factly he suggested that I would have to hire a man to be the nominal head of the project and that I would have to work in the background. I, of course, took the opposite view.

Supper was almost over when Anwar entered the tent and came over to Brydges. He leaned over and whispered something and I noted he appeared agitated. Brydges gestured for him to sit down and waved to Harris, beckoning for him to join us. Harris was there in the other chair in a moment. "Anwar says some of the men are leaving," Brydges said briefly.

"Hell and damnation," Harris said, completely forgetting my presence. "I was afraid of that." He rose quickly. "How many?"

"Only two or three now," Anwar said, rising as well, "but I think more may go."

Brydges looked after Harris and Anwar as they went out into the evening. "By all means, join them," I said to him. "In fact, your presence may act as a deterrent to the others and convince them to stay." Brydges shot me a look of gratitude and dashed off.

Actually, as soon as the word spread, all the men went out to see what was happening, leaving the women in the mess tent. Flora seemed as worried as I, Aunt Hen seemed somewhat relieved not to have to talk to Uncle Harley any more, and Mrs. Drummond seemed unbelievably petulant that her tête-à-tête with Lymond had been interrupted. "I'm sure Robert would prefer to stay here," she said, "but he does feel constrained to show an interest in this project." She smiled at the rest of us. "What can you tell me of him? He's such a fascinating man."

Aunt Hen, of course, immediately began to wax eloquent

about her favorite male (other than Uncle Harley), and I left in disgust. If Mrs. Drummond heeded Aunt Hen, she would soon be convinced that Lymond was the marital catch of the century. Furthermore, I said to myself as I stalked to my tent, if Lymond was taken in by an obvious fortune hunter such as Mrs. Drummond, then he deserved what he got.

I paced my tent for a while, thought about taking a walk for a while, actually stalked around the outside of my tent in the wind and the sand for a while, then went back inside and sat down on my bed. It was the first time I had been able to use my bed since Aunt Hen arrived. I stared at the top of the tent for a few minutes, then decided to use my time writing some letters. I searched for my wooden box with my addresses and scraps of paper in it, and began to write some letters. When they would be posted, I didn't know. That activity soon paled, but I did sort through my addresses and clean out the box so it would once again hold the book of sermons. Just picking up the book reminded me of my promise to Livvy and I quite resolutely sat down beside the small lamp to read more about obedient wives, but managed only a sentence or two. With another fleeting hope that Livvy didn't subscribe to such nonsense, I closed the book with a sigh; it was beyond my powers of concentration right now and, with a guilty feeling of relief, I put it inside the box and put the whole thing on the table next to my bed.

With nothing else to do, I decided to open my trunk and examine the mirror and its wrappings. Carefully, I removed the key from the back of the miniature, opened the trunk, and extracted the mirror. I moved over next to the door where the light from the pale evening moon was best, put a pillow on the floor, sat, and proceeded to examine both the wrappings and the mirror carefully.

The outer covering was market-variety striped cotton, but there was another layer of linen inside. It looked very old and brownish. When I examined the papyri, I discovered that it evidently had been all of a piece at one time. I got a clean cloth, spread it out, and began trying to assemble the pieces of papyri, fitting the pieces together like a puzzle. Some bits were missing, but for the most part, they fit enough to show me that the papyrus had been a single sheet. The writing was clear enough to read, but I had no knowledge of Egyptian, either modern or ancient. The writing was strange, appearing to be a combination—there were hieroglyphs on one piece of the papyrus while the other contained inscriptions in some kind of alphabet. I had no idea if the inscriptions were two versions of the same thing or two entirely different writings. I would have to ask an expert—just as soon as I could locate one.

I carefully left the papyri on the cloth and folded it over where it joined so it would be as flat as possible, then put it carefully back in my trunk where it wouldn't be damaged and turned my attention to the mirror.

The mirror was not at all attractive, not golden or shiny, not even reflective. I held it by the handle and looked at it, then retrieved a soft cloth and began to try to clean it. I had learned enough working with the pottery to know that this process could not be rushed. At the end of an hour or so, I had some of the front cleaned, but hadn't touched the back. It was covered with some kind of bas-relief that looked rather like triangles and squiggles. It was getting too dark for me to see what was there, much less work as I wished. I would await another day for that. In the meantime, I wondered if Harris or Brydges might be able to assist me with the markings on the papyrus.

Carefully I folded the mirror in the soft cloth, then the

striped cloth and put it back into my trunk. Without thinking, I put the key in my pocket, picked up part of the papyrus, and went out into the early night in search of either
Harris or Brydges.

I found Harris in the tent we used to clean and catalogue
the findings. He was smoking his pipe as he squatted on
the ground looking at a pattern of squares and dots on what
appeared to be a map. The flickering oil lamp threw his
shadow onto the sides of the tent, giving the scene a surreal
quality. I hesitated, then went firmly inside. "Good evening, Mr. Harris. Am I interrupting?"

He glanced up at me and then back down at the map.
"I've been doing some reading about the work of Sir Rich-
ard Colt-Hoare, and decided to block off the area into sec-
tions, so I'm just looking at a grid of the camp I've
prepared. I have Miss Rowe to help me." He looked up
into the darkness. To my surprise, Flora sat there, sketch
pad in hand. Evidently I *was* interrupting, but it was too
late now. Instead, I pulled the piece of papyrus from my
pocket and plunged ahead.

"I wondered if you could tell me what this says?" I proffered the scrap carefully. I had put the backing from Papa's
miniature against it so it wouldn't bend.

Harris stood, put the lamp on the table, and sat down
next to Flora so they could peruse the scrap together. "Do
you wish me to sketch it?" she asked, pencil at the ready.

"It would be a good idea." Harris examined it carefully
and shook his head. "I don't know what it means," he said
mournfully. "This is one of the great mysteries of the
ages—what does this writing mean? I read that the Swedish
diplomat Akerblad deciphered some Egyptian hieroglyphics back in 1802, and that Thomas Young is working on it
now, but, as far as I know, no one has been able to make a

real alphabet out of it. Some of the French are working on it as well, but I don't know what's been done there—Anwar knows more about the French than I do—and says they're making strides. When we do decipher hieroglyphics, then we'll know so much more." He spoke fervently.

Flora busily reproduced each line on the scrap, as Harris measured it carefully and called out the measurements to her. "There's so much we don't know," she said, smiling.

"More we don't know than we do," Harris agreed. "I only hope scholarship intervenes and keeps the study of Egypt from being a treasure hunt." He paused. "That's what it seems to be now."

"Brydges?" I asked as Harris nodded agreement. "Then why do you work for him, Mr. Harris? If you don't agree, why don't you go out on your own where you can follow your scholastic bent?"

Harris was blunt. "Money. Brydges has money; I have none. It's that simple." He paused as someone outside the tent called his name. "Excuse me a moment," he said, leaving us.

I regarded Flora working over the scrap. "I was certainly wrong about Harris, wasn't I? I can't believe I made such an error since I usually have an infallible sense of character. I suppose we didn't meet under the best of circumstances."

Flora smiled at me. "He's wonderfully dedicated and cares very much about preserving what is found. He studied history until he became fervidly interested in archaeology. He knows a great deal about Egyptian history—he's studied extensively with a man who was here in ninety-eight with Napoleon." She finished her sketch and folded her sketchpad.

I lifted an eyebrow as I wrapped the papyrus. "You seem

to know a great deal about Mr. Harris, Flora." She blushed
so that it showed up in the light from the lamp as Harris
reentered the tent, Brydges behind him.

"Working late?" Brydges smiled at all of us and sat
down. "Tell me, Harris, are we going to find anything?
I've already reserved space on the next freighter to England
for whatever we find. Atherton assures me that we're close
to something valuable."

A look of irritation swept across Harris's face. "If we
do find anything, it may take months to get it out, studied,
and packed. Perhaps you should wait."

"Dam . . . drat it, man, I don't want to wait!" He leaned
forward in his chair. "I've read all the accounts. Almost
everything I've read tells of treasure all over Egypt."

"I've read many histories as well," I remarked. "Even
Herodotus was impressed, but that was millennia ago. I
would imagine that anything like gold had been melted
down long ago."

"I hope not," Brydges muttered, standing. "Tomorrow
is another day and who knows what we may discover? By
the way, Harris, Edward and Atherton are going to the village again tomorrow to try to find out if there are any antiquities there. Edward swears he saw some tiny funeral
figures in the marketplace."

"He probably did," Harris said wearily, "and they may
have come from here, they may have come from God
knows where." He turned to Flora. "Would you like me to
escort you to your tent, Miss Rowe?" He caught himself
and looked at me. "And of course, you, Miss Sydney."

"Never mind," I said. "I'm not particularly sleepy and
I may go for a short walk. I brought my shawl." The desert
cooled down considerably at night, sometimes approaching
cold weather.

"Would you like me to put your . . . that in your tent for you?" Flora asked, looking at the wrapped papyrus.

"Please." I had almost forgotten I had it. "I'd hate to lose it while I was walking."

Brydges looked at me and offered his arm. "Perhaps you will do me the honor then? I, too, would like a stroll around the camp. I need to see that everything is in order." We blew out the lamps and went outside, under the spangled sky.

"After Mustapha's . . . after last night's tragic occurrence, I feel I need to check everything. Edward is standing guard tonight—we were unable to get any natives to do it, no matter what we offered. I imagine we'll have to take turns at watch."

"I imagine so. Have you discovered anything about Mustapha's death?"

Brydges looked at me briefly. "His throat was cut and there were no signs of a struggle, so either he was surprised from behind or knew his attacker. What I can't figure out was why he was over in the rocks when he was supposed to be standing watch."

"He was on watch earlier, and doing an excellent job."

Brydges sighed. "He was one of my most reliable men. Several of the others have gone now. They say the camp is cursed."

"Superstition comes easy in a land such as this one."

We walked on in silence for a short while; Brydges took my arm to assist me and didn't let go. Finally, we sat down on a rock where we could see the camp below us and talked of the difficulties of such an expedition. I did my best to convince Brydges that scholarship should be the end result of such a foray, but he was too caught up in finding riches and fame. Still, I thought I could convince him, given time.

I finally suggested we should get back to camp and we started down the path. "I do want you to know, Miss Sydney, that I'm glad you've joined us. I know the circumstances are somewhat unusual, but I would like to further our acquaintance." He paused a second. "I've survived the Marriage Mart and London mothers because I always preferred a woman of substance." He stopped and looked at me. "I don't mean riches—I have more than enough, but I've always wanted to meet a woman of intellect who was also beautiful and charming." He smiled at me in the moonlight. "Imagine my surprise at meeting her here in Egypt!"

Overcome, I didn't really know what to say. I'm not facile at accepting compliments during the best of times. Fortunately, Brydges didn't seem to expect an answer. Instead he continued, "I do hope you'll stay long enough for us to come to know each other."

"Thank you, I do intend to stay a while."

Brydges took my hand and we started down the path again. I was musing over Mustapha's death and I realized I had forgotten to tell Brydges about the white wraith·that had frightened Bue into running. I opened my mouth to tell him as we rounded a curve in the trail, but stopped as we saw two figures in the distance standing face to face, almost touching. They were vividly silhouetted against the bright Egyptian moon. "My goodness," Brydges said in a whisper, "could that be Harris and Miss Rowe? I do believe they're taken with each other."

"No." The word came out through stiff lips. There was only one woman in the camp who was that slender and elegant and who had hair the moon turned to silver spangles—Cecilia Drummond. As for the man, I'd know those gestures and that physique anywhere: he was Lymond.

Ten

I hardly knew what I said to Brydges as he walked me to my tent. I'm sure I was cool and collected on the outside, but inside I was a mass of angry emotions. Even when Brydges squeezed my hand and murmured that he hoped we became very good friends indeed, I was able to give him some kind of answer. I think I said I hoped so; I really wasn't paying much attention. I couldn't wait to get inside my tent and throw something.

Once I was inside, I saw that Aunt Hen was there, reclining in my bed. "Oh, there you are, Roxanne, dear. I wondered where you had gone. Miss Rowe came by and left this for you. She said you were out walking about the camp." She handed me the papyrus. "Really, dear, you shouldn't go wandering about without an escort. Would you like me to walk with you tomorrow?"

I took the papyrus in my fingers to keep from crushing it. Right now I felt like harming something. Instead of putting the scrap in my trunk, I opened my now empty presentation box and tossed it inside, then put the key in its hiding place and returned the backing to the miniature. "I don't think you need to worry about Cecilia Drummond snatching Uncle Harley away from you," I said, falling against one of my pillows Aunt Hen had thoughtfully put on the floor for me. "She seems to have other prey in mind—I saw her all over Lymond."

"Bless the boy," Aunt Hen said, "I knew he would help me in my hour of need." She rolled over and pulled my sheet up under her chins. "Thank you for setting my mind at rest, Roxanne."

I pummeled my pillow with my fist. "You're welcome."

Things were no better the next morning. When I arrived at breakfast—at dawn, an hour civilized beings are still abed—Lymond was eating with Cecilia Drummond. She *still* looked as if she'd stepped from a pattern card, drat it. After my night on the floor, I looked rather as if I'd stepped from the confines of a dungeon. I ate with Woodbury and Henry while Bue snuggled next to me, waiting for some buttered bread. The very thought of being next to Cecilia Drummond was intolerable and I resolved to get away.

"Henry," I said, "I'd like to take Bue and go to the village to explore the marketplace. Would you go along to translate for me?"

He bowed slightly. "It would be an honor."

Woodbury looked at me in alarm. "You can't go there with that dog!"

I stood. "Of course I can, Woodbury. Is there anything you want from the village, or would you like to go along?"

Woodbury elected to go along, more I thought because he wanted to browse the marketplace than because he wanted to assist me with Bue. In a crisis, I'm really the only one who can handle Bue.

It was still rather cool when we reached the village. It was farther away than I had thought, and it was also larger than I had anticipated. Even at the early hour, the market-place in the center of the village was bustling with activity. Merchants had piles of goods and called out to passers-by to buy wares, haggling was going on everywhere; there were stacks of woven goods, baskets by the score, vegetables and fruits in neat piles, and even animals for sale. The animals seemed to be limited to donkeys and camels. The donkeys were quiet, biddable animals, but the camels were another matter entirely. I supposed camels were necessary, but they were ill-tempered beasts, spitting at prospective buyers and refusing to display any cooperation whatsoever. The stench was not to be described.

Near one stall, I saw Edward and Atherton fingering some tiny pottery pieces and we walked over to them. "Good morning," I said cheerfully. "Have you made any discoveries?"

Edward picked up a small figurine. "This is from a tomb. I just don't know if it's ours or came from somewhere else."

I rather took exception to the 'ours,' but let it go. We were the intruders here, although I was sure neither Atherton nor Edward would agree. I held the tiny figurine in my hand. It looked like a female slave. The man who ran the stall began chattering and waving his arms. Henry launched into discussions with him, then asked me if I planned to buy the tiny statuette. At my nod, Henry resumed his negotiations and soon the tiny slave was wrapped in a scrap of cloth and safely tucked away. "You shouldn't buy them," Atherton said. "It just encourages tomb robbing."

"At least I'm paying the natives money for it," I replied, stung, "which is better than simply digging things up and walking away with them."

Atherton flushed a dark red under his tan. "You have no idea of what's involved here, Miss Sydney. If you knew what was good for you, you'd go back to England and tend to your embroidery."

I fought down the urge to slap him right there. "Perhaps,

Colonel Atherton, I'm thinking of what may be good for others rather than what's good for me. Good day." I turned my back on him and stalked off to look at some woven things on the other side of the marketplace. Henry came to stand beside me. "Good for you," he murmured.

My hands were almost jerking as I flipped through the materials. "Why do you say that, Henry? I thought most men around here agreed with Atherton."

Henry shook his head. "Atherton isn't a good man. It's true that he—what do you say?—clears the way for many trips and purchases, but he isn't loyal to those for whom he works. He can be bought."

"Do you mean he's greedy?"

"Yes, that's the word."

I had to agree with Henry. However, one of the best ways to deal with the Athertons of the world is to ignore them, so I turned my attention to the marketplace.

As I stood at one stall, I felt something tugging on my skirt. Looking down, I recognized the child that Bue, Lymond, and I had found. To my delight, he held his chubby arms out to me and I picked him up, cuddling him to my shoulder. His grandfather, Abdullah, came immediately from behind a stall and began speaking. "He is honored that you should visit and take an interest in the boy," Henry translated.

"Tell him I'm delighted to see the boy in good health," I told Henry. We talked, through Henry, for a few moments and then I put the boy down and started to leave. I remembered Lymond's comments about the difficulty of getting reliable information in the village, so I had Henry ask if Abdullah if he had heard anything of the casket containing the papyri. To my surprise, his answer to Henry was long and involved many gestures and whispers. Henry turned to me. "He says that he saw the casket once and it was a lovely thing—a gift from the old gods. His grandfather had it briefly and told the family he was going to hide it in a special place. According to Abdullah, the grandfather told them on his deathbed that he had left instructions showing them the way to the casket. If they ever needed to sell it for any reason, they knew where it was."

"So he knows," I said in wonder.

Henry spoke to Abdullah further, then turned to me again. "No, he doesn't know. They searched far and wide to discover the message the grandfather had left for them. The casket has never been found."

"Could he describe it, Henry?" I asked.

Again Abdullah was animated. Just watching him, I had no doubt that he had actually seen the casket. He told Henry that it was of shiny metal, he thought probably gold, and was decorated with enamelwork and jewels. He held his hands to indicate the size. It appeared to be about the size of my wooden box. I had thought of a large casket, but Abdullah indicated something about the size of a fairly large book.

I had Henry thank him in his language, and I thanked him profusely in English. He invited us to return, and I promised I would. With that, Henry and I wandered on down the street. I wanted, I confided to Henry, some cool clothing such as the natives wore. Henry pointed out some things, and after a morning of haggling on Henry's side, I started back to camp laden with purchases. I had my figurine, several pieces of fresh fruit as well as some dried dates and figs, and some pieces of native costume, including the loose robe, the galabeah, and a headdress, the keffiyah. I had foregone the rusty black gown and heavy veils usually worn by many of the women and had settled for a long tan and white striped robe and a piece of white material that made up the keffiyah. I had hesitated on my purchases, but as I mopped the sweat that trickled down my neck, I decided it was time to forego fashion for comfort.

About halfway to camp, Henry and I ran into Lymond and Cecilia Drummond, heading to the village. Mrs. Drummond was dressed in pink and looked fresh and cool under a frilly parasol. She was daintily picking her way among the rocks in thin pink slippers. Lymond was holding her elbow. I surreptitiously wiped some sweat from my face and put on a smile. I would be pleasant if it killed me.

It almost did. Mrs. Drummond was cloying. Throughout the entire conversation she kept touching Lymond on the arm and looking up into his eyes. He had to dodge a time or two to keep from having his eyes poked out by the parasol ribs, but she didn't seem to notice that. "We're going to the village to see if we can find some papyri," she told me. The woman smiled continuously.

I thought for a second of telling Lymond what I discovered, but didn't want to say anything in front of Cecilia Drummond. Worse, Lymond was looking down at the woman and smiling in that way he has. He didn't even look at me as he spoke. "It won't hurt to ask again. Who knows what we may find?"

"Why don't you just post a sign, Lymond, and save yourself the trouble of walking? 'Papyri wanted.' You'd probably get an assortment that would satisfy Uncle Harley. He can't read the language anyway."

"You know that Uncle Harley isn't interested in the papyri as much as he's interested in the casket they're supposed to be stored in. It's rumored to be exquisite." He pulled his watch from his pocket and looked at it. "Aunt

Hen has been looking for you for quite a while," Lymond said. "She said you had abandoned her when she was practically prostrate from the heat."

"If it wasn't the heat, it would be something else." I sighed as I started for camp. Behind me, I could hear Mrs. Drummond pretend to hurt her pretty little foot on a rock. I risked a look and saw her clasp Lymond as if she were drowning. He sat her down on a rock and looked at her foot while she sat under her parasol. It rather seemed to me that he lingered overlong with his fingers on her ankle. The woman was dangerously close to being fast.

The camp seemed a little quieter as we came in. I looked up at the excavations and saw Harris, with Flora sitting there on a stool, sketching. It didn't seem to me that there were nearly as many workers as there had been. Harris's worst fear seemed to have come to pass—after Mustapha's death, the workers had been leaving in twos and threes, melting into the rocks and desert. One minute they were there, the next minute gone. It was clear that the project was short-handed and everyone was going to have to work. Even Brydges was there working, wielding a shovel. I was surprised and impressed—perhaps I had thought the man too much the dilettante. Uncle Harley was there as well, doing his usual thing: he was standing around giving suggestions and orders. As best as I could see, everyone was politely ignoring him. That didn't stop him one whit.

Aunt Hen was just the same, lying on my bed fanning herself. "Have they pitched your tent yet, Aunt Hen?" I asked. "You'd be more comfortable there, I'm sure." I directed Henry to put my purchases on the floor and he left to join the others.

"Harley assures me that it'll be up by afternoon," Aunt Hen said languidly. She turned to me, tears in her eyes.

"Whatever can we do to get out of this place, Roxanne? We're going to die here! Harley told me those silly rumors that you knew the whereabouts of a cache of gold are still circulating. Roxanne, we could all be murdered in our beds for that!"

"Don't be theatrical, Aunt Hen. There is no cache, or if there is, I certainly don't know anything about it. Any reasonable person would know that. As for how long we'll be here—I intend to stay for a while. You may be here for a few weeks as well; I understand that Uncle Harley is enjoying himself immensely."

Aunt Hen began to moan and reached again for her vinaigrette. She stopped, however, as I unrolled my galabeah and started unbuttoning my dress.

"Surely you're not going to wear that!" Aunt Hen was so overcome that she sat bolt upright. "Whatever would George say!"

"Papa would probably say that this was the sensible thing. Don't worry, I'm not going to wear it out in public. I intend to keep this in the privacy of my tent." I shook the robe down and moved around in it. The cloth touched my skin here and there, feeling wonderful. I could see why this type of attire had evolved here. I fell down against my pillows and looked at Aunt Hen. "You should get one of these, Aunt Hen. What have you been doing with yourself while I've been gone?"

She held up the book of sermons. "I'm delighted you've been improving yourself with these, Roxanne. I've enjoyed them tremendously." She picked up the presentation box and put the book inside. "An excellent choice for reading material."

"I'm glad you liked them, Aunt Hen." At least, I reflected, someone was getting some benefit from the sermons. I took the proffered box and put it on the small table beside my bed, taking out the papyri I had tossed in there the night before. This time, I put it in my trunk.

Outside, I could hear the workmen coming back into the camp to eat. Afterwards, there would be a quiet period—everything stopped during the heat of the day while the workers sought shade or took a short nap. I had fallen quickly into the habit of a short nap in the middle of the day. Uncle Harley stuck his head into the tent. "Going to eat, Henrietta?" he asked. "We're going to get our tent up after it cools off a bit."

Aunt Hen came alive. She got to her feet, a smile on her face. "Of course, Harley. Just give me a moment to tidy my hair." In a second, she was gone with him out the door. I lay on my pillows in my galabeah and weighed the thoughts of eating against taking a nap. I had eaten some sweetmeats in the village and really wasn't hungry, and my pillows really were very comfortable, I wouldn't have to give any explanations as no one would miss me—the others would think I was still in the village. I curled up on the floor amongst my pillows and drifted off to sleep.

The noise wasn't loud, just enough to make me realize that I wasn't alone. I had been deeply asleep and couldn't seem to get awake. I opened my eyes and caught a glimpse of someone going out of my tent. At least I thought it was someone—it was merely a glimpse of a white robe and headdress. I couldn't see anything else. I closed my eyes, then opened them again and saw nothing except my tent as it should be. Perhaps I had been dreaming. I shook my head to clear it and sat up, looking around. Everything looked as it should; it must have been a dream.

I stood and stretched. The freedom in the loose robe felt wonderful, but I couldn't go out wearing this, so I changed and walked to the mess tent. Almost everyone had eaten and gone back to work, although Uncle Harley and Aunt Hen were still sitting there with Lymond and Cecilia Drummond.

"The papyri are real, I think, but the jeweled casket is probably a myth," Lymond was saying.

Uncle Harley frowned. "If that's the case, the damned things are probably worthless except as a curiosity. Who can read the stuff anyway?"

I pulled up a chair and sat down between Aunt Hen and Lymond. "Harris tells me that people are working on deciphering hieroglyphs. Wouldn't they be valuable even as some kind of record of the past?"

"Not if you don't know what's on them," Uncle Harley pointed out. "The damned things could be a grocery list for all anyone knows. No, it's the casket that's valuable, no doubt about it."

"Harley, your language!" Aunt Hen looked at me and rolled her eyes. "There are ladies present."

"I *am* watching my language, Henrietta."

I turned to Lymond just in time to see Cecilia Drummond run her fingers up his bare arm to the point where he had his sleeve rolled up. The woman was flirting with being *beyond* fast. I forced myself to look at Lymond's face and keep my composure. "Why do you think the stories about the casket are false, Lymond?" I thought of Abdullah's face and was convinced that he had seen the casket.

Lymond glanced down at Cecilia's fingers resting lightly on his arm, then looked at me in reply. "Several things make me think the rumors are false. One, there are about a dozen different descriptions of the casket, varying in every particular from size to appearance. Two, I can't find anyone who has really seen it. Everyone knows someone—

a friend of a friend or, more likely, a cousin of a cousin who has seen it, but I never get a name or a concrete sighting. Three, if something this valuable had been floating around for the past hundred years—which is the story—I would think that someone would have already claimed it, tossed the papyri away and taken the casket somewhere. Four, as best as I can discover, these stories have been around for years and no one has discovered a thing. If it were real, I think someone, somewhere, would have discovered something." He smiled at me. "Enough?"

I nodded. "Very convincing, Lymond. But if it's false, then why are the stories going around?"

Lymond shrugged. "Probably some tomb robber trying to get some advance money from some gullible collector."

Uncle Harley choked on his tea.

It took several minutes before Uncle Harley was able to speak, and then Aunt Hen suggested they retire during the midday heat. He agreed, and they both headed off to my tent. "Looks as if you're going to have to nap in the mess tent, Roxanne," Lymond said with a grin, standing. He looked at Cecilia. "I promised Brydges I'd go over some maps with him, so I'll see you later this afternoon." With that, he went out, leaving me there with Cecilia Drummond.

"I believe I'll work on packing the pottery," I said, beginning to rise. Mrs. Drummond stopped me.

"Please," she said, "wait a moment. I have a question or two I'd like to ask."

I sat back down and she continued. "I talked to your Aunt Henrietta about Robert, but she really didn't give me many particulars. You've known Robert for a while, I understand, and I wanted to know if he's attached."

I stared at her. The woman was as bold as brass. "Attached?"

"Yes," she said, leaning back in her chair so she could look directly at me. "A handsome man like that must have some sort of attachment in England. I thought surely you'd know. Robert tells me that the two of you are acquaintances."

"I'm not sure you could call us *acquaintances,* Mrs. Drummond. Actually, Lymond rents part of my house."

Her eyebrows lifted. "Oh?" There was a wealth of meaning in the syllable.

I tried not to be angry. "It's a perfectly respectable arrangement, I assure you. The house is much too large for me to live in alone." I caught myself and wondered why I felt the need to explain myself to her. "As for attachments, Lymond has none that I know of. However, I must warn you that I know little of his private life." With a sudden jolt, I realized this was perfectly true. Lymond might have been engaged a dozen times. I had never known of any attachments, nor had his family ever mentioned anyone, but what did that signify? The man could have put Byron in the shade for all I knew.

Cecilia all but purred. "What can you tell me of his family? Are they well-to-do? His uncle seems to be quite wealthy."

"The family is comfortable. I suppose you already know that Lymond is the youngest brother of the Earl of Rywicke. I'm sure the family has made provisions for all its members." I tried to keep my voice even, but it was a struggle. I stood up and headed out of the mess tent. "I really must be going. If you need to discover anything else about Lymond, I suggest you ask him."

"I'll certainly do that." Her laugh followed me out into the heat of midday.

I was still fuming when I got to the tent where I discovered Harris and Flora working. They were working closely, literally. His head was mere inches from hers as they pored over a sketch she had done. His fingers touched hers and they looked at each other in surprise. I had a choice of interrupting them or leaving. I chose to back quietly away from the tent. Whatever they discovered about each other certainly wasn't for a third party to observe.

My tent was occupied by Aunt Hen and Uncle Harley; Flora and Harris were not to be disturbed in the collections tent; and I certainly wasn't going back to the mess tent. I wandered around for a moment, thought of commandeering Lymond's tent since he was with Brydges, then decided to walk up to the excavation itself and perhaps descend the stairs and explore. I hadn't been down there at all and I wanted to see what a real tomb looked like.

Edward was watching over the stairs, stationed just on the bottom stair where it was shadowed and cooler. "We looked at the seals this morning and discovered that Harris was right, they had been broken. We opened the door and went inside, but there was nothing of value there." His voice was full of disgust. "Just some pottery and the remains of some wooden chairs and so on."

"That sounds interesting," I said, peering around him. "May I go in?"

"Go on." He gestured to the door. "Nothing of any value in there at all. I don't even see the need to guard it, but Harris is insistent. He thinks what's in there is valuable."

I went on inside, poking around in the clutter. It looked as if someone had been in there searching for something and had been surprised. Everything was thrown topsy-turvy. All I was carrying was a small lamp, and it threw giant shadows on the walls, giving the items an unearthly appearance. The tomb was hot and musty with, it felt, very little air. The dust of centuries was all over everything and I sneezed when I moved a chair. I touched what looked like a small boat and some figurines like the one I had purchased in the village. Looking around, I saw no gleam of metal.

There was a crash at the door and then the darkness closed in around me completely. I have never been in darkness like that. My tiny lamp flame flickered and I picked it up and blew gently, trying to fan it. It kept burning and I made my way out of the room I was in to the tomb door. At the entrance, I could see one tiny sliver of light where I supposed the door had been forced. I fell to my knees and tried to look outside, but couldn't. The light there was only the faintest glimmer. For a moment, I was disoriented, wondering if this was truly the door or if it were merely part of the wall and I was imagining that minuscule sliver of light. I could easily have missed the door and the faint sliver been a reflection of my lamp off of something shiny in the rock. I put the lamp down and felt along the edges where I thought the door was located—sure enough, there was an indentation where the door was cut and there were flakes of rock at my feet where the door had been forced. "Edward!" I cried, "Edward, open the door!" There was no answer.

Panic seized me for a moment. I have never been afraid of the dark, but being in a tomb in such darkness wasn't exactly what I would choose as a way to pass the time. I forced myself to be calm. After all, I did have my light and surely someone would open the door. Perhaps Edward had merely gone somewhere and the door had shut of its own accord. As soon as the workers return, they would reopen the door. I tried again, beating on the door with my fist and calling out to Edward. I realized quickly that this was futile and the flickering of my small lamp forced me to recognize that I needed to make preparations to stay in here for an hour or so. The workers might not return until late in the afternoon.

I picked up the lamp and made my way back to the room where I had been. Clearing a small spot next to the wall, I put the lamp carefully on the floor, afraid I might set alight the wood that had dried for two thousand years.

The lamplight flickered again and seemed pale and feeble in the darkness. Already I felt I had been in there for hours. I lay down on the floor; hunger was beginning to be a problem. After all, I really hadn't eaten anything at midday and the sweetmeats and fruit I had in the village were past being a help. For one of the few times in my life, I felt like crying. However, I reproached myself, it would do no good at all.

I made myself sit up, hearing the creak of something in the room with me. I held my breath as I listened again, almost waiting for the Pharoah to come striding into the small circle of light. It took me a moment to realize that I was partially leaning against a chair which had moved under the pressure of my shoulder. I shook my head and put my face into my hands while I tried to control my thoughts. My hands felt gritty and I looked down at them—they were black with dust and dirt. I rubbed at my face, feeling the grime embed itself in my skin. Asking myself if it really mattered at this moment, I made myself put my hands in my lap, lean back, and take a deep breath. Somehow, propped up there, I drifted off to sleep. When I awoke, I was in utter darkness, a darkness such I had never even imagined. It seemed to close in on me from all sides and make even breathing difficult. For a moment, I was seized by complete terror and felt around for my lamp. It had gone out while I was sleeping. I had no way of knowing how long I had been trapped inside the room. I fought down the urge to scream, realizing it wouldn't help and tried to formulate some sort of plan. There was none. All I decided to do was crawl to the door and wait for someone to come. Surely someone would miss me.

I had crawled halfway across the floor when I heard a noise. This time, I wasn't touching anything except the floor, so I knew I hadn't made the noise. Terrified, I stopped and listened. Every ghost story I had ever heard came flooding back. Every rumor that had crossed my path about curses from the pharoahs and priests engulfed me. I cringed against the wall and waited in terror. There was a flash of light that almost blinded me and I saw the white wraith Lymond and I had seen the night of Mustapha's death. The swirling white robes and headdress hid the face and body from view. I tried to be still as I caught a glimpse of the wraith, but before I could help myself, I screamed, as much, I like to think, in surprise as in fear.

The wraith dropped its lamp and fled out the door, the source of the light that had almost blinded me. It was only moonlight, but it looked as bright as the sun to me. As I crawled out into the way leading to the door, I picked up the lamp, then looked out the open door at the moonlight Egyptian night. I almost cried in relief.

I took great lungfulls of the cool evening air and told myself how lucky I was. Better, as I emerged from the tomb, I saw Bue trotting across the sand to greet me. We fell together, rolling around on the sand, and I lay there, breathing in deep gulps of air and looking up at the stars pocking the clear night sky.

I had never seen anything that looked better.

Eleven

Bue and I wandered back to the camp in time to see everyone gathered around tables in the mess tent. Edward was there, his head bandaged. "Did you miss me?" I asked, falling down into a chair. There was dirt and sand all over my hands and arms and my clothing was filthy and smelled. I was sure my face looked as black and knew I must look terrible, but I didn't care.

Brydges looked at me and, for an instant, horror crossed his features, then he composed himself and acted as if we were having in tea in Brighton. "Have you been in the village? We wondered where you had wandered off to," he said, his eyes focusing everywhere but on me. "Did you fall?"

I was devastated—after all I had been through, the least they could have done was worry about me. I related my adventures, looking to Edward for confirmation. "I don't remember." He shook his head slowly. "I was watching your dog chase something on the sand, and then there was a crash and everything went black. I don't remember a thing. Since you mention it, I do recall now that you went into the tomb, but I had forgotten. I'm so sorry."

Brydges patted my hand. "Are you all right now? That must have been terrible for you."

"It was," I agreed. I told them of the white wraith that

was in the tomb, and they looked at each other skeptically. "You know it exists, Lymond," I said, looking at him. "We saw it the night of Mustapha's death."

Lymond nodded. "We saw something. I can't be sure if it was real or a sand devil or what."

Atherton came in to join us. "I've checked the entrance. Everything seems normal." He looked around at all of us. "What's going on?"

I had to relate my tale again, and Atherton suppressed a polite titter. "Really, Miss Sydney," he said. He turned to Brydges and began discussing the next day's work. I was enraged. I got up to go to my tent, taking one last look across the sand before I went inside to clean the black filth from my body and to change into my comfortable native robe. I stopped as I thought I saw a movement and, sure enough, there, going down the stairs to the tomb, was the white wraith. I ran back to the tent. "I saw it! It's there now if anyone wants to go find out what—or who—it is!"

They looked at me blankly. "The white wraith! I just saw it going down into the tomb!"

Aunt Hen got up and put her arm around me. "Come, dear, let me get you some strong tea and some laudanum drops. I'm afraid this has all been too much for you."

I shook her off. "Thank you, Aunt Hen, but I happen to be fine." I turned to the others. "I've done my duty—I've told you about what I saw. You may do something or nothing—I don't care. I'm going to my tent." I turned and stalked away. As I walked, I took another look at the tomb entrance in the distance and saw nothing. Surely I hadn't been hallucinating.

The next day was uneventful. I saw nothing unusual at the tomb entrance and no one spoke of anything odd. Harris returned to the room inside the tomb and, with great difficulty, restrained Brydges and Atherton. Of course, both of them were disgusted after Harris ascertained that the mummy and any gold or silver articles had been stolen long ago.

I went back to the room in the tomb for a few minutes and it looked perfectly unthreatening in the light and with other people there. Harris was methodically going through the items inside and Flora was there as well, diligently sketching. Shaking off the terrified feeling of the night before, I picked up a chair and began calling out measurements to Flora.

Late that evening, after the moon was up and the desert was cooling rapidly, Brydges asked if I wanted to walk with him. I started to refuse, but a glimpse of Cecilia and Lymond wandering off together changed my mind. "Of course," I said with a smile. "The air will do me good." Brydges waited while I went to get my shawl as the evenings turn quickly from cool to chilly. I stopped to tell Aunt Hen I was going out and to collect Bue. He had become comfortable enough with our surroundings to run without his leash. Woodbury was most grateful.

Rather than walking towards the rocks, we wandered slowly towards the river, talking of ancient times. "I think you're making a convert of me, Miss Sydney," Brydges said. "I've told Harris to note everything in the tomb and preserve it. Perhaps I'll give part of it to a museum."

"I'm glad," I told him, trying to stifle a smile. I knew Harris was insisting on such a procedure. "Papa always said that the everyday life of a culture said more about it than its gold and jewels."

"Your father must have been an interesting gentleman."

"He was." We went on in silence for a moment as the boat came into view. "Do you think this scene was the same thousands of years ago?" I asked, looking at the light on the water, the dahabeah gently rocking at the shore, and the shadows of the crew on the edge of the river.

"Quite probably. Who in the devil is that?" Brydges pointed to the shadows on the deck of the boat. "It looks like a woman."

"I thought they were some workers you had left to guard the boat." I peered at them in the growing darkness. There was light on board the boat, but not enough to identify the two figures. As we got closer, I recognized one figure by the hair that gleamed silver-gilt in the moonlight. She was certainly close to the other figure, and he wasn't putting up any resistance. So little resistance, in fact, that in moments they were embracing and kissing each other. I spun around.

"Take me back, please," I said to Brydges through stiff lips.

"Who is that?" he asked, still looking.

"I'm sure it's Lymond and Cecilia Drummond." I had walked several paces away from him. "If you'll excuse me, I need to be getting back to my tent."

Brydges couldn't resist that male chuckle that seems to be a mixture of congratulation, envy, and pride in the male sex. He turned, casting one last look over his shoulder as we left. As usual, he was the perfect gentleman, walking me back as he chatted about such inconsequentials as London society. At the entrance to my tent, he held my hand for a moment. "I do hope, Miss Sydney, that you haven't felt I've been neglecting you. I apologize for yesterday. I was so worried about Edward and I didn't know you were in the tomb. I assure you that if I had known, I would have moved heaven and earth to rescue you."

I smiled at him. "I realize that, and I thank you. No, I

haven't felt at all neglected. We've all been far too busy for that and I know the expedition is a heavy responsibility for you."

"Thank you for recognizing that. Harris does most of the work, but the planning and finances are all mine." He paused. "You've added a great deal to the expedition, both professionally and personally." With that, he leaned over and gave me a quick kiss. "Good night, Miss Sydney. I hope we may continue our walk tomorrow evening." With that, he turned and went off towards his own tent.

I stayed inside my tent for a short while until I heard voices outside. The muffled giggle told me that Cecilia and Lymond had returned. Hating myself for doing it, I peered outside, just in time to see Lymond entering Cecilia's tent. For the first time, I realized the cathartic effect of profanity. I caught myself and retreated inside my tent. I couldn't believe what I had just seen, but, no matter which way I looked at it, there seemed to be only one explanation.

I paced my tent for a while, but there wasn't room to vent my feelings properly. Disgusted with myself and unable to quell my emotions, I tried to go to sleep. It was futile. I utilized everything I knew, but nothing worked, not counting sheep, not concentrating on how tired I was, not deep breathing. In desperation, I lit the lamp and decided to read some of the sermons in Livvy's book. I searched all over the tent and couldn't find the box. I supposed Aunt Hen had taken it with her when she moved into the tent the workers had erected for her and Uncle Harley. After all, she had enjoyed reading them.

I rose late the next morning as it had been almost daylight when I finally went to sleep. I skipped breakfast and brewed myself some tea in the mess tent, then went to the collection tent to work on some of the things that had been removed from the tomb. I didn't want to speak to anyone.

Lymond came floating in after I had been working about an hour. His greeting was cursory and his only comments were about the weather and Bue sleeping at my feet. He went off then, whistling, no doubt to join Cecilia Drummond for the midday meal.

Brydges came in to take me to eat. I joined him at his table with Harris and Flora. "We may have to shut down if workers keep disappearing," he said grimly. "Two more left this morning. They asked for their pay and told me that they had heard in the village that the camp was possessed by demons."

"Surely not!" I could hardly believe my ears.

Harris nodded in agreement. "Superstitions are rampant. What we need to do is figure out a way to convince them that there are no demons here, only good spirits."

"Perhaps Abdullah could help us," I suggested. "He told me that he'd do whatever he could for me—us."

"The grandfather of the boy you rescued?" Harris frowned. "It might work. Do you think you could go see him this afternoon?" He looked at Brydges. "You and I could go as well, and we could take Henry or Anwar to translate."

Brydges thought a moment. "Perhaps it would be better to let Miss Sydney go with Anwar and Henry. If we go, it might look like coercion."

I risked a glance at Lymond and Cecilia who were eating with Uncle Harley and Aunt Hen. Cecilia had her hand on Lymond's arm and was leaning towards him as he spoke. "I'd be delighted to go to the village this afternoon," I told them. "It may help, and it certainly can't hurt."

The trip also gave me the opportunity to talk to Anwar.

When I told him I was thinking of financing an expedition, he discouraged me, but then when I told him that I felt Egyptian antiquities should be used for study and should stay in Egypt, he changed completely. "This is our heritage," he said in his heavily accented English.

"It certainly is, and it needs to be preserved. I'm shocked at the attitude of many who come here. These things should be used as objects of scholarship." I paused at a bend in the path to the village. "If I can get everything together for next year, Anwar, would you consider helping us? I believe Harris might be working with us as well."

"And our finds stay here?"

"Certainly. These things should be sketched, of course, and documented, but I firmly believe they should stay here where they belong."

To my surprise, Anwar sat down on a rock. "I am overcome," he said, looking at the ground. "It is what I have always hoped."

"Then plan to join us," I said. "Harris tells me that you are extremely knowledgeable."

"I must think on it," he said, rising and looking strangely at me. "I will tell you soon."

Satisfied, I continued to the village where Henry, Anwar, and I talked to Abdullah. He said he had heard the rumors, and that he knew that many men were leaving. "Ask him if he knows why the rumor started," I told Henry.

Henry translated to me. "He says it is because of the ghost that walks at night. Several have seen the afreet and say it killed Mustapha. The men say it will kill whoever gets near it."

"Tell him that I have been near the white ghost and I am still here. The ghost is not real."

Henry and Anwar looked at me in amazement. "You could recognize it?" Anwar asked.

I nodded. "I saw it the night Mustapha was killed, then again when I was in the tomb. I frightened it away then, so it can't be too evil." I thought for a second about the flash of white I had seen in my tent as I woke up, but I didn't mention it.

Henry translated and Abdullah spoke excitedly. "He is amazed that you frightened it," Henry said, "and he says that you must have powers of your own."

I nodded. "Tell him that I do, Henry. I am on the side of good."

Henry spoke, then Abdullah looked at me and bowed slightly, speaking. "He will tell those concerned in the village that you have frightened the ghost," Henry said, "and that you have power."

We left at that, but not before I convinced Abdullah to allow me to give his grandson some sweetmeats. I was beginning to feel a proprietary interest in the child. His mother came out to see us, holding the child who smiled at me and held out his chubby arms. "He is called Faoud," Henry translated.

I cuddled Faoud and played with him for a few minutes while the mother and I exchanged pleasantries, translated by Henry. The mother was dressed, as most of the women were, completely in black with veils covering her face. She, too, thanked me. I tousled Faoud's hair when I left and he smiled sweetly at me and waved. I was going to have to rein in these strange maternal feelings.

That evening, I worked late to make up for my trip to the village. To my surprise, Lymond came in alone as I was working. "I understand you've been asking in the marketplace about the casket," he said without preamble.

"What I discuss and where is my business," I answered, not looking at him.

He sat down beside me, his hands on the table in front of him. I couldn't stop myself from looking at the scars on his hands and remembering how they had gotten there. Lymond today differed greatly from the Lymond of that day. "Did you discover anything?"

"Why? You've been making inquiries. Didn't you tell me that you were convinced that the casket didn't exist?"

He ran his fingers through his hair. "Dammit, I don't know. Some of the descriptions are so detailed that I think someone must have seen the thing, but then, what happened to it? Surely something that valuable would have been noticed on the market."

"Perhaps everyone isn't as observant as you, Lymond." I concentrated on cleaning and cataloguing the item I held—it was a wooden spindle for spinning.

"Will you put that thing down and talk to me!" Lymond's hand closed over mine and he moved closer to me.

I stopped and looked at him. In the waning light, his skin, which had bronzed in the sun, looked swarthy and his eyes were dark. With a little imagination, he could be a reincarnation of an ancient Greek or Egyptian. "I didn't realize we had anything to say to each other, Lymond," I said coolly. "Perhaps you need to go talk to Mrs. Drummond."

He drew back and regarded me for a moment. I forced myself to meet his eyes, my chin lifted. "All right, I'll just do that," he said, getting up with such force that he overturned his chair. I watched him stride across the sand out of my line of vision, wanting to call him back, but too proud to do so.

A few minutes later, I heard a noise behind me as I

worked. I turned, expecting Lymond to be there, but it was Anwar. He came over, picked up the overturned chair, and sat down in it. "You do a careful job," he said, by way of opening the conversation.

I put the spindle carefully in some packing and put it in a box. "It's tedious work, but I've found it quite rewarding. I'd like to continue, but the light is gone."

Anwar lit the small lamp on the table and put it between us. "Did you mean what you told me today? That you may finance your own expedition?"

I nodded. "Yes. I have means of my own and I can't think of a better way to use them. My father collected antiquities from Asia and from Egypt because he was afraid that others would destroy them. I've always worked with antiquities, but never any this fascinating."

"You would leave things here?"

"Yes, Anwar, it would be as I told you." I looked at him, puzzled. "Are you unsure of what I say?"

"Most English come here only to rob and take our valuables back to their country."

I raised an eyebrow. "Just the English? Then the French left here with empty hands?"

Embarrassment flooded his face. "I apologize. I am tied to the French through my father, but I assure you I have no love for them. For thousands of years, the world has looked to Egypt as a place to plunder."

"I agree, Anwar. Perhaps you and I could begin a movement to stop that. It will be difficult."

To my complete amazement, he seized my hand and kissed it. "I believe you," he said. "Abdullah told me you could be trusted. He said you had extraordinary powers. He said the people in the village are calling your tent the Dahr El Sytt."

I looked at him curiously. "Dahr El Sytt? And what does that mean, Anwar?"

"That is the house of the princess."

I didn't know whether to laugh or not. Afraid of offending him, I merely smiled. "I may be many things, Anwar, but I am certainly not a princess."

"The villagers think you have powers." He looked at me. "There is something . . ." He paused.

"I am not unusual at all, Anwar," I said firmly. "I merely try to keep my word. As soon as we can, perhaps we can meet with Mr. Harris and discuss some plans. I would like to have everything in place before I leave Egypt. That way, you and Mr. Harris can go ahead and purchase what you need." I rose and looked at him. In spite of my reassurances, he appeared troubled. "I give you my word on this."

He sprang to his feet. "It is not that, Miss Sydney. I cannot tell you what this opportunity means to me. It is . . . it is something else. I must tell you of it, but I cannot right now. I need to . . . to . . . to speak to . . ." His words trailed off into nothing. "I thank you for giving me this chance."

We went out of the tent together. "I'm pleased that you accept, Anwar. If you need to tell me of something, come to me whenever you wish, and we'll discuss it. In the meantime, I'll tell Harris that you will work with us next year."

Anwar bowed slightly and went off into the darkness, his white galabeah visible for a while in the dying light. After he went out of sight, I looked around in the darkness but saw nothing or no one. There was no light in Cecilia Drummond's tent. There wasn't one in Lymond's either.

Flora was in my tent when I returned. She was mending the hem on one of my dresses. "I've neglected my duties to you, Roxanne," she said, tying off her threads.

"You have no duties to me, Flora. I do appreciate the

mending, however. You know what my sewing looks like."
We sat in silence for a moment. "Have you seen Lymond?"
I asked casually.

"I saw him walking out with Mrs. Drummond." She
poked through the small mending basket to find another
color of thread. "They were going towards the river." Flora
turned to look at me. "I don't dare say anything to Alex,
but that woman is *fast.*"

"I suspect he knows it." I smiled at her familiar use of
Harris's first name.

"He says she's spoiled and demanding and he has no
idea why she wanted to come here in the first place. He
thinks she's on the dangle for an eligible match."

"Just any man who's eligible?" I asked.

Flora nodded. "Alex is embarrassed by her behavior, but
doesn't know quite what to do about it." She tied off her
thread and shook out the gown. "There! That looks much
better." She picked up my native garment. "I didn't know
what this was."

I explained about my trip to the marketplace and told
her how comfortable the native galabeahs were. "Except
those heavy looking robes and veils worn by the poor
women," I said, folding the robe. "I don't see how they
wear all that black in this heat." Flora agreed, but gently
refused to try on the robe.

Flora stood and left, bidding me goodnight. I tried to go
to sleep, but I wasn't successful. I was uncomfortable and
eventually got out of bed, lit my lamp, and changed into
my galabeah. At least I could be comfortable while I tried
to sleep. I blew out the lamp, lay down, and waited, but
sleep still eluded me. Evidently, I wasn't the only one.
About midnight, there was a whisper at my tent door. I relit
the lamp so Aunt Hen could come in.

"I can't sleep!" she cried, falling down on my bed. I was forced once again to sit on the floor pillows. "Roxanne, I thought having our own tent would ameliorate Harley's foul mood, but it certainly hasn't. Tonight I had to make him go outside because he began cursing poor Robert for not turning up that miserable casket."

"I thought Lymond had convinced him that it didn't exist."

"Harley's decided that it does. Not only that, he's convinced himself that riches await the man who finds it. Atherton has told Harley that he can help find it."

"For a fee?" I asked cynically.

"How did you know? Really, Roxanne, there must be some truth to what they're saying. Did you know the cook told me that you had special powers?"

"Good Lord."

"That's why I'm here," Aunt Hen said, sitting up.

She had completely lost me in the conversation. "Why, Aunt Hen?"

"The Lord. I thought I'd read some more of those edifying sermons. They're so soothing when one is distressed."

I leaped to my feet. "You don't have them?"

"Heavens, no, Roxanne. I certainly wouldn't take something without asking! What do you think of me!" She rose and yawned gently. "I'll even return them to you tomorrow if you wish." She looked at me sternly. "It would be wise if you took those lessons to heart. Since you've been in Egypt, you've become quite . . . quite *independent,* Roxanne."

"Aunt Hen, I don't have them." I began to pace the floor, going over the events since I had last seen the presentation box and the book of sermons.

"Well, who does?"

I sat back down. "I don't know, Aunt Hen." I frowned. "There's only one possibility I can think of." I told her of waking up and seeing the flash of white. "I convinced myself that I was dreaming," I concluded, "but it must have been a thief stealing my box. And the book." The answer to one puzzle eluded me, however. "Why on earth, Aunt Hen, would anyone steal a box containing a book of sermons?"

"God works in mysterious ways," Aunt Hen intoned. "Perhaps someone here needed the Word." She stood. "If they're gone, I might as well go back to bed. Do you have anything at all here to read?"

I knew exactly what she wanted. Opening my trunk, I pulled a volume from the Minerva Press out of it. I occasionally read those things when I need to go to sleep.

"Bless you, Roxanne." Aunt Hen pressed the book to her bosom and padded out the tent door. In a few moments, I could hear Uncle Harley roaring as Aunt Hen fell over him when she reentered her tent.

Since my trunk was open, I reached inside and got out my mirror. I had polished the smooth side and looked at my image by the light of the flickering lamp. In the golden bronze, my skin and hair looked like rich honey. The image was somewhat distorted, but, in the absence of silvered glass, I could see how Egyptian women would prize such an item. As I held the mirror and looked, I wondered what woman thousands of years ago had done the same. Slowly I turned it over, looking at the back of it which I hadn't cleaned. Since I was wide awake, I got out my soft cloth and set to work. The back was much more difficult than the front since it had several raised markings on it, as well as several deep scratches. As I held it up to the lamp and looked more closely, it appeared that the mirror was in two layers—it looked almost as if someone had cast the back separately and fastened it on. The more I cleaned the back of the mirror, the more intrigued I became. I couldn't really see closely enough to decide if the mirror was in two parts. There was a large magnifying glass in the collections tent and I decided to go there and look at the edges of the mirror through it. I glanced down at my clothes, then poked my head out of my tent. There was no one around; the camp was as quiet as a cemetery.

Clutching my mirror, I walked over to the collections tent, still wearing my galabeah, the stones on the ground sharp through my thin shoes. In the tent, I had difficulty lighting the lamp, and finally had to go outside and try to do it by the pale light of the moon. I wasn't helped by Bue constantly rubbing against me and trying to leap up whenever the lamp flared. "Sit!" I demanded, and he went just inside the tent and flopped down to sulk.

When I finally got the lamp lit, I went back inside and looked carefully through the magnifying glass. I was right—there were two separate layers. From what Harris had told me, the pieces were usually done in one casting, so I thought this might make my mirror unusual. I would have to show this to Harris in the morning.

I was almost ready to leave when Brydges came in, a pistol leveled straight at me. "Halt there!"

"I've halted," I said with a gulp. I recognized his voice although I couldn't see his face in the darkness outside the pool of light from my lamp. Just seeing the pistol was enough.

He dropped the pistol immediately. "Miss Sydney! I'm so sorry. With all the problems we've been having, when I saw the light in the tent, I naturally assumed that someone had come in here to steal something after we'd all gone to sleep."

"I couldn't sleep," I said.

He came into the pool of lamplight. "I'm sorry. Have all the goings-on around here upset you?"

I had been upset, but not for reasons I could explain to Brydges, so I merely nodded my head. "I'm sorry I got you up," I told him, "but I . . ." I glanced down at my clothes at the same time he did. I was definitely not dressed for conversation and Brydges looked at me curiously, then carefully tried not to look below my neck. "I need to get back."

"Certainly, let me walk with you. It *is* late."

I certainly couldn't deny this, so I picked up my mirror and blew out the lamp. We started for the door. Bue stood and leaped right on Brydges before I could warn him, and Brydges staggered right into me. I fell back against the table, trying to hang on to my mirror. Brydges fell right beside me and I felt the mirror thunk into something.

"My . . . my mirror," I gasped, trying to free myself. All I managed to do was pull my robe so that Brydges rolled over on top of me. "Dear God," he mumbled, trying to get up. Bue banged against him and he lost his footing again, crashing right down on top of me again. "A thousand apologies, Miss Sydney," he gasped.

We were still in the process of untangling ourselves when I heard a noise and peered across Brydges' shoulder. There was a silhouette in the door and I shoved Brydges aside as much as I could and cried out, "Someone's there! Look!"

"You don't need to worry," Lymond said from the doorway, "I won't tell anyone of this. I beg your pardon for the interruption." His voice would have frozen water poured on the sand.

By the time we stood and I got my galabeah straightened out, Lymond had disappeared into the darkness.

"Oh, good God," I moaned as the full import of the scene hit me.

Brydges took a deep breath. "I'm fully aware of the danger to your reputation, Miss Sydney, and I don't want you to think that's the only reason I am now saying this to you. The thought has been in my mind since the very first moment I saw you. Miss Sydney, will you do me the honor to be my wife?"

Twelve

I could think of only one thing to say. *"What?"*

"Miss Sydney, will you marry me?" He glanced at Lymond's figure stalking away and disappearing into his tent. "Please believe me that I'm not asking you because Robert saw us in a . . . a compromising, uh, position. I'm asking you because I have regarded you highly since I first met you. We seem to have the same interests, the same sort of background, and so on. In short, Miss Sydney, I think we would be perfectly matched."

I tried not to stare at Brydges. The darkness helped tremendously. He sounded as if he were selecting two horses to breed. "I'm just overcome," I said truthfully. "Please give me some time to think of this."

Brydges took my arm. "Of course. I know this is sudden and you need to ponder of every facet. As to finances, I assure you that I—"

"I'm sure," I said hastily. "However, this is so unexpected that I need time to consider."

"Of course." he said gallantly, offering me his arm to walk me to my tent. We paused there for a moment and I looked up into his face. "You seem to be bleeding slightly," I said. It sounded silly to me; I could imagine how it sounded to Brydges.

He touched his lip. "In the fracas, I believe you hit me with whatever object you were carrying."

"I'm so sorry." He had a dark line along his cheek and into his lip where I had hit him with the edge of the mirror.

"It isn't bad," he said with a smile. "I'll show you." Then, before I could move, he put his hands on my shoulders, drew me to him, and kissed me. To my surprise, I kissed him back. On the clear, night air I thought I could hear a noise from Lymond's tent. It sounded like something breaking. I must have been mistaken as I looked in that direction when Brydges released me and I saw nothing.

"I hope you don't think me forward, Miss Sydney, but I've been wanting to do that since we met." He touched his lip gingerly and grimaced. I must have hit him harder than either of us had realized. "Please consider what I've asked you and do not hesitate to ask me anything you wish about my family." He smiled again, a little lopsided this time so he wouldn't move the injured side of his mouth. "Good night, Miss Sydney."

I watched him for a moment, then almost fell backward into my tent. Once inside, I sagged down on my camp bed. "Oh, good God!" I said to Bue as I collapsed against my pillow. "Whatever will Lymond think?"

Bue had no answer other than to flop down beside my bed and let me know it was time for sleep. Getting no help from that quarter, I replaced the mirror in its hiding place, locking my trunk carefully and hiding the key. After the disappearance of my box, I was inclined to believe Lymond when he said that not very many things in the camp were safe. However, I wanted to show the mirror to Harris tomorrow and get his opinion about it. The man knew his antiquities.

I lay a long time thinking of Brydges' proposal. I had

joked with Lymond that Lady Brydges might not be a bad title, but I hadn't been serious. It would be more than that— it would be *quite* a title. Brydges and I did, as he had pointed out, have the same interests, but there was something missing—something, *je ne sais quois.* We would rub along as friends and grow old together, much like Aunt Hen and Uncle Harley. The thought made me shiver.

Finally, I was able to put the whole thing out of my mind and drift off to sleep, my only accompaniment Bue's gentle snoring. However, when I awoke the next morning, the whole scene was the very first thing to flash into my brain. The second thing to hit my brain was intense pain. I had the culmination of all headaches I had ever had in my life.

I didn't make it to breakfast or to work. In spite of my protests, Aunt Hen insisted on sitting beside my bed and reading to me from the book she had borrowed from me. It concerned an extremely idiotic girl locked up in a castle in the Alps. As if the story weren't bad enough, Aunt Hen insisted on reading with 'meaning.' My head was pounding before she got to the end of Chapter Three.

Aunt Hen also insisted that I drink some lemon water. It tasted rather strange to me, and later I deduced that she had laced it with laudanum, because when I awoke, it was almost time for the evening meal. My headache was gone and I was ravenous.

"I knew exactly what you needed," Aunt Hen said happily. "Sleep. What's that Shakespeare said about sleep— sleep that knits sleeves." She nodded sagely. "If anyone should know, he should. At least, that's what Harley says." She frowned. "Although I could never quite figure out what Shakespeare meant. What in the world does sleep have to do with sleeves?"

"It's 'sleep that knits up the raveled sleeve of care,' Aunt

Hen," I said gently. "He meant that when you wake up, your cares are lessened."

"I knew it was something wise." Aunt Hen nodded again then got on to more important matters. "I have enough water here for you to sponge off, Roxanne. I knew you'd want to bathe and dress for the evening meal."

I gave her a hug. "Aunt Hen, whatever would I do without you?" I could see it pleased her. For a brief moment, I thought of sharing Brydges' proposal with her, but I wanted to think on it further before I mentioned it. I was sure Brydges would make no reference to it in public which was good; the second Aunt Hen got wind of it, she would be pressuring me to marry the man. Aunt Hen was deathly afraid I was going to be on the shelf for the rest of my life.

Brydges was waiting for me when I entered the mess tent. Everyone dressed somewhat for the evening meal. The general theory was that one should carry convention and manners along as far as practicable. It did seem to almost bring a touch of home to this faraway place.

"Mrs. Sinclair said you were ill," Brydges said, a worried frown on his face. "Are you all right now?"

I nodded as I sat down. To my horror, Brydges seated us at a table with Cecilia Drummond and Lymond. Lymond looked at me coolly and, quite deliberately, I thought, put his hand on Cecilia's. "To have been ill, you're looking remarkably fit, Roxanne," he said.

"Aunt Hen drugged me and I slept all day," I said with a laugh I didn't feel. "Do tell me what I've missed."

"You didn't know about the dead worker?" Cecilia asked. "It was shocking!"

I looked from Brydges to Lymond. "No. Who was it? What happened?"

"One of Anwar's men," Brydges said. "It was terribly

unfortunate, nothing at all like Mustapha. This was an accident. The man was up on the side of the mountain and evidently lost his footing and fell a distance right on to more rocks. He lived a short while, I understand."

"How is Anwar?" I asked.

Brydges shook his head. "Taking it very badly, I'm afraid. I doubt he'll be able to help us for several days."

I looked directly at Lymond. "Was it an accident?"

"Of course," Lymond answered. "What else could it have been?"

The conversation drifted off to more general topics, with Lymond and Brydges doing most of the talking. Lymond was talking, that is, during the few moments when either he or Cecilia weren't touching each other. It was disgusting. I was glad when the meal was over and we all went outside to sit for a while and talk. With everyone there, Lymond had to sit with Uncle Harley and Aunt Hen. Cecilia, however, didn't waste any time—she spent the remainder of the interval talking to Colonel Atherton. She talked, he leered, and Lymond glowered at them both. I could almost feel another headache coming on.

"Do you know where Anwar might be?" I asked Brydges, touching his arm briefly to interrupt a conversation with Harris.

Brydges shook his head, but Flora spoke. "I saw him at the entrance to the tomb before we came to eat. The poor boy was just sitting there sifting sand through his fingers."

As soon as the group broke up, I dodged Brydges and went into my tent to change into my everyday clothes and shoes. Then I collected Bue and went in search of Anwar. The boy—for that was what he was in spite of his size and age—didn't need to be alone if someone close to him had

died. Besides, I had my own theory about this and I wanted
to find out if Anwar really believed this was an accident.

I took a lantern with me so I could see as I walked across
the sand. It wasn't just sand, it was sand mixed with rocks,
some of them quite sharp. As I got close to the tomb entrance, I couldn't see anything. Bue bounded in front of
me, sniffed around the entrance, then sat down and looked
around. "I was counting on you to locate him," I told Bue
as I, too, looked around. I saw nothing. "Where could he
be?"

"Were you searching for me?" The voice came from behind me and I turned quickly, lantern in hand. Anwar appeared
as if from nowhere. Actually he had been sitting in the deep
shadows of the rocks, but I hadn't seen him. He walked up
to me slowly and, even in the darkness, I could see the sorrow
on his face as he leaned against a rock.

"I just heard that one of your friends died today, Anwar.
I came to offer my condolences." I put the lantern down
on a convenient rock and sat down. "This must be very
difficult for you."

"Feisal and I grew up together," he said, sitting on the
other side of the lantern.

We sat in silence for a moment, then I could wait no
longer. "Lord Brydges said it was an accident."

"Yes, he fell from the rocks." His voice was toneless.

"But he lived for a while. Were you able to be there with
him?"

"Yes."

I put the lantern aside so I could face him without blinding him with the light. I sat it down on the sand behind us
and it cast strange shadows on the rocks, giving them an
eerie glow interspersed with the blackest of shadows. "Anwar, this is very important. Did he say anything to you?"

He hesitated. "Yes."

"Was it an accident?"

There was a long pause. "What do you think?" he finally asked.

"I didn't talk to the man, but in view of the other things that have happened around here, I think it might not have been accidental. Perhaps it might have been the ghost. The white wraith."

Anwar laughed, a short, bitter laugh. "It was not the white wraith, I can assure you."

"Are you sure?"

He made a derisive noise. "I am sure. That was one of the things I wished to tell you—*I* am the white wraith, Miss Sydney."

For the second time in as many days, I was speechless. *"You,* Anwar? Surely not!"

"Yes, I." He looked at me and I knew he was telling the truth. "I will not say more about it except I was wrong. However, I did nothing evil; I assumed the disguise merely wished to frighten some of the workers."

"But why? You work here. Surely you have the good of the expedition foremost in your thoughts."

He shook his head slowly. "I was afraid we were going to find something. My . . . my friend convinced me that Brydges knew where some very valuable antiquities were located and intended to take everything back to England."

"That may have been true, but I think I am changing his mind."

"I thank you for that. However, I felt justified in assuming the disguise at the beginning because I didn't wish to see valuable things leave Egypt. I felt using the idea of a ghost would be harmless."

"But I saw the white wraith when Mustapha was killed. I thought . . ." I let my words trail off.

"You thought I had killed him. Or that the white wraith had killed him."

I nodded. "What were you doing? Why were you there?"

"Delivering a message from my friend. Nothing else." He tossed a pebble into the sand. "I don't want to tell you anything else until I . . . until I talk to another."

"So you think Feisal was killed?" He hadn't actually said so, but a leading question often brings results, so I tried it.

He nodded. "He told me so. Someone pushed him."

I thought about this for a moment. "Someone trying to discredit the expedition? Has something been found that might be stolen? I see no reason to frighten Brydges enough to cause him to pack up and leave. All he's found is a rather empty tomb and the wages he pays should endear him to every villager here."

"I know nothing much has been found, but with these types of excavations, you never know what lies ahead on the next day." Anwar was still tossing pebbles down. "I tried to frighten the men because I was afraid something would be found and taken away from Egypt. I never intended for anyone to be harmed."

"And you didn't harm anyone," I said, "so don't blame yourself for your friend's death. That's what you're doing, isn't it?" He nodded miserably. "Who is the other person you've mentioned, Anwar? Why is he doing this?"

"I cannot say yet because I do not know for sure that it was he who pushed Feisal." He paused. "After Feisal is buried, I intend to speak to him. I will tell you then." He looked at me, his eyes enormous in the darkness. "Until then, I ask you please not to divulge what I have told you."

"But Anwar, they need to know! You could be in danger yourself."

He shook his head. "There is no danger for me. The other person does not know that Feisal spoke to me." He stood. "I very much regret doing what I have done." There was almost a catch in his voice as he continued, "I hope you do not think the less of me for what I have told you. I would like very much to be a part of your expedition."

"I understand, Anwar and, no, I do not think less of you. My plans are the same. Perhaps, after your friend is buried, you, Harris, and I might meet to make some preliminary plans." I could think of nothing better to get his mind turned from his grief.

Anwar bowed slightly. "Thank you, Miss Sydney. I will do nothing further to tarnish your trust in me." He turned and I watched him go up the path towards the village, his head bowed. I did understand why he had tried to frighten the men, given his feelings about antiquities being taken from Egypt. I might have done the same thing myself.

"Let's go, Bue," I said heavily as I picked up the lantern and headed back to the camp. I wanted to share this information about the white wraith and Feisal's death with Lymond. I hadn't promised Anwar not to tell anyone, but I didn't want to tell Brydges—he wouldn't understand. Lymond would. I headed towards his tent.

I smelled the cigar smoke and saw the glow from the tip of Lymond's cigar before I got to the tent. He was sitting outside, beside the tent, leaned back against a chair. "Slumming, Roxanne?" he asked as I walked up. Bue ran over to him and nuzzled his leg while Lymond absently scratched him behind the ears.

"Hardly, Lymond." I sat down beside him. "Do you think we can talk here without being heard?"

"Why? Are you afraid Brydges will know you've spoken to me?"

"I'm not worried about Brydges."

He looked at me through half-closed eyes. "After last night, I don't suppose you have to worry about him. Did he come up to scratch?"

"You really misinterpreted things, Lymond. What you saw was perfectly innocent."

"Of course, I see things like that all the time."

I was stung. "No doubt every time you spend the evening in Cecilia Drummond's tent."

He looked at me again, his eyes half-open and glittering. His voice was a purr. "Of course, Roxanne. Why else would I be there?"

I felt sick. Visions of Lymond and Cecilia doing unspeakable things floated in front of my eyes. I looked at him smiling at me like the cat that ate the cream and I refused to give him the satisfaction of an answer. In just an instant, my body turned cold and then hot and my eyes refused to focus. I stood and walked away on unsteady legs, although I made it a point to hold my head high. I was afraid I wasn't going to make it into my tent; thank goodness it wasn't far. I was almost there before I stumbled on a rock and I realized I had left my lantern sitting on the ground beside Lymond. I left it and walked on—I wouldn't have gone back to get it for anything.

Once inside, I pulled the tent flap together and tied it so no one would enter. Then I very carefully arranged the pillows on my floor, changed into my galabeah, and lay down. Then and only then did I allow myself to let go. I wanted so to cry, but tears wouldn't come. Instead, my body gave itself over to dry, racking sobs. Lymond and Cecilia Drummond! It wasn't possible that Lymond could be taken in by nothing except a pretty face. And a lush body, I had to admit. Nevertheless, he surely could see what kind of person she was: a shallow fortune-hunter.

Then the opposite reaction set in. To think he had accused me of something improper when he was carrying on in such a way! The man judged everyone by his own life. How dare he! I would show him how little his taunts had affected me.

By this time, I had another headache. This was becoming a way of life for me, it seemed. For me, who had never had the headache more than a dozen times in her life.

There was a glow of light outside my tent. "Roxanne," Lymond said, "are you in there?"

"Go away," I said wearily.

The light in the lantern went out. "Roxanne, I need to talk to you." He was speaking in a hoarse whisper.

"I no longer wish to speak to you, Lymond. Go find Mrs. Drummond if you want conversation."

"Dammit, Roxanne, open this tent flap. I don't intend to stand here all night trying to whisper to you through the side of a tent."

"Good, because I don't intend to let you in. You might as well leave now."

"You left your lantern and I merely wanted to return it." His voice sounded stiff and cold.

"Just put it beside the tent. I'll get it in the morning." There was a sound as he put the lantern down with a soft thud and then I heard him walking away, his boots crunching on the sand and rocks. He was muttering to himself. I listened intently, but I couldn't tell if he went to his tent or to Cecilia's. I had my own ideas about his destination.

I crawled into my narrow bed and tried to sleep, to no

avail. In just a few minutes, I heard a whisper outside my tent. "Roxanne are you all right?"

"I'm fine, Flora. Do come in." She scrabbled around the outside of the tent before I realized I had tied the tent flaps, so I had to get up and untie them. She came inside. "I heard a noise, and thought something might be wrong."

"It was just Lymond returning my lantern." I leaned out the front of the tent and retrieved it. As soon as I had it lit, I invited her to sit.

"So many things have been happening, I thought I should check on you," she said. "I realize I haven't been the best of companions. I seem to have largely left you to your own devices."

"Exactly the way I prefer it," I reassured her. "I would call you the perfect companion." I smiled at her. "Tell me, are you enjoying your work?"

"It's wonderful! I never dreamed that I could enjoy anything so much. Alex says that I'm useful as well, so what could be better?"

I laughed. "I'm glad your trip to Egypt has been successful."

"More so than you realize." She paused. "I have wonderful news to share with you! Alex and I are going to be married. I'll stay with you as long as possible, of course."

I gave her a hug in the same way I would have done one of my sisters. "Flora, I'm so glad. This is wonderful news. Perhaps you and Harris will be married by the time our proposed expedition takes place."

"That's what we plan." She paused. "And you, Roxanne?" she asked gently. "What are your arrangements?"

I shrugged. "I'll go back to England, then return here for the expedition next year. I think with you in the camp, that I should be able to stay here without a companion of any sort. Surely Aunt Hen can't complain." I grinned. "Although I'm sure she would if she knew what I plan."

Flora giggled. "I agree." She looked at me again. "I know I've been busy, but not too busy to notice that you've been preoccupied lately. Is anything the matter?"

I hesitated. I had confided often in my sisters, but they were all gone. I knew I could trust Flora. "I've been distressed," I told her. "Between Lymond and Brydges, I hardly know where to turn. First, you do know that Lymond has been spending a great deal of time with your future sister-in-law."

Flora nodded. "I don't think he really cares for her, though. I believe Mr. Lymond has deep feelings for you, Roxanne." She paused and shook her head. "As for Cecilia, I can't believe how she's thrown herself at poor Mr. Lymond."

"Poor Mr. Lymond!" I snorted. "Flora, the man is as bad as Cecilia. If she's thrown herself at him, then he's *hurled* himself at her. He has no morals whatsoever."

Her expression was shocked. "How can you say that, Roxanne, when he cares so for you?"

"The only person Lymond cares for is himself."

She leaned towards me. "You can't believe that, Roxanne. He cares for you, I know he does."

"Then why did he spend the evening with Cecilia in her tent?"

It was Flora's turn to be speechless. "He did that?"

I nodded. "I saw him entering her tent. I didn't wait around to see how long he stayed."

"It doesn't matter, Roxanne. There has to be a reasonable explanation. Mr. Lymond cares for you. I know it."

"I fear you're mistaken, Flora." Those in love often

imagined everyone in love. I had seen the same effect with my sisters.

She leaned back against my pillows. "I don't think so. I just hope things work out for you, Roxanne. Did you say there was a problem with Brydges as well?"

"Not really a problem." Briefly I related the earlier events. "So he proposed to me and I told him I had to think about it," I concluded.

"Lady Brydges! How wonderful for you, Roxanne!" She looked at me. "But you're not happy about it, are you? That's why you put him off."

"I don't understand it, Flora. I should have said yes immediately and settled things. I just thought about how he phrased it—that we had similar interests and so on. He might have been interviewing for a secretary." I hesitated. "I'm not making sense, I know."

Flora smiled at me. "You make perfect sense to me. There isn't that spark between you and Brydges, is there? The second Alex spoke to me, I knew I had fallen in love with him. I wanted nothing more than to be next to him for the rest of my life, and when he proposed, I said yes almost before he finished speaking."

"I'm so happy for you, Flora. Perhaps someday I'll know the same thing."

Flora reached for my hand. "I hope so, Roxanne. Please think about the two men—Lord Brydges and Mr. Lymond, that is—before you do anything. I know Mr. Lymond cares about you."

"I know he cares, Flora, because of everything we've been though in the past, but I can't delude myself into thinking that he *cares*. There is nothing there beyond the boundaries of friendship." I sighed. "No, I suppose I'll give Brydges my answer soon. I just wish he had offered under different circumstances. I don't wish to marry a man who felt obligated to offer for me." I smiled at her. "Who knows? Someday I may meet someone as fine as Harris and fall in love."

Flora stood, her face glowing. "He's a wonderful person, Roxanne. I'm so glad you have enough faith in his methods and his character to hire him for your expedition. Because of that work, Alex told me we'd be able to marry."

"It will be good to be together again next year, won't it?"

"Yes, except I'll be married to the most wonderful man in the world." She paused at the tent door. "Are you sure you're all right?"

"Positive. Go back to sleep. That's what I intend to do."

Just think, I said to myself as I settled myself in bed, Flora had discovered both her husband and her life work here in the deserts of Egypt.

At least, I thought, as I tossed futilely on my narrow camp bed trying to go to sleep, someone was going to be happy.

Thirteen

The next morning, I was almost out of my tent when I remembered my mirror. I wanted Harris to see it and to give me his opinion of it. It looked much better since I had cleaned it, and he might be able to tell me something about it. I got it out and, to my surprise, discovered I had bent the side. Evidently I had struck poor Brydges on the mouth much harder than I realized. Looking at the edge, I could clearly see that the mirror was in two pieces, the second one completely covering the back, and it looked as if there were some kind of markings on the part under the overlay. This was intriguing. I wrapped the mirror in a cloth and took it with me.

When I went into the mess tent, I glanced around. Neither Lymond nor Cecilia Drummond was there. Brydges tried to smile at me, but his upper lip was swollen and there was a blue bruise running from his chin to the side of his nose. "Don't mind my brother," Edward said cheerfully. "For the first time in his life, he's having trouble talking. Seems he had a run-in with a tent pole."

"Those can be dangerous," I murmured, taking a seat with Flora. I smiled at Brydges by way of thanking him for covering up last night's scene. I hadn't even thought that the others would notice his injury and ask questions. The poor man tried to smile back, but it was impossible. I ran to the collections tent and got some paper and a pen. "Here," I said, "presenting it to him. This should see you through the day. By tomorrow, perhaps you'll be able to speak, but you really shouldn't even try today." He nodded gratefully. Edward spent the rest of breakfast gleefully teasing his brother.

Harris was heavily involved with Atherton, Edward, and Brydges, so I was unable to speak to him until we were dispersing to go to work. I wouldn't have caught him then except he paused outside to let the others go on ahead. As soon as he was alone, Flora stepped up next to him and he took the time to smile down at her and say something that was quite obviously of a private nature. I hated to interrupt them, but I did want him to take a look at the mirror.

"Two pieces?" he said. "That is curious. I'll take a look at it."

"I have it here," I said, giving him the wrapped parcel.

He moved the cloth aside and the polished brass caught the sun. "I see you've done some work on this since I last saw it," he said. "Let's go inside where we can see it properly."

We were walking as we talked, so I directed them to my tent and we all went inside. Harris sat down on the edge of my bed after I explained that I used it as a sofa during the day. The man was surprisingly modest, considering the deportment of his sister.

He unwrapped the mirror again, and looked at it. "Two pieces! I've never seen that before!" He ran his fingers around the edges of the mirror. "What happened to cause this dip on the edge? I don't recall this."

"I did that," I said with a sigh. "I accidently hit Brydges with it. He was kind enough to say it was a tent pole, but it was my mirror."

Harris looked at me a moment, then stifled a chuckle.

"I won't ask for particulars." He turned his attention to the mirror, as did Flora and I.

"Look," I told him as I pointed, "at the side. I just glanced at it, but it appears that there's something written or embossed on the under layer. I wondered if this part had been added at a later time. It doesn't look the same. It won't even polish up as well."

Harris peered at the edge. "It's definitely two different kinds of brass. I think you're right: this overlay doesn't seem to be anywhere near the quality of the reflective surface." He pulled a knife from his pocket and held the blade, ready to insert it into the indentation I had made. "Do you mind? I'll be careful."

"I don't mind at all," I said, peering over his arm as he worked. Flora was looking at the other side, sketchpad at the ready.

"This upper brass is much softer," Harris said, prying gently with his knife. "You're right, there are markings on the under surface." He moved the knife blade a little. "What's this?" To our amazement, a scrap of paper floated from between the layers. "Since it's your mirror," Harris said with a grin, "I'll give you the honor." He handed me the scrap. I opened it carefully, making sure that I didn't crumble the paper.

"This is much later," I said automatically. "This scrap is paper, not papyrus." I smoothed it out carefully, trying to contain my excitement. We all looked at it as Flora sketched rapidly! "What is it?" I asked, bewildered. It looked like a series of pictures tied together by squiggles.

"Let me have it a moment so I can make an accurate copy," Flora said. I handed her the scrap as Harris probed further with his knife.

"I have no idea what it means," Harris said, "but it must

be valuable. Why else would someone go to the trouble of hiding it in such a manner?" He looked back at the mirror. "I'd like to look at this more closely when I have time to do it justice—perhaps this evening, with you there as well. If we think it warrants, we might want to remove the backing and see what, if anything, else is there. At least we might see what was on the original backing."

"Of course." I took the drawing back from Flora as Harris handed me the mirror.

"I'd be sure to put those in a safe place," he said.

After he and Flora had gone, I did as he suggested, hiding the copy of the drawing in my clothing, replacing the mirror in my trunk, and secreting the original drawing in the back of Papa's miniature along with my trunk key. I felt like a conspirator in one of Aunt Hen's gothic novels.

When I went outside, there was major consternation. No workers had shown up at all. "It must be because of Feisal's burial," Brydges said. "Atherton told me that the Egyptians manage to take a day from work for the slightest excuse. I certainly believe it now." He sighed. "Sometimes all the baksheesh in the world can't move them."

"Perhaps," I suggested, "we should attend part of Feisal's burial just to show our respects. After all, he was a worker here. I don't think they'd want us there for whatever they do, but Anwar might appreciate our support."

My suggestion was taken by Brydges and Edward; the remainder elected to stay in camp and take care of mending, letter writing, or whatever. I wished to go to the village, more to let Anwar know he wasn't alone than pay my respects to an unknown worker. I asked Henry to accompany us so we could express ourselves. The four of us, Brydges, Edward, Henry, and me, arrived at the village to witness a scene of terrible wailing, hair-pulling, and agony. "Don't be alarmed," Henry whispered to me. "It's merely the normal form of laments for the dead."

Anwar was there and we paid our respects. He seemed distant and preoccupied, neither effusively acknowledging our presence nor taking part in the native ceremonies. Rather, he sat apart, his sorrow evident on his face. We didn't press him, rather we told him we were sorry, then took our leave.

"At least," I remarked to Brydges as we made our way back to the camp, "he knows we recognize his sorrow. At heart, I think Anwar is a good person."

Brydges smiled at me and touched my arm lightly. "I have noticed that you seem to find the good in everyone," he said.

I thought of my own feelings about Cecilia Drummond and didn't answer him. Instead, I began asking him about his plans for shipping the items in the tomb to England and discovered that he had already made arrangements to ship most of them to the British Museum. "They're nothing like what Elgin brought in, but they're a start," he said.

"What about keeping them here?"

He looked at me and laughed. "I remember your concern about that, Miss Sydney. I am leaving part of what we find, but think of the many Englishmen who will never get to travel to Egypt. Is this not an excellent way for them to see the wonders of the land?"

He had me there.

Back at camp, I went to my tent and busied myself with mundane things like letter writing, getting my laundry together, and so on. After I had completed that, the day still dragged on. I opened my trunk and got out the mirror and the scrap. Flora's copy was perfect, down to the last detail. I put the scrap down and looked at it closely. There were some circles of varying sizes, all in a heap on one side, and a squiggle leading from there to the apex of the scrap. There the drawing looked like the tops of triangles; there were no bottoms. Another squiggle connected those with another triangle that had a circle in it and what looked vaguely like a star inside the circle. I looked at it for the better part of an hour and couldn't figure out what it meant. I was still trying to decipher it when Flora came to my tent. I folded the copy and put it under a book beside my bed.

Flora was furious. "I just had a visit from Cecilia," she said, shaking all over.

I hunted up a small brandy bottle from my trunk. "Lymond didn't know about this one. I thought we might need fortitude," I said, pouring her a small amount. "A visit from Cecilia Drummond would seem to require both fortitude and assistance."

"I really don't need spirits," Flora said, trembling.

"Of course you do. Here." I gave her the glass; no more than two tablespoons were in it, but it seemed to brace her somewhat. "Now tell me what transpired."

"She came in and bluntly said that she thought I was getting entirely too familiar with her brother." Flora grimaced and I could see the forbearance it had taken for her to leave Cecilia's lovely neck alone. "I told her that we planned to marry. That was when she became livid." Flora stood and began pacing the tent, all of four steps either way. "She said that Alex couldn't marry; he was supporting their mother and her, and he simply didn't have the extra money to take on a wife. Her exact words were 'Alex simply can't be encumbered with you, Miss Rowe.' " Flora sat down. "Can you believe such!"

"I certainly can. Not of Alex—of Cecilia. I'm sure there's a reasonable explanation." I looked at the brandy bottle but judged she didn't need it. "Flora, you certainly aren't going to let her change your plans, are you?"

She shook her head. "I don't know, Roxanne. If Alex really can't afford to marry, why has he suggested it? He knows I have no money of my own. I don't know what to do."

I stood and took her arm, pulling her up. "I think the first thing you need to do is talk to the man. It has been my experience that most misunderstandings are caused because two people don't talk and clear up these contretemps before they get out of hand. Go to Alex right now and tell him what you've told me."

Flora looked at me anxiously. "What if . . . ?"

"You must go, Flora," I said gently. "If you don't, you'll never know."

"You're right, Roxanne. I'll do it."

"Good. Harris is an honorable man. If he had prior obligations, I don't think he would have proposed to you. I'm sure this is all in Cecilia's head."

That seemed to cheer her and she left to go find Harris, while I sat and thought about Cecilia's visit to her. Why would Cecilia be planning on Harris's support? There could be only one answer: she wasn't going to be able to bring Lymond up to scratch. The thought brought a smile and, for the first time in a long while, I relaxed. I even picked up a book and read for a short while. Flora came back in, her face glowing.

She threw her arms around me "You were right, Roxanne! It was nothing. Alex says that Cecilia and his mother have always come to him for money. Last year, his mother married for yet another time, and Alex informed her that he would no longer give her funds. Cecilia has a small legacy from her husband. Alex implied that the legacy was

smaller than Cecilia had hoped, but was still more than
ample to keep her up if she lives a modest life. Cecilia,
however, isn't interested in such a life and feels she needs
to move into the higher reaches of society. Alex said Cecilia
was frank about the fact that she plans to marry again, and
marry for money."

"So your wedding plans are still proceeding?"

"Yes! Yes!" She twirled around my tent and went back
to join Harris.

I noticed a scrap on the floor and when I picked it up, I
realized it was the copy Flora had made. I had been careless
with it and knocked it to the floor. I started to put it back,
but glanced at it one more time, tracing the squiggles with
my finger. I had looked at it for over an hour before, not
being able to figure out what it might be, but on this look,
it practically leaped out at me. It was a map.

Excited, I sat down and tried to find words hidden in the
drawing or landmarks I might recognize. The circles had
to be rocks and the squiggle was some kind of path or road
to some mountains, represented by the bottomless triangles. Then there was a road to another mountain. I puzzled
for a few minutes over the circle with a star in it, finally
deciding that it was a cave in the mountain, and the star—
with a sudden flash it all came together. The star could only
be one thing. This was the fortune Abdullah's grandfather
had hidden for them: the casket for which Lymond, Uncle
Harley, and dozens of others had searched so long.

I almost ran out of the tent to tell Lymond or Brydges
of my find, but stopped myself. I didn't know about approaching Lymond; Brydges, in spite of what he said,
would find the casket and ship it to the British Museum.
No, this prize belonged to Abdullah and his family. It would
lift them from poverty and ensure a future for little Faoud.

I had to go to the village and tell Abdullah about it. Besides, I thought as I looked down at the map again, I had no idea where these rocks, mountains, or the cave might be. Abdullah, having grown up here, would know instantly. I ran to fetch Henry to go with me to translate. I should, I thought to myself, get Anwar to go with us when we talked to Abdullah; it would cheer him immeasurably to know that such a priceless antiquity was helping a local family.

Henry and I made our way to the village for the second time that day. Henry, bless him, asked no questions and I offered no explanations. When we arrived at the village, the place was quiet and there were few people to be seen. We did see Colonel Atherton in the village and talked to him a few minutes. In contrast to his usual demeanor, he was overly familiar. He actually put his hand on my shoulder and leaned so he was next to my face. I felt soiled.

"Have you seen Anwar?" I asked him, stepping back.

Atherton shrugged. "Hardly. He's with the rest of these natives, I'd say, moaning and carrying on. Watch what I tell you—they'll take four or five days off from work to get over this." He moved next to me again. "The less you have to do with him or any of the natives, the better off you'll be. Sorry lot, all of them."

"Thank you for your advice," I said, glancing at Henry. He was standing there, his face completely impassive. I knew he had understood every word. "We really must be leaving, Colonel Atherton. Good day."

We walked a great distance away before I spoke to Henry. "I apologize for my countryman," I told him.

"Everyone knows Atherton," Henry said, "and we pay no attention to him." In spite of his words, I could hear an edge of anger in his tone.

"Let's go see Abdullah, Henry. I want to tell hir

thing but not yet. I want Anwar to be there when I do. Perhaps Abdullah can tell us something of Anwar's where-abouts."

Abdullah was, as usual, glad to see us and gave us directions to Anwar's house. I asked if I could speak to him later, after I found Anwar, and he again told me that his life was mine to command. Henry and I took our leave and Henry led the way to the very fringe of the village. "There," he said, pointing. "That is Anwar's house." The area was lonely, bounded by rocks and blown by sand.

We called, but no one answered. "Let's go around back, Henry," I suggested. "Perhaps he hasn't heard us." This wasn't likely as the house was small, but I wanted to be sure. I didn't think we'd find him easily if we had to look in the village.

As we went to the back of the house, I stopped. "Henry," I asked in alarm, "what's this?" I pointed to a trail in the sand of sticky liquid. "Is it going that way?" I started down the trail of drops towards some rocks, bending and touching a drop. "Unless I miss my guess, Henry, this is blood. Do you suppose Anwar has met with . . . ?" I couldn't go on. Henry and I scrambled across the rocks to try to find Anwar.

We found nothing except a scene that told a story. There was blood splattered on the rocks, and one particularly large rock that had been tossed aside was covered with blood and bits of hair. "I fear the worst, Henry," I said anxiously. "Where could he be?"

"It might not be Anwar," Henry reminded me.

"True." I stood and looked around. "I think we came the wrong way, Henry. The drops seem to be going back to Anwar's house." I began following the trail more carefully than I had before. We came to the back of Anwar's house where a stout door barred our way. Henry couldn't budge it, but he went around the side, and in a moment, I heard him on the roof, then inside the house. He opened the door for me.

"It doesn't look good," he said, gesturing to a heap on the floor. "I think he dragged himself in, closed the door, and collapsed."

That appeared to be the case. Anwar had been beaten senseless. If we hadn't known who he was, I doubt we would have recognized him. He was in terrible shape. I washed him gently as best I could and sent Henry to get Abdullah. There was no way he could be moved far, but I thought he might need some kind of protection. I told all of this to Abdullah when he arrived and asked if someone might come stay with him. Nothing would do Abdullah except to have Anwar moved to his house where he could be tended and watched. Henry and I stayed with him for a long time, but he didn't regain consciousness. We finally left him in the care of Abdullah's family and went back to camp to tell the others.

Colonel Atherton, Lymond, and Woodbury caught up with us as we walked back from the village. Lymond looked grave as we told him about Anwar. "Feisal might have been a coincidence, but this certainly isn't. Someone is deliberately trying to sabotage the expedition," he said, frowning.

"Nonsense," Atherton said. "These natives are always getting drunk and beating their wives and each other. He probably just got caught up in the celebrations. Where is he, by the way? I'll try to stop by and see him."

"He's with Abdullah's family." I looked at Atherton. "This was not an ordinary beating, Colonel Atherton. Someone tried to kill Anwar."

"That bad? I'm surprised. Do you think he'll pull through?"

I shook my head. "I don't know. He's unconscious and we won't know anything until he wakes up. I told Abdullah to come get me whenever Anwar woke up."

"My apologies, Miss Sydney," Atherton said gravely. "I didn't realize the boy was in that kind of shape. I'll be glad to help if I can. Do keep me posted on his condition."

"Keep all of us posted," Lymond said grimly. "We've got a murderer somewhere in our midst."

Abdullah still hadn't come the next day and neither had a single worker. Brydges was anxious and yelling at anyone and everyone who was near. "This damned trip has cost me a fortune," he said to Edward as they were sitting in the tent. He wasn't speaking to me, but I could hear him even though his bruised face made it hard for him to talk. Actually I was on my way to see Aunt Hen and just happened to stop behind the tent. It wasn't really eavesdropping. "Atherton gave me an estimate of future expenses yesterday and I don't know where all the money has gone. Between bribes and baksheesh, it's costing a king's ransom."

I would have heard more, but Woodbury came up to stand beside me and I had to move. "Mr. Lymond has suggested that I stay with you," he said formally. I noticed that Woodbury was carrying a pistol.

"This is hardly necessary, Woodbury. I have my own pistol and Bue to sound the alarm if I'm disturbed." I glanced down at Bue piled in a heap at my feet, prostrate from the heat. At least he had lost weight.

"Mr. Lymond gave me strict instructions."

I started to remind Woodbury that he didn't work for Lymond, but it was easier to let it go. Woodbury is naturally

very protective. "Very well, Woodbury. Let's go get Henry
and go to the village. I want to check on Anwar."

Woodbury mopped at his sweating brow and followed
stoically.

Anwar was still unconscious and showed little sign of
improvement. I was beginning to wonder if he would regain
consciousness. Abdullah was worried about him as well.
"It is in the hands of Allah," was all he would say. For a
moment, I started to ask Abdullah about the map, but hesitated with everyone around. Instead, I asked him about his
grandfather, the one who had secreted the casket. "A beautiful thing," Abdullah said. "My grandfather said he had
left careful instructions to show us where he hid it, but
we've never been able to find anything."

Again words sprang to my lips, but again I hesitated. I
wanted to talk to someone else before I revealed the map.
"The casket seems to be public knowledge," I said.

"Oh, yes," Henry translated. "Everyone in the village
has heard about it. Some of the older ones even saw it many
years ago."

"I may be able to help you find it, Abdullah," I said in
a low voice. "I don't want to say much until I'm sure, but
I may have an answer."

Abdullah stared at me. "The power of the Sytt. It is a
wonderful thing." I could have sworn he bowed his head
slightly.

Uncomfortable with such unwarranted adulation, I motioned for Henry and Woodbury, and we left. I could see
that the two men were bursting with questions, but I discouraged them. Woodbury was quite miffed about it and
fell behind us, muttering to Bue. I knew Lymond would
have a full report in minutes.

When I went into my tent, I was horrified. There were

things everywhere. My bed had been turned upside down, bedclothes strewn all over, my books and papers had been torn to bits and, from the appearance of the lock on my trunk, someone had tried to open it. I searched the floor for Papa's miniature and, with a sigh of relief, discovered it unharmed and, apparently, unopened. Before I could open it, Flora came in.

"I talked to Alex—" she began, then stopped. "What happened, Roxanne?"

"I appears that some unknown visitor ransacked my belongings. Did you see anyone enter or leave?" I opened the back of the miniature and breathed a sigh of relief. The trunk key and the small map were there. I removed the map and put it in my pocket. If someone else suspected its existence, then I needed to discuss this with Lymond right away.

I was just putting the miniature back in its place when Aunt Hen came barging in. "Roxanne, dearest, have you finished with—" She stopped and looked. "Whatever has happened?"

As gently as possible, I explained that my things had been ransacked, hoping that Aunt Hen wouldn't overreact. It was a vain hope. "A spasm!" she cried, clutching her chest. "I'm having a spasm, Roxanne! What if you had been in here! You'd be dead! We'll all be murdered in our beds!" With that, she fell into a swoon, almost knocking both Flora and me down. Aunt Hen is not a thin woman.

As soon as we had revived her, I called for Woodbury to help me take her to her own tent. "Yes, I must rest," she gasped, staggering between us. "This country will be the death of us all, just wait and see." Woodbury helped her to bed, gave me a pitying look, and fled. I tried Aunt Hen's vinaigrette, burned feathers, and gave her sips of ratafia to no avail. I finally decided that laudanum drops were called for in this case. Aunt Hen had none, and I had to return to my tent for mine. I found Flora straightening up my tent— she had the bed made and was folding some other things. I snatched up the drops and was just leaving when Cecilia Drummond came to the tent door. "Miss Rowe," she called around me as I tried to leave my tent, "I know you're in there and I want to talk to you."

"Do come in," Flora said sweetly. "I'm sure we have many things to discuss."

I hesitated, but Flora seemed able to take care of herself. I remembered well her determination when she left her brother. Not many women would have set out alone and on foot for Brighton. If she could do that, she could handle the likes of Cecilia Drummond. I went on to Aunt Hen's where I gave her the drops and sat with her until she dozed off to sleep.

It was dusk by now and I still had the map in my pocket. I went outside to Lymond's tent and stood there a moment, wondering how to best approach him. It wasn't necessary—he approached me; he and Uncle Harley came walking up.

"Henrietta calm now?" Uncle Harley asked. "Women!" he said to Lymond as he walked off without an answer.

Lymond grinned at me; he knows Aunt Hen well. "Have you had your hands full?" he asked as he lit a cigar, the smoke curling up to blend in with the dusk. His face looked strong and bronzed in the flare of the light.

"Yes, but not with Aunt Hen." I fingered the map. "I need to talk to you, Lymond. Privately."

"While I'd love to entertain you inside, Roxanne, I think the others might frown on such." He glanced around and nodded towards the rocks near the tomb. "Let's go over there."

We walked together to the rocks and I pulled out the map, explaining to him how I had come by it "I didn't recognize it at first, Lymond," I said, pointing, "but it has to be a map. See, these are mountains, this is a path or trail and this has to be a cave or a hiding place with the casket in it."

"So you believe in the casket?"

I nodded. "Abdullah says he's seen it."

"So do half the men in the village, some of them too young to have ever seen it if the chronology is correct."

"I believe in it. I also believe that it should be found and given to the owners."

Lymond laughed briefly. "Roxanne, the owners died two thousand years ago or more. This thing is probably a case of finders, keepers."

"It needs to stay in Egypt. It belongs to Abdullah's family."

"If it exists," Lymond added. We turned and leaned against a rock. The lights from the camp outlined the tents nicely, giving everything there a cozy glow. Remembering that Flora and Cecilia were in my tent, I cast an anxious glance that way. I didn't wish to return and discover everything in shreds again.

Suddenly I grabbed Lymond's arm and pointed. "Look, Lymond! There in the desert beyond my tent!"

There, in the distance, in the faint glow from the light, it was easy to see a struggle going on, but it wasn't between two women. Rather there seemed to be five or six men holding two struggling bodies. Immediately I knew what was happening: "Someone's trying to kidnap Flora and Cecilia!" I gasped.

Lymond shoved me aside and began running, shouting as he went to arouse the camp. I heard him call out Cecilia's name as well.

Fourteen

The whole camp was in an uproar. Colonel Atherton stood next to me as we looked at the tracks in the desert. "The natives. I can't imagine what they want with our ladies. Are you sure you're all right, Miss Sydney?"

"Yes," I said shaken. "Are you going to join the others?"

"Of course. Don't you worry, Miss Sydney. We'll find those ladies." With that, he finally rushed off to join the others and left me alone. Lymond came over. "We're not far behind them, so I think we can catch up." He looked around carefully. "I've asked Woodbury and Uncle Harley to stay here and watch you and Aunt Hen." He paused an instant. "Flora and Cecilia might not have been the targets, Roxanne. After all, didn't you say they were in your tent?"

I nodded, my lips numb.

Lymond put his hand on my shoulder. "Promise me you'll stay in Uncle Harley's tent with the others. Don't go out for anything until I get back." I said nothing and Lymond's grip became tighter. "I know you, Roxanne. You'll be out wandering around the countryside and into every tomb here. Promise me you'll stay with the others." He glanced over his shoulder as the other men called to him to hurry.

"I promise, Lymond," I said. "Just try to find Flora."

"Don't worry." He smiled down at me, his smile warm

in the lantern light. He ran off to join the others, and I plodded along to Aunt Hen's tent. Woodbury and Uncle Harley were there, pistols drawn, so that I walked in to face two firearms trained right at me. The firearms weren't as frightening as knowing what Woodbury and Uncle Harley might do with them. Aunt Hen, bless her, was sleeping right through everything, snoring gently.

I took up a position beside the door where I could look out and observe my tent. I didn't think that I was the object of the kidnapping, but someone might take advantage of my absence to search my tent again. If at first you don't succeed, et cetera.

The men returned before daylight, dejected and without the two victims. "We lost them in the rocks on the other side of the village," Lymond said as he sat down heavily. "Atherton thought he found a trace, but it was nothing. We became separated and didn't find each other for hours, so that was time wasted. We'll resume the search tomorrow." He looked at me with weary eyes. "I don't want you to stay alone in your tent or to walk out alone. Have someone with you at all times."

"I have my pistol and I'm perfectly capable of taking care of myself, Lymond."

"God," Lymond said with feeling. I didn't know if it was a prayer or a mild expletive and thought it better not to ask.

I had to spend the remainder of the night with Aunt Hen as Lymond slept by the tent door. I thought this was a little much, but nothing would dissuade him, so I gave up. I did take his advice and try to sleep—heaven knew I had had little enough sleep lately. About the time I dozed off, the laudanum wore off and Aunt Hen woke up and promptly went into hysterics when she heard what had occurred. Aunt Hen is not the best in a crisis.

After breakfast, the men gathered and went to resume the search. Lymond again extracted a promise from me that I would go nowhere alone. I persuaded him to leave Henry with me. Although I certainly didn't tell Lymond, I had decided that, as soon as the men were gone, I was going to the village and see how Anwar was getting along. That was my excuse, at any rate. What I really wanted to do was enlist Abdullah's help in locating Flora and Cecilia.

I had to wait for a long time after the men departed before I could leave. Aunt Hen was protesting, having regular attacks of the vapors, and anything else she could think of. Uncle Harley finally left us and went outside to talk to Woodbury.

"To leave me in my hour of need!" Aunt Hen said, holding her handkerchief to her nose. "Roxanne, I was not made to stay in this country."

I silently agreed, but asked if she wanted me to read to her. I read for the better part of an hour, then fetched her some lemon water. I paused outside the tent to lace the lemon water with some laudanum drops. I tried to do it secretly, but Uncle Harley saw me and asked what I was doing.

"Just some laudanum so Aunt Hen can rest," I told him, stirring the drink briskly.

Uncle Harley nodded. "Good. Henrietta's at her best when she's asleep." He paused. "Nothing derogatory intended."

"I understand perfectly, Uncle Harley."

"Good girl." He patted me absently on the arm and went back to his conversation with Woodbury. They were discussing Napoleon, with Uncle Harley being devil's advocate. He relishes that role.

Aunt Hen was asleep before long, and I excused myself

to go to my tent. Uncle Harley and Woodbury wandered off to the mess tent after telling me to call them if I needed anything. I agreed, lured Bue into my tent and fed him until he, too, dozed off, then hunted up Henry.

"Do you think it wise to leave the camp?" Henry asked.

"I have my pistol, Henry, and I'll get one for you if you like. I think we need to enlist Abdullah's help in finding Flora and Cecilia. After all, the village men know these rocks and valleys much better than we. Besides, I need to check on Anwar."

Henry finally agreed after I fetched a pistol for him. I didn't tell Woodbury or Uncle Harley that we were going since I knew they would try to scotch my plans. Instead, Henry and I set off. Unfortunately, we had to leave in the hottest part of the day, but I did take some water with us. It really wasn't far to the village.

We had gone perhaps a little over half way when it happened: two ruffians attacked us. One leaped on Henry from above while the other dashed from behind a rock and tried to grab me. Henry and I both fought the men and, for a moment, I thought we were going to subdue them. However, just as the scuffle was turning our way, there was a pistol shot from up on the mountain in the rocks. It ricocheted off a huge rock next to me and rock chips flew. One hit my cheek and cut it. Blood began to run down my cheek and, in the dust and uproar, I couldn't see whether Henry had been hurt. The only thing that penetrated was his shout "Run, Miss Sydney, run! Hide yourself!"

I hit my attacker with the butt of my pistol and he reeled backward. That gave me a moment to see Henry, blood streaming down his face, fall to the ground. The third attacker was climbing down the rocks to get to us. "Run!" Henry yelled as he fell.

I ran. I dashed by one man and started towards the village, but saw that the man on the rocks was heading diagonally to the path to cut me off. I rounded a bend in the rocks and realized they were unable to see me for a moment, so I veered to the right between two rocks and began climbing. I had no idea where I was going. I was trying to be quiet. I didn't even look behind me—it was no use. Either I could get away from them or they would catch me. I had to concentrate on the terrain and make every effort to hide myself as best as I could.

I climbed and moved to the right for the better part of an hour, I judged. I was exhausted, my cheek was throbbing, and I felt giddy. I crawled down into some shadows among some rocks and tried to make myself invisible. I still had my pistol and the small jar of water I had brought with me. I took a small sip, holding it in my mouth to make it last. I wanted to gulp down the whole jar, but knew I'd better ration it. I did take my handkerchief from my pocket, dampened it, and tried to wipe away the blood that had dried on my cheek. It hurt very much and I gently touched it. Part of the rock chip was still embedded and I pulled it out, gritting my teeth so I wouldn't screech with pain. The blood began again and I had to hold my handkerchief to the wound for a while before it stopped.

By this time, the afternoon was wearing on. I listened intently and thought I heard voices in the distance. The men must be searching methodically so I wouldn't be safe for long. My best hope was to circle around and try to get to the village from the back. Abdullah would protect me if I could just make it there.

Reluctantly, I came from my hiding place and looked around. I saw nothing, so I clambered out and began rounding the mountain, going in the direction I thought the village to be. Periodically I could hear the faint echo of voices in the distance. Every time, I hurried my pace, trying to get farther away from them. After dark, I heard nothing. I knew the natives were afraid to get out at night because of the afreets that roamed then but, with these men, it was too much to hope that they had abandoned their search; they had probably made camp, so I needed to get farther away.

I looked up at the sky, trying to get my bearings, but could recognize nothing. Finally, the terrible truth dawned on me: I was lost. I had no idea how to get to either the village or the camp. For a moment I panicked, but then gathered my wits about me. The moon was on the quarter, so the light was minimal. I decided to try to put some distance between the men and me during the night, but I would have to be careful and not fall. One slip could injure me enough so that I wouldn't be able to walk and I might be trapped here until . . . I didn't even want to think about it.

The sky was unfamiliar to me. The stars certainly didn't look as they did when I looked up in Brighton so I couldn't locate the Pole Star and get my bearings. I believed the village was off to my left, so I headed that way. I traveled about two hours and then the rocks gave way to desert. Perhaps, I thought, if I skirted the desert, I would find the village. I had two more sips of water and decided to hide in the rocks until morning. I was exhausted. I looked around until I saw a gap in the rock cliff and started inside, but my fear of snakes reasserted itself at that point, so I searched until I found a large rock aslant another. I crawled inside, drew my knees up, and leaned back. I hurt all over and thought I would never sleep, but I was so tired, so very tired. The next thing I knew, it was morning.

The small water jar was almost half empty and I allowed myself only a taste. It might take me hours to reach the village, and I would need every last drop. I crawled from my hiding place and had a terrible time getting to my feet. I was wearing the boots I had purchased in Cairo, and my feet felt swollen and blistered. For that matter, I was stiff and sore all over my body. There was not a part of my anatomy that didn't ache and I was light-headed from hunger. For a moment, all I wanted to do was crawl back into my hiding place and cry.

That would be a waste of time and effort, I reminded myself. Right now, I had to reach the village somehow. I looked up at the sky; already the sun was moving up into the cloudless blue and the heat was beginning to gather. I started walking, stopping every half hour or so to listen, but I didn't hear anything, not even the howl of an animal. It was just me, the sun, the heat, and the desert.

At what I judged to be midday, I could go no farther. I could feel my skin redden and tighten with the sun and sand, and my feet were swollen until they felt squeezed in my boots. I sat down and couldn't even get my boots off; even tugging at the boots was painful. I relaced them and gingerly tried to stand. I was close enough to the cliff of the mountain to see shadows, so I went to the base and propped myself there. I got out my water bottle; I had allowed myself three sips during the morning, but the level in the bottle seemed to have gone down alarmingly. At this rate, I would have drunk all the water by nightfall. I had to ration myself further, even though my body cried out for water.

I sat in the shadows for a while, listening, but hearing nothing but the wind and the sound of sand hitting the rocks. I thought I might hum to myself to keep up my spirits, but my lips wouldn't work. I touched them and discovered they were swollen and parched. My cheek was throbbing like fire; I was afraid sand had blown into the wound.

The shadows offered little protection from the heat. Still, I sat there for a while and dozed off, holding on to my water jar with both hands so I wouldn't drop it. The pistol was heavy in my pocket, but I could lose it better than I could lose the water jar.

I woke up in the middle of the afternoon, looked longingly at the pitiful amount of hot water in the jar, but denied myself. Instead, I forced myself to stand and start to walk. My feet were so swollen and blistered now that each step was painful. It was difficult to go on and I could see why some people just sat down and died—it was tempting.

The rocks and the cliffs lost all substance as I walked. They dissolved and faded into the heat waves, then loomed up again, hot and dry. I fell down several times and wondered if I would ever get up again, but I managed to get to my feet each time. I knew if I stayed down, I would die. I clung to my pathetic store of water with one hand, terrified each time I fell that I would break the jar. Those few mouthfuls of water were all that stood between me and certain death.

By the time the afternoon was wearing on, I had taken two tiny sips of water and I judged there were perhaps two more in the jar. I couldn't go on and fell against some rocks. I felt my skin and it was raw to the touch, the wound on my cheek throbbed and it was full of sand and dirt so I moistened my handkerchief and tried my best to soothe it. Then I looked at the jar and took the last swallow of water, holding it on my tongue and savoring it, trying to make it last.

Looking at the empty jar, I knew it was all over. Still, I had to keep trying. No Sydney has ever given up against odds, no matter how great. I forced myself to get to my feet, feeling blood squish between my toes, and started walking again, tossing the empty jar aside where I heard it crash and break against a rock.

How far I went, I will never know. As the first fingers of the sunset appeared, I fell again. This time I tried to rise but couldn't. I crawled for a while on my hands and knees, and managed to get close to the rocks. I knew it would be getting cold as night fell and the rocks offered some stored warmth. I would worry about tomorrow when it came.

"Roxanne!" I thought I heard someone shout. I listened again and decided it had been an illusion. I closed my eyes and huddled against the rock as the sun set. Then I made myself stand and look at the sunset in all its glory. It might be the last one I would ever see.

That lasted for all of a minute. I could stand no longer and fell back against the rock. "Roxanne!" I heard again. I could have sworn it was Lymond's voice.

Dear Lymond, I thought to myself. Never to see him again, never to argue with him again, never to speak to him again. That was the worst part of all of this. My sisters were taken care of; Aunt Hen was happy; Bue would survive. And Lymond would turn to Cecilia Drummond. A tear ran down my cheek and mixed with the sand. Angrily, I wiped it away. I would not feel sorry for myself.

"Roxanne! Where are you?" It was no illusion. I tried to get up. "Here," I croaked, but I could hardly hear myself. I crawled on my hands and knees out into the sand where I could be seen. "Here," I tried to say again, but the only sound was a rasping noise in my throat. They won't know where I am, I thought wildly. I could be rescued, but no one can hear me call. I fell down on my face in the sand.

There was a thud and a familiar noise in my ear as Bue began lapping at my face. "Stay, Bue," Lymond said, running up to me. He turned me over and took me into his arms. "Oh God, tell me it isn't too late! Roxanne, Roxanne!" He brushed my face and held his face down to mine to see if I was breathing. I lifted my hand and tried to speak, but I couldn't. Lymond made a strange noise in his throat, like a sob, and held me tightly against his chest, rocking me for a moment. Then he released me, got out a large waterskin, and gave me a sip. "Don't drink much now," he said. "There's plenty. Just small sips now."

When I had drunk a few sips, he looked at my face in the light from the setting sun, then wet his handkerchief and sponged my face. "Aunt Hen will have something to say to you about your complexion," he said with a chuckle. Then as darkness fell, he picked me up and moved over to the rocks. He put me down gently, then fired his pistol twice into the air.

"I apologize for everything I've ever said about Buecephalus," he said, lighting a small lantern and giving me another stingy sip of water. "He was frantic, pacing around and we finally tied him while we looked for you. I was afraid you'd been captured. I finally thought to untie Bue and let him have his head. I thought there was a slim chance he could help us find you."

Bue curled up beside me and his tail thumped regularly in the sand. I scratched him behind his ears as best I could. He answered by licking my arm with his large, rough tongue.

"Thank you," I tried to say to Bue and Lymond.

"Don't try to talk yet, Roxie," Lymond said, holding me close. "I hope they heard those pistol shots. I have my map and a compass just in case." He looked around at the darkness. "We're going to have to spend the night here anyway. You certainly can't be moved in this condition."

"At least," I said faintly, my voice returning, "in this condition, my reputation is in no danger."

Lymond laughed. "Try convincing Aunt Hen of that."

"Flora and Cecilia?" I croaked.

"They're safe. We didn't find them—the kidnappers set them free near the camp." His arms tightened around me. "I was right in thinking you were the target. Flora told me she heard a man cursing the others for abducting the wrong person. They were supposed to get you."

Something didn't seem right about this explanation and I finally hit on it. "Flora understood . . . ?" I whispered.

"The man in charge is English. He was swearing in English, then switched to the native tongue. Flora said there was no doubt." Lymond looked down at me and touched my face. "I have a good idea who he might be. Right now, you don't need to worry about a thing. You're safe." He settled back against the rock and snuggled me down in his arms. "Just go to sleep, Roxie. I'll be here all night."

I didn't think I could sleep, but for the first time in days, I felt comforted and safe. Being in Lymond's arms was *right* somehow. I reached down and patted Bue on the head, then, with a sigh, put my arms around Lymond's waist and went to sleep.

Sometime in the middle of the night, I awoke thirsty again. Lymond gave me some sips from the waterskin and looked at my cheek again. I sat upright while he worked on it. "I'm feeling much better, Lymond," I said. "I think my feet are still a mess, but for the first time in a while, I think I'm going to be all right."

"I was worried, Roxie," he said, as he washed the wound. "This is going to be all right. I think you may have a small scar here, but nothing disfiguring." He touched the place where the rock chip had been embedded.

"It isn't that I ever planned on being the beauty of the ball," I said. I looked at him with more than heartfelt gratitude, remembering my feelings when I thought I would never see him again. "Thank you, Lymond. I . . . I appreciate it." I touched his arm with my hand.

To my surprise, he clasped my hand and kissed the palm. "Isn't it time we stopped playing games, Roxanne?"

My heart lurched. "What do you mean, Lymond?"

"I mean that I care for you, Roxanne. I always have."

A strange feeling washed over me; I wanted to tell him how I felt, but there was one thing I had to know first. "What about Cecilia Drummond? I saw you go into her tent one night."

"I was afraid of that. You and Brydges were out walking that night near the dahabeah and I saw you then. I'm ashamed to say I used the woman shamelessly to make you jealous. When we got back to camp, she said her camp bed was broken and asked me to come in and tighten it for her. I didn't find anything wrong with it and left. Nothing happened." He looked chagrined. "I implied it did because I wanted to make you jealous. Every time I looked, you and Brydges were together. And when I stumbled onto that scene in the tent . . ."

"Nothing went on, Lymond," I assured him as I explained what had happened.

"I wanted to kill him, and maybe you as well. Did he offer you a proposal of marriage?"

I felt myself blush. "Yes, but it was only because he felt the obligation."

Lymond hesitated. "Did you accept? You once said Lady Brydges would be quite a title. I own he'd be quite a catch on the marriage mart."

I shook my head. "I don't love Brydges."

Again there was a pause. I was surprised as I had never known Lymond to be hesitant about anything. "Do you love . . . someone, Roxanne?" he asked very softly.

Feeling flooded over me as I realized what I had been hiding all this time. "I love you, Lymond. Very much. I think I have since the first moment we met. I just never admitted it to myself until this afternoon when I thought I might never see you again."

Lymond took me into his arms. "And you let me dangle all this time?" he said with a smile as he pulled me to him. "I shudder to think what might have happened, Roxanne. What if Bue and I hadn't found you?" He smiled that melting smile at me. "I can't begin to tell you how much I love you."

I started to answer but was prevented by Lymond kissing me quite thoroughly. By the time he stopped, I had forgotten what I was going to say. Instead, I touched his face and said, "Do that again."

"I'm going to. Again and again forever."

Fifteen

Early the next morning we started slowly back to camp. I looked back at the rocks where we had spent the night. If I could have, I would have marked it some way so I could return there time and again. "Do I need to carry you?" Lymond asked.

"I'm going to try to walk," I told him. I leaned heavily on his shoulder as Bue wandered along beside us. Lymond pulled out his map and compass, consulted them, then looked at his pistol. Brydges and Woodbury shouldn't be too far away, he thought. He loaded his pistol and shot it once in the air, the sound ringing and echoing from the nearby cliffs.

We hadn't gone far when we saw Woodbury running towards us. "Miss Sydney," he said, almost in tears. "I was so worried."

Woodbury has been with me since I was born. I hugged him as best I could. "I was worried too, Woodbury. If Lymond hadn't found me, I shudder to think what might have happened." I leaned against Lymond. My feet just wouldn't cooperate with my body. Lymond scooped me up and walked to a shady rock as Brydges came into view, leading a donkey. "We thought we might need transportation for you," Lymond said lightly. From the look on his face, I knew the donkey had been brought along to take my body back to camp.

"Do you know who tried to abduct you?" Brydges asked as we headed back to the camp.

"No, I had never seen them. They were dressed in native dress. How is Henry?"

"He's fine," Lymond answered, moving to one side of me so he could hold me. Woodbury was on the other side, while Brydges led our little procession. "He was knocked unconscious, but aside from being sore all over, he seems to be all right." Lymond chuckled. "Henry said he was going to stop going places with you—he was injured every time you dragged him off somewhere."

"The nerve of the man!" I could laugh, but this was the second time Henry had tried his best to protect me. I could never thank him enough.

Back in camp, the men decided I should go on to the boat and I was only too glad to comply. I felt fine until I looked in a mirror. Lymond must love me, I thought, to have told me so when I looked this way. My face was beet red and scoured by the sand, the wound in my cheek looked terrible, my lips were parched and cracked, and the sun had bleached my eyebrows and eyelashes. I was a mess, but I didn't really care. I was alive and Lymond loved me. Nothing else mattered.

Flora and Aunt Hen came to the boat and helped me bathe. They put lotion on my sunburned skin, dressed the wound on my cheek, and forced me to eat a little. Then they put me to bed, full and content. I don't know how long I slept, but when I awoke, it was dark except for the light of one small candle. Lymond was sitting beside my bed. "Ssshhh," he said, putting his finger over his lips. "Aunt Hen doesn't know I'm here."

I reached out and took his hand. "I'm glad you are, Lymond."

He leaned over and kissed me. "I needed to ask you something else." His eyes were sparkling in the faint light. "I forgot to ask you to marry me," he whispered, "and I knew I needed to correct that oversight immediately."

I held out my arms and he leaned to fit right into them. "Go ahead, Lymond."

"Go ahead?" He grinned wickedly. "Just what do you have in mind, Roxanne? Have you recovered more than I thought?"

I had to wait until he finished kissing me before I could answer him. "No, Lymond, I'm waiting for your proposal. Isn't that why you came here?"

He nuzzled my neck and whispered in my ear. "Roxanne, love, will you marry me?"

"Yes, oh, yes!" I whispered back as I ran my fingers through the hair at the back of his neck and smelled that wonderful scent that was Lymond.

"When?" he asked.

Before I could answer him, Bue came shambling in and jumped up on the bed. "I suppose," Lymond said moving a little, "that the dog comes with the agreement?"

I scratched Bue lazily behind the ears. "Of course."

A few minutes later, Lymond sat back up and looked down at me sternly. "I hope I'm never as frightened again, Roxanne. Whatever made you go off to the village?"

"I wanted to talk to Abdullah about Flora and Cecilia. Thank goodness they're safe." A thought hit me and I sat up in the bed. "The map, Lymond. We need to show it to Abdullah. If anyone could find the casket, he could. Those villagers know almost every rock in this valley. I'm sure he could go right to it."

"I'm ahead of you, Roxanne," Lymond said. "I went to the village and looked around, map in hand. I think I have the landmarks puzzled out, and, what's better, I think the map may be roughly to scale. Woodbury, Jem, Henry, and I are going tomorrow to see if we can find it. We thought we'd leave a little before daylight." He looked at me. "Don't even say it, Roxanne. You definitely are *not* going."

I felt my bandaged feet, still swollen from the walking I had done, and sadly agreed with him. "But you will come right here and tell me if you find anything, won't you?"

Flora came in and told me that supper was served on the deck if I could walk there; if not, she would bring me a tray. When I opted for supper on deck, Lymond waited outside until Flora had helped me comb my hair and put on a prettier dressing gown. Then he came in and insisted on carrying me to the table. Aunt Hen was there, and with Flora, we made four at the table. After supper, I felt I could walk along the deck, so Lymond and I wandered away from the others. In the shadows that hid us from the others, he kissed me again and told me what I wanted to hear. Somehow the ties on my dressing gown had come undone and I had to stop and make repairs before we joined the others.

I felt I could have stayed there forever, but Lymond had to return to camp since he was going out in the morning. He insisted on making sure I was in bed with Flora watching me before he left.

Brydges came to see me the next day. He sat down in the chair beside my bed, a worried frown on his face. Flora brought us some lemonade and sat down nearby with her needlework. Brydges fidgeted for several minutes, looking from Flora to me and back again. I took the hint and asked Flora to go up on deck and get something for me. With a look of understanding, she nodded and left, promising to be back in a quarter of an hour.

"I'm glad you're all right," Brydges said nervously. "We—I was worried."

"Flora will return in a moment," I said, knowing what was on his mind. "There is something I must tell you while we have a moment."

"I—" he began, but I interrupted him.

"I'm sorry, but I cannot accept your offer of marriage."

For just an instant, he broke into a grin. The man could have at least looked sorrowful. I had been right—he had offered for me only out of a sense of obligation. "I thought there might be . . . I was afraid you might not," he said, "but I would have been honored if you had." He grinned at me again. "Is it Lymond?"

I nodded. "I thought as much," Brydges said. "He's a lucky man." He leaned back in his chair and sipped his lemonade. "I wish I could say the same for me." He sighed. "This trip has cost me a small fortune and I have nothing to take back with me except some chairs and pots."

"I imagine a trip of this magnitude would be expensive." I was rapidly calculating costs in my head.

"Frightfully so. That was one reason I was in Cairo when we met. Costs were so bad I thought I could purchase supplies myself cheaper. And I did, but between what Atherton needs to run things and all the baksheesh, I've overstepped my budget." He sighed. "I'm going to have to go back to London for a while."

"Atherton? I thought he merely acted as a local liaison."

"Oh, no. He actually does everything. Harris runs the camp and the excavations, but Atherton buys everything and takes care of the locals. I couldn't do without him."

Flora returned and Brydges left, telling us he was going

to Cairo, but would be back in a few days. He appeared dejected, but at least I knew I wasn't part of the cause. If anything, he was probably glad he wasn't going to have to marry.

It was almost dusk the next day before Lymond returned. After the preliminaries, which I enjoyed tremendously, I asked if his trip had been successful. In answer, he reached for a package he had brought in. Unwrapping the cloth covering, he held up the casket for me to see.

I was terribly disappointed. It was much smaller than I had anticipated and certainly wasn't made of gold. "What is it?" I asked Lymond.

"Bronze, I think. This is all enamel work. But look here." He put the casket near the bed and opened it gently. There was a quantity of glass beads inside, faience from their appearance. Lymond moved them aside and lifted out a slim gold necklace and a golden ring. "These seem to be the valuable things here."

"Good," came a voice from the door. "Just put it all back and give it to me." I stared past Lymond to see Atherton in the doorway, a pistol in his hand, aimed right towards Lymond's back.

"Give it to him," I said. "Please." Nothing was worth Lymond getting hurt.

Lymond dropped the golden necklace and ring by my hand and I swept them under the covers. He replaced the cover, turned, and handed the casket to Atherton. "I thought you might be behind all this," Lymond said. "It all fit together."

Atherton shrugged. "I'd squeezed all I could from Brydges, but still needed money. I thought the rumors of the cache of gold might be true. That's why I took the box."

"You!" I said. "You were the white wraith I saw that day and you took my box."

"Nothing but a damned book of sermons. I even read the things, hoping to find some kind of code." He spat on the floor. "What a waste. Give the casket." He looked at us. "I suppose dispatching two more won't make any difference, will it?"

Atherton took the casket from Lymond's hand, looked at Lymond, and then down at his pistol. Just as I saw his hand jerk slightly, I leaped from the bed and knocked Lymond down. We were a tangle of arms, legs, and bedclothes on the floor as Atherton's pistol went off. Atherton slammed the door and ran. By the time we got untangled and Lymond went up on deck, he was gone.

I followed Lymond up on deck, trailing my dressing gown as I hobbled. "You're hurt," I said, seeing the blood on his arm.

"I'd be worse than hurt if you hadn't pushed me," he said, taking me in his arms. "How did you know he was going to shoot?"

"I saw his hand jerk. I just acted without thinking."

Lymond kissed me. "You could have been hurt, Roxanne." His voice almost shook.

"But I wasn't." A thought struck me. "Good Lord, Lymond! We've forgotten Flora!" I called out her name and heard a muffled response. Lymond went ahead and found her tied, a gag in her mouth. In just a few seconds he had her free, and it took both of us to get him to sit down and have his arm tended.

It was just a graze, so we disinfected it and wrapped his arm in a bandage. "I need to get Atherton," he said, standing.

"Lymond, why don't we go see Abdullah? I think native

justice might be better in this case. They could find him and retrieve the casket." I stood and tried walking across the deck, but my feet were too sore to use. "I'll go get dressed and send for a donkey to ride. I need to see Anwar, anyway."

"No, indeed," Lymond said firmly, sitting me down. "The locals won't go after him tonight anyway. I'll get a donkey for you and we'll go to the village the first thing in the morning."

Aunt Hen came up to us. "I was sleeping and heard a noise," she said, patting her hair down. It stood out in all directions. "What happened?" She looked at Lymond's arm. "Robert, you've been hurt!"

We looked at each other. There was nothing to do except tell Aunt Hen what had happened and prepare for another attack of the vapors. She surprised us. "Atherton! I could have told you. I told Harley that man was up to no good!" She nodded and turned to Lymond. "Do you think Harley plans to come to the boat this evening?"

"I'll persuade him if I can," Lymond said gravely as he left. He must have done it, as I heard Uncle Harley just as I went to sleep for the night. "Giving it all up, Henrietta," he was saying to Aunt Hen. "Too many damned nuisances in this country. Going to stick to book collecting." I couldn't hear Aunt Hen's reply, but I was sure it was one of relief.

Lymond made the trip from camp to collect me the next morning. I rode on a donkey while he and Henry walked beside me. In the village, Abdullah greeted me with emotion. "He was afraid you had died," Henry translated.

"Tell him about the casket and Atherton, Henry," I said. Henry did and Abdullah's face underwent a series of changes. He spoke rapidly to Henry. "He's going to get some men right now. He thinks he knows where Atherton is," Henry told us. Lymond and I wished Abdullah Godspeed as we went into check on Anwar.

To our delight, Anwar had regained consciousness. A tall man dressed in native dress was there, talking to him. Lymond shook the man's hand like an old friend, then introduced him to me as Mr. Monroe, the local Methodist missionary. I informed him that my sister had married a Methodist missionary to America, and we chatted for a moment before he left. Lymond followed him out for a moment, then returned. "Your friend Monroe seems to be a nice man," I remarked to Lymond before we sat to talk to Anwar.

"He is. Unlike many others, he's dedicated to his work. And, as you noticed from the dress, he seems to have assimilated quite well. I don't think he's making many inroads as far as converting the natives, but he does a great deal of good."

"Just like my brother-in-law," I said smiling as I turned to Anwar. "I'm glad to see you doing so well," I said to him. His face was still puffy, but he was able to speak to us. "I heard about your misfortune," he said.

"It turned into good fortune," I told him, with a glance at Lymond. "Not only that, we've recovered the casket. But it's been stolen."

"Atherton?" Anwar asked.

Lymond nodded. "Is that who did this to you?"

Anwar nodded and told us of his involvement with Atherton. The man had preyed on Anwar's feelings about antiquities being looted and taken away, and convinced him that Brydges was there for no other reason. "Atherton wanted the trip to fail and Brydges to get discouraged and go home," Anwar told us. "Atherton had taken all the money Brydges had given him. He had no more for other things. There is a word for it . . ."

"Embezzlement?" I asked.

"That's it." Anwar sat up and tried to sip some water. "Before he died, Feisal told me that someone had pushed him onto the rocks. I put everything together and concluded it must be Atherton. Right after I confronted him, his hired brawlers beat me and left me for dead." He looked at me gratefully. "If it hadn't been for you . . ."

"We were all concerned about you, Anwar," I told him quickly. "Do you know anything else about Atherton?"

"Just that he had the same men kidnap Miss Rowe and Mrs. Drummond. I also would say they were the same men who tried to harm you. Were there three of them, one short and wiry, one taller with a scar, and one larger man?"

I nodded. "Exactly. Do you know where they are?"

"I know." Anwar grimaced. "Abdullah discovered what they had done. They will never do anything again. Trust me."

I looked at Lymond. "If Abdullah gets Atherton, he may not have to face the authorities."

"I guarantee it," Anwar said, "but he'll never harm anyone again."

"And Abdullah will have the casket. If he wishes to sell it, Anwar, be sure he gets a fair price for it. I have some jewelry that belongs with it."

We left Anwar and went back to the boat. Uncle Harley and Aunt Hen were there, Aunt Hen singing and humming. "We're on our way back to England," she said, smiling. "Of course, you're going with us, aren't you, Roxanne? Brydges said for us to take the boat on into Cairo. Mrs. Drummond has already gone."

"She has?"

Aunt Hen nodded. "Yes, she decided to go overland with Brydges and his brother when they left. Most improper! I don't think Harris is too pleased, but he doesn't seem to be able to control his sister." She frowned. "I really don't think Brydges will come up to scratch there. I could have told the poor woman that she was wasting her time. I'll wager we'll see her in London, chasing after some member of the *ton,* hoping for a wedding."

"That's a wager I wouldn't accept," Lymond said. "however, how would you like a wedding right here?"

Aunt Hen and I both stared at him. Lymond put his arms around me and gave me a kiss right in front of Aunt Hen. "I don't want to wait, Roxanne. It will be weeks, maybe months, before we can marry if we go back to England. I talked to Monroe and he said he'd come here tonight and perform the ceremony if we wanted him to."

"Impossible!" Aunt Hen said with a gasp. "Married? Roxanne is getting married?"

"Yes, Aunt Hen, to me." Lymond seized her and whirled her around.

"A dream come true," Aunt Hen said, starting to cry. Suddenly she wiped her eyes and looked straight at me. "I think you should, Roxanne."

"Should what?"

"Should get married tonight. What about a license?" Such practicality was unusual for Aunt Hen.

"Not necessary here, Monroe tells me." Lymond turned to me. "I even have a ring." He produced the heavy, gold ring we had found in the casket. "What could be more fitting?"

"Good," Aunt Hen said. "I'll get Harley, Flora, and Harris. Roxanne, go get ready."

"I can't believe this, Aunt Hen. You, the soul of propriety

and doing things by the book! Why are you agreeing to this?"

Lymond laughed before she could answer. "For the same reason I want to do this now: she's afraid you'll change your mind." He gave me a quick kiss on the forehead. "Monroe will be here around eight."

At dusk, with the boat gently rocking on the Nile and the Egyptian sun painting a picture in the west, Lymond put the ancient gold ring on my finger and we each said I do. It was better than a ceremony in Westminster Abbey, better than a wedding with all of London society in attendance.

However, I must confess that the very best part came later.